MERGED

Jim and Stephanie Kroepfl

Month9Books

Month9Books

To each other.

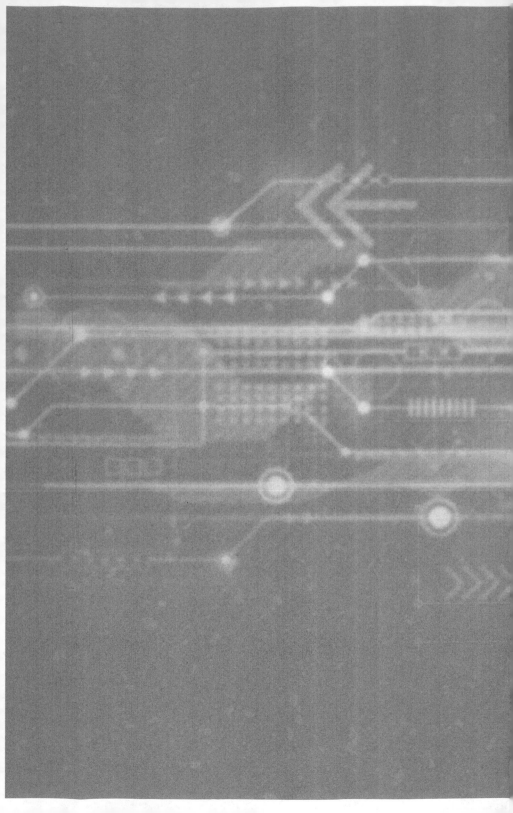

Prologue

"As we feared, Mr. Wakowski, there is no hope."

It's what I expected, but it's still a shock to hear it in his detached, clinical tone. As my body has become more and more useless, so have my doctors. *We* aren't dying. I am.

I blink a series of commands, and the computer responds in the French accent I programmed to amuse me. "Thank you, Doctors. Goodbye."

The day's last sunlight streams into the living room as they leave. The room that hasn't changed since Mom died. I've created entire worlds in cyberspace, but haven't left my house in years. That's about to change.

I stare at the van Gogh on the wall, the one he painted just before he died at thirty-seven. What would art be like now if he'd lived longer? What would everything be like if Vincent had had more time to influence the world?

Time to make the call. I blink, and the computer dials the number the man in the gray-blue suit provided.

"Darwin Corporation," a flinty, no-nonsense voice greets.

I blink again, and the computer recites the pre-recorded message in my own voice. "Bartholomew Wakowski. Procedure M-sixteen. Confirmation code zero-alpha-four-nine. Art."

"Thank you, Mr. Wakowski. We do require a verbal consent, as per your instructions."

This is the reason I have to do it now. I don't know how long it's been since I've spoken, and in a few days, it won't be possible. I give it all I've got.

"Bat!"

It comes out in a whisper. It's good to hear the name I call myself, even though it's only me saying it.

"Thank you, Mr. Wakowski. The procedure is confirmed. A transport team will arrive within twelve hours, and the chosen subject will be prepared. If you have any additional—"

I blink the line dead. Life is too short to endure polite conversation. If all goes as planned, though, and the man in the gray-blue suit is telling the truth, I will soon have all the time in the world.

Orfyn

Depending on your point of view, I'm either famous or infamous. I'm called by many names: Ward of the State, Orphaned, Foofool (only by Sister Mo), and Kevin. That last one makes me feel like I'm wearing someone else's clothes. Tight and loose in all the wrong places. So, I came up with my own name, though no one has ever connected it to me. The identity of street artists should never be revealed.

I flick turpentine at a rat that's getting a little too curious about my brushes. The alley smells like something died, making me wonder if there's a body in the dumpster. Michelangelo cut up dead people to better understand how we're built. If he was willing to do that for his art, I can endure this stink for one night. I breathe through my mouth and get back to work.

After four straight hours, the painting is coming along great, and I know I can finish it before people start heading out for their nine-to-five jobs. I paint madly, getting lost in the scene, moving from figure to figure, jersey to jersey. It's my best work yet, and I want this one to last.

At least, for a few days.

I take a moment to admire the shading on the faces. Peter's skin is a little dark, but the rest are just right, especially Jesus. I initially wanted to paint him with missing front teeth, but he isn't smiling in da Vinci's version—nobody is—so it would be too cartoonish. The stern glare of a defenseman is perfect.

I did give Judas a black eye, though. Who wouldn't?

It's three in the morning in Brooklyn, and I'm glad I brought the ratty tarp to conceal me from the street. Sister Mo would've called it divine intervention. I call it experience. I've been caught in the act before, but not found out. There's a big difference.

I don't want to brag, but not many painters can recreate a da Vinci on cold brick in one night. If anyone who knows anything about street art sees my half-finished painting, my anonymity will be history. And if people start to think St. Catherine's Home is sheltering delinquents, not only could I be thrown out, but the nun who's lovingly cared for me the past sixteen years, Sister Mo, could be in serious trouble.

"Can I see?" I hear a girl ask.

I pray she isn't talking to me, but I know better. There's no one but me hanging out in this alley. I look up and spot a Latina girl, a couple years younger than me, leaning over the rickety fire escape. *Damn.*

How long has she been there? I'd scoped out this location and didn't see any late-night activity in the apartments looking out onto the alley. Big mistake. One I can't afford to make.

I should get out of here and paint somewhere else tomorrow. But the da Vinci is coming to life, and I can't abandon it. Except for this girl, no one has seen me. Not even one close call. I hear Sister Mo's disapproving voice in my head. *Don't start what you don't finish, you.* But she also loves to spout, *Pride goeth before a fall.* Which nun's proverb should I follow tonight?

"What's your name?" I ask, barely above a whisper.

"Rosa." She gives me her name as if daring me to try to take it from her. There's mischief in her eyes: the need for something exciting to happen, the innocence of not knowing what could. I can't help but think about painting the defiance in her face.

"Rosa, can you keep a secret? A big secret?"

"I'm great at secrets."

"If I let you watch me paint, will you promise not to tell anyone you know who I am?"

"How could I? I don't know your name."

"You will tomorrow."

Rosa looks down at me and crosses her arms with more attitude than a girl her age should possess. "I can watch you?"

She should've been asleep hours ago, but I understand the loneliness that clings to people in the middle of the night. "You can if you keep my secret."

Rosa scrunches her face like she's really thinking it over. "Okay."

A blast of excitement hits me. I actually get to see how my painting affects someone. I might regret it later, but at this moment, when it feels like we're the only people in the entire city, I choose to trust her. I dive back into the painting. Mixing colors, abusing my brushes on the brick, making motion and light where there weren't any before. And it's nice having Rosa to talk to. Being alone in an alley at night is more than a little scary. But how long could I paint in Times Square before getting arrested?

Knowing that Rosa will soon discover my street name makes me want to tell her more: who inspired me, why I have this need to leave my mark on these grungy walls, and how I dream about painting for a living. I also come to understand why her mom isn't aware that Rosa is on the fire escape in the middle of the night, hanging out with a stranger.

Instead of distracting me, Rosa keeps me focused. I become absorbed by the Disciples' jerseys, shading the folds to look right, cheating just a bit. You've got to find a way to make it yours. Almost everyone in da Vinci's version is wearing blue or red, so it's perfect

3

for my home team. Sister Mo might not approve of Jesus in a hockey jersey, but there's not much she won't forgive when it comes to the Rangers.

I finish all their names on the silver base of the Stanley Cup sitting between Jesus and John. Then, in the most Gothic-looking letters I can style, I paint the title on the table's edge: *Take This Cup.* Finally, I reach for my signature orange paint and tag my work with the name my followers know me by.

"Orfyn?" Rosa asks. "Is that your real name?"

"One of them."

Her look tells me I'm not the only one who understands about hiding in the shadows.

"Is it done?" she asks.

I step back to soak it in. It's closer to the image in my mind than anything I've ever painted. The geometry is accurate, as well as the positions and expressions of the thirteen men. And twenty-three hands. Twenty-three! No small feat in just one night.

I spend another moment examining my work. "Yeah, it's done." The exhaustion of a night's worth of painting begins creeping through me. "Want a closer look?"

Rosa climbs down from the fire escape as if she's been doing it all her life. When she takes in the whole painting, she gasps. Her face shifts from shock to fascination to awe. I no longer wonder whether I got it right.

The risk was worth it, and I'm glad I let her be a part of my best painting yet. My New York Rangers version of *The Last Supper* and Rosa's rapt expression make the space between the tarp and the brick wall feel almost like a cathedral.

"You're amazing!"

"I had a good teacher," I say, as if being able to pull off a da Vinci in a dark alley—or anywhere—is something that can be taught.

"Are you famous?" I swear I can see the colors as the words leave her mouth. Warm yellow, Mars orange, a splash of deep gold.

"What fun would that be?" I say, trying to sound cool.

The truth is, I don't want anyone to learn my true identity. Within minutes of someone posting the news that they've found a new Orfyn, people will flock to take photos before it's ruined or removed. When this painting hits social media, even more people will learn about my art. But they'll learn nothing about me, which is how I like it. Admired, yet mysterious.

"Will I ever see you again?" Rosa asks, suddenly acting shy, even though she knows more about me than pretty much anyone. Except Sister Mo.

"If you keep your promise."

"I'll never tell."

I want to believe her. So I do.

There's a reason I stumbled across this particular alley. Rosa will get to see *Take This Cup* every day … or for as long as it lasts. Most of my paintings have disappeared. Stolen and sold. Destroyed. Tagged over. My last painting was cut out of the side of an old couple's house and sold at an auction. I don't care; really, I don't. I hope it changed their lives.

I painted this one on a brick wall, hoping it lasts longer, but you never know. One thing for sure, this *Last Supper* isn't going to make it five hundred years, but a few weeks would be nice. It would make Rosa happy. I think she deserves that.

Then I get an idea. "Rosa, how would you like to be famous?"

Her face fills with excitement.

"Do you want to be the one who discovers my painting?" I say. "You'll get a lot of attention for a day or two. I promise."

She gives me a look no one has given me before. As if I could work miracles. I suddenly feel braver. More important.

Rosa takes a few photos of my painting, agrees to post the one we chose, and promises—four times—not to betray me. I know I'm taking a big risk. No one can predict how fifteen minutes of fame will affect someone, but something inside of me trusts that she'll keep her word.

The sky is brightening, and when the second person obliviously passes the alley, I know it's time to go. I pack up my stuff and pull away the tarp to reveal *Take This Cup* to the world. Or, at least, to this gritty alley in Brooklyn.

"I'll come by again," I promise.

"You better," she answers, with an attitude half as hardened as it was earlier.

I steal one last look at my painting, peer around the corner, wave good-bye, and sprint down the street. I'm exhausted, but there's no way I'll be able to sleep. I'm already thinking about my next painting.

The Darwinians

"I've found the boy," the man in the gray-blue suit reports to the woman and two men arranged on the opposite side of the highly polished, mahogany conference table.

One wall is lined with framed portraits of serious-looking people, most of them etched with decades of wrinkles. Their eyes hold the cool confidence of aptitude and accomplishment, although each gaunt face betrays the fact that none of them are well.

"*The* boy?" the man with a perfectly trimmed, white beard asks.

"Yes. I'm certain."

"Will there be complications?" asks the man with slick, raven-black hair.

"There's no reason to believe he'll be a hostile recruit. The situation is favorable."

"Are you sure they'll keep it confidential?" the woman with the helmet of gray hair asks before turning away to cough. An ominous, gurgley cough.

"It's a good arrangement … and I've uncovered a few things. They won't betray us."

"I would like to underscore my opposition to this plan," the white-bearded man says, firmly. "Including Art debases our core disciplines."

"We had no choice," the raven-haired man says. "We needed that grant. Still, every subject is a risk, and doubly so with that kid." He shakes his head in disgust. "He's a street punk."

"He's an *orphan*," the woman says. "That doesn't automatically make him a hoodlum."

"And you're certain this is the one he insisted on?" the bearded man asks.

"Unconditionally," the man in gray-blue answers.

"Perfect." The raven-haired man slaps both hands on the conference table. "Let's proceed."

Orfyn

After sleeping off my exhaustion, I go into Sister Mo's office and turn on the ancient computer to look for posts about *Take This Cup*. On Rosa's page, as I instructed, is my painting with the caption, *A New Orfyn*.

The blues and reds stand out well, and the Stanley Cup looks almost three-dimensional. The flesh tones are lifelike, and the glares of Jesus and his disciples make them look badass.

Then I see it.

A reflection in the dirty window next to the painting. Lampblack hair cut in a fade, and a streak of Cardinal red paint slashing across the guy's light brown cheek.

It's clearly me.

Rosa posted the *wrong* photo. My stomach twists so hard it nearly bowls me over. Beads of sweat sprout on my forehead. My identity is blown. I want to believe it's not disastrous, but I know better. The mayor offers a reward for turning in people like me, and it's only a matter of time before someone needs the cash. The thing is, no matter how beautiful my paintings are, or how much people like them, it's still vandalism. Officially, criminal mischief. I could be facing up to a year in jail and some serious fines I could never pay.

How am I going to tell Sister Mo? My recklessness will damage the reputation of St. Catherine's Home for Children—something Sister Mo takes very seriously. When word gets out that one of her orphans was arrested, it'll prove to those people who think we're no-good that they were right all along.

I am so screwed.

Rosa has to delete that post. I start to message her, but then the site acts funny. When I refresh it, not only is the post with the incriminating photo not there, all of her previous posts have disappeared.

She must've noticed my reflection, but why would she remove everything about herself? I search every site that's ever posted anything about Orfyn. No alerts about a new painting. No slightly blurry but recognizable photo of me in the window. No *Take This Cup*. No Rosa. No nothing.

The last thing I should do is go see her. The surest way to get caught is to return to the scene of the crime. But I have to. There's bound to be a bunch of people there taking photos, so I get into disguise, which pretty much means covering my T-shirt with a hoodie.

By the time I get to Rosa's neighborhood, I'm feeling twice as nervous as I did in the alley. My hastily-made plan is to loiter in the bodega up the street and case the scene from there. That is, if the store owner lets me hang out without buying anything. When I get near, I'm surprised there's no crowd. Is it possible no one noticed something that colorful? I stroll by the alley, trying not to seem like I'm obviously looking for something, pushing my hoodie slightly to the side.

It's gone! *Take This Cup* is gone.

The brick wall is still intact, though it looks like it's been acid-washed, leaving not even the slightest haze of color. It's as if my painting was never there. I'm used to my work being ruined, but not this quickly. Or thoroughly. Why would someone go through the trouble of erasing *Take This Cup* from an alley wall?

I look up at Rosa's fire escape. Maybe she saw what happened. I count the windows and figure out which apartment is hers. After making my way to the front of the building, it only takes a few random buzzes on the panel before someone lets me in. The entryway smells like urine. I make my way up the sticky stairs, and pass an old man sleeping on the landing between the second and third floors. The sound of gunfire blares from behind a door, and I'm seriously hoping it's coming from their TV. My unease grows with every step.

Rosa's door is ajar. I push it open a crack. "Hello?" I'm greeted by silence. I push the door open a bit further and peek in. "Rosa?"

Even from the hallway, I can tell they've moved out. And in a hurry. There's the stuff you take and the stuff you leave. Her place is strewn with the things that weren't important enough to pack up.

Then it hits me. No painting. No Rosa. Abandoned apartment.

I need to leave. Now.

>>>

"I have to tell you about something I did."

I lead Sister Mo into her office as dread latches onto me. I shut the door, sit in the chair in front of her desk, and tell her what happened, not daring to leave anything out. I brace myself for her reaction.

"There is a chance no one saw that photo," she says in her thick, Kingston lilt.

I want to believe her, but it all happened too fast to be a coincidence.

She crosses herself. "Good Lord willing."

I follow her example, needing all the blessings I can get. Lesson learned: street artists and photo ops don't mix. *I'm sorry, Rosa. I thought I was doing something nice for you. And yeah, I admit it. I was showing off, too*. My pride getting in the way again. I can only pray she's okay.

Sister Mo studies me with her deep-set eyes, and I swear she's been aware of every thought I've ever had. "The girl who saw your painting, did she say she was leaving today?"

"No." Rosa would've told me. We talked about everything.

"Does she know who you are?"

My stomach clenches as I think it over. "I never told her my real name or where I live."

Sister Mo gets a distant look, as if she's seen the ghost of someone who used to piss her off. "Don't go back to that place, you. I'll call the Chief, and we'll learn what we can learn."

She means this. The family tree of St. Catherine's includes a council member, two state senators, more than a handful of lawyers and, yes, the Deputy Chief of the New York City Police Department. Couple that with a bishop who owes Sister Mo a few favors, and you get the idea of her pull.

But because of me, she needs to admit all is not right at her orphanage. If they discover I'm a vandal who stays out all night, people may start to question if Sister Mo is properly watching over her wards.

If it's the last thing I do, I'll make sure this doesn't screw things up for her or St. Catherine's.

Lake

My eyes snap open. I'm not dead.

I blink a few times to erase the blur. Two people wearing white lab coats and anxious expressions are focused squarely on me. I squint at the blinding light overhead.

The male scientist says, "Her occipital lobe is functioning properly."

Good to know. And I can still hear, which means my temporal lobe is also operational. My racing heart begins to decelerate.

"What is your name?" the woman asks me, over-enunciating each word.

I summon the answer, although it takes longer than it should. "Lake Summers."

She makes a note in her tablet, looking more than a little relieved. Then I remember why. Losing one's self-awareness was on the long list of risks in the *Informed Consent Agreement* I'd signed.

My throat constricts, and I blink back tears. My brain hasn't become inert matter, but I should know the woman's name. It isn't coming to me.

"Water," I croak. "Please."

The pock-faced male scientist places a straw between my lips, and I suck in the warm, chalk-flavored liquid. I can still taste; my parietal lobe is undamaged. Since I have the capacity to inventory my senses, my reasoning and problem-solving functions must also be intact. The nerves in my face convey to my brain that a tear is sliding down my cheek. It slips between my lips, and I savor its saltiness. *I'm still here.*

"Can you move your fingers and toes?" the woman asks.

I wiggle on command and smile in relief. The motor neurons in my spinal cord fired and successfully transmitted a message from my brain to my extremities. I rub my index finger against my thumb. I'm able to feel the scar, which is reassuring. Touch is the first of the five senses to develop in a human embryo, and it plays a crucial role in physical and mental health.

"How old are you?" The woman asks.

This answer comes more easily. "Sixteen."

"Perfect."

High praise, considering most two-year-olds can tell you their age.

The woman's chestnut-brown hair shines in the light. My brain can recognize colors, so the connection between my retinas and brain hasn't been damaged.

"Will you let my dad know I'm okay?" I ask, surprising myself. The final phase of the procedure—the most intrusive, since it involved the transfer of emotions—must have loosened the nails in the coffin where I normally bury my feelings about him.

The male scientist's frosty, gray eyes briefly meet mine, and it feels like the temperature dips five degrees. "We'll contact your father once you've merged."

His clipped English accent unleashes my memory. Cecil is his name, and I distinctly remember not liking him. But he's correct. I need to merge before anything else. A wave of nerves flutters through me. I take a deep breath. *I can do this. I can merge.* And once I do, my new life will unfold.

And so will hers.

I shut my eyes and search for some sense of Sophie Weiss. An awareness to let me know she's in there. A tingling sensation resulting from our compounded thoughts. Something that feels different. But there's nothing. The pings of my heart monitor betray me. I feel a touch on my shoulder and refocus on the woman's kind face. She's from Wisconsin. If I can remember that, why can't I recall her name?

"You feeling okay?" she asks.

I nod, even though my feelings are as chaotic as an unstable biochemical reactor.

"Why don't we let you sleep?"

Even though her tone is caring, she's not saying this just to speed my recovery. The dream state is where Sophie and I will work together. The loss of my own dreams is a small price to pay for what we'll accomplish.

They wheel me to a subterranean room that feels about as cozy as a gas station bathroom. The woman scientist assured me that once I'm a Nobel, they'll move me from this square, cinderblock cell to a lovely room with a window.

I squeeze my eyes shut and try to sleep. The electrodes stuck to my head don't exactly help. I tug a few strands of my long, auburn hair from the sticky adhesive, then begin listing the elements in the Periodic Table. My body slowly relaxes into the orderly world of chemistry, where everything reacts as it should.

Deborah. That's her name. The beaker-sized knot in my stomach loosens a little.

Eventually, I fall asleep. But I don't dream. The next night, it's the same. The Darwinians tell me not to worry. They explain that it may take a little time before my mind learns how to process Sophie's thoughts along with my own.

Despite their assurances, dreams continue to elude me.

5

Lake

I turn my head at the *click* of my door's lock releasing. I've been told this precaution won't be necessary once I've merged with Sophie—which still hasn't occurred.

"Take a walk with me," Deborah says.

She refuses to tell me if I'm the only Candidate who hasn't merged, but I must be. If there were others, Cecil wouldn't look at me the way he does each time I admit another night has passed dreamlessly. It briefly crossed my mind to lie, but I'd skew their results. I may be desperate, but I'm not a cheater. Or a saboteur. To me, the Scientific Method is as sacred as the Ten Commandments.

I set aside my book and leap to my feet. "Where are we going?"

"I'll explain when we get there."

About now, I'm up for cleaning toilets in a boy's locker room if it means escaping these four depressing walls.

Dr. Deborah Duvaney is my assigned Guardian during my awake-life. We've spent a great deal of time together this past week, trying to determine why I can't dream. Last night, she brought me a cup of warm milk with nutmeg. Since milk has tryptophan, an amino acid that induces sleep, I'd been hopeful. It was delicious, but it didn't work.

Deborah passes her crystal keycard in front of the reader to unlock my door. I follow her click-clacking heels down the white, unadorned hallway. This secret research facility used to be a school, and its opulent exterior hasn't been altered, but beyond the entryway they've eliminated every vestige of The Flemming Academy's old-world charm.

"Here we are," Deborah announces in front of a white door labelled *Sanctuary*.

It seems we're now trying meditation. Or prayer.

She steps aside, and I blink in surprise. The room appears vintage, making me feel as if I truly *am* a student in an elite boarding school in upstate New York. The ceiling is adorned with dark, wooden beams, and the fireplace's ornately carved marble mantle is stunning. One of the walls is lined with books that appear to have actually been read, and I yearn to revel in their titles. There's even a plaid, wool blanket draped across the back of a worn, leather couch, and a vase of real-looking, white roses on a coffee table

Deborah clears her throat. "We find a more relaxed setting tends to help in these situations."

My stomach clenches. *These situations? Am I being released from the Nobels Program?*

The room's ambiance transforms from tranquil to its true purpose: a place to console. When Grandma Bee was first diagnosed with Alzheimer's, the doctor delivered the news in a similar setting. As he explained that Grandma Bee was already in the middle stage of the disease, my dream of graduating high school early and taking the full-ride scholarship to Stanford University vanished.

While researching the horrors my grandma would experience in the late stage, my new reality took root. I vowed she wouldn't be displaced from the only home she's ever known. Dad wasn't there for Mom while she was sick; it was Grandma Bee who'd cared for her daughter-in-law. Now, it was up to me to be my grandma's caretaker.

I'm not complaining. I love her. I have to keep reminding myself that the disease is responsible for her personality changes. Still, caring for her was the most demanding thing I've ever done—and it's only going to get worse.

Deborah gestures to the couch.

I select the stiff-backed chair and trace my scar. The nine-year-old memory flickers to life. It was the first time my grandma trusted me with a sharp knife. In less than a minute, I slashed open my thumb, bloodying the carrots. Grandma Bee held my hand tightly while they stitched me up. I don't remember where Dad was, but he wasn't the one promising chocolate ice cream afterward.

"Lake, it's been more than a week, and—"

"I've been thinking about her soul," I say, before Deborah has a chance to do the deed.

She blinks a few times. "Excuse me?"

"Sophie's soul. What happened to it after her body and her consciousness were separated?" If Sophie exists in my mind, but I'm unable to merge with her, is she stuck between this world and the next?

"That's not something you should concern yourself with."

From Deborah's pained look, she wants me to drop it, but this could be the final time we ever interact. "I read about an experiment where a body was weighed before and after the person died. There was a twenty-one-gram difference, which was attributed to the soul leaving the body."

"This isn't approp—" she cuts off her own words with a frown. "Is this what you've been thinking about?"

"If there is a heaven, Sophie is going to need her soul."

Without empirical evidence, it's difficult for me to embrace the concept of heaven, but Grandma Bee has never questioned her belief that she'll be going to a better place. We stopped letting her drive after she got lost going to the church she'd attended her entire life. Dad promised to take her there after I left.

Dad promises a lot of things.

I wince when recalling all the times I'd believed him as a kid, like how he'd figure out a way to keep us from getting evicted from our house. Then there was the time he told me the kids at school wouldn't notice I only had one pair of shoes. And, the band will call any day now to ask him back. His favorite: none of the jobs he applied for were worthy of his talent.

Before I left, I asked Pastor Mayer to call Dad if Grandma Bee didn't show up for church. I know the nurse could bring her, but it means so much to her when she can show off her family. Dad owes her this. We'd have been homeless if Grandma Bee hadn't taken us in.

Deborah begins to pace across the richly-colored Oriental rug, halts abruptly, and faces me. "Lake, do you believe Sophie is already dead?"

Deborah told me Sophie selected me because I rated in the highest tier for tenacity—which I *think* is a compliment. That trait had never failed me. Until now.

"Please, Lake. I need you to answer truthfully."

My eyes drop to my chewed fingernails. "When I first woke from the procedure, I assumed Sophie made it, too. But now, after all this time … I'm no longer certain."

Deborah's forehead creases into an exclamation point. "I need a few minutes." She rushes out, and the lock clicks into place.

When the man in the gray-blue suit offered me this opportunity, it felt like my family had won the lottery. I'd just been awarded first place at The American Chemistry Club for the second year in a row, which is what probably put me on the Darwinians' radar. But if I don't merge, Dad will no longer receive their huge payment. That money allowed us to hire a full-time nurse to live with Grandma Bee, freeing me to come here and do miraculous things.

The ticking clock on the mantle marks each passing minute as my thoughts spiral into freefall. If I had merged, Grandma Bee would've been cared for by a professional with the skills needed to deal with late-stage dementia. If I had merged, Dad could've had another chance at making it in the music business. And, not unimportantly, if I had merged, Sophie would've had a second lifetime to discover how to end the ravages of Alzheimer's. Maybe, just maybe, in time to cure Grandma Bee.

Together, Sophie and I would've made life-expectancy tables obsolete.

Instead, I let everybody down.

The Darwinians

"Impossible!" the raven-haired man says. "Protocol requires that they remain isolated until they merge."

Deborah stands across the conference table from her three bosses. "Lake is spending too much time alone. That's why I want them to meet."

"This could easily backfire," the white-bearded man says. "The girl is questioning if Sophie is dead, while the boy already believes Bjorn has detached. We have to take extreme caution not to magnify any subconscious beliefs." He takes a moment to gaze upon one of the portraits. A woman with salt-and-pepper, curly hair. "It may not be possible for the subjects' minds to overcome such obstacles."

"They have names, you know," the woman rasps.

"It's prudent at this point not to foster emotional attachment."

"But what if they can help each other figure out how to merge?" Deborah asks.

"They're strangers," the bearded man says.

"Strangers who have something unprecedented in common."

The bearded man nods at the door. "Give us a minute please, Doctor."

"I believe they'll be less anxious if they realize they're not the only ones experiencing difficulties," Deborah says with determination.

They hold their discussion until her footsteps trail off.

The raven-haired man speaks up first. "It's quite concerning that Sophie hasn't appeared yet."

"Have you ever known her to give up on anything?" the bearded man asks. "One way or another, she'll break through."

"I'm starting to have my doubts."

"Don't be so insensitive," the woman says. "Sophie is more than a test subject."

"I apologize. I didn't mean to imply … I blame the girl."

"The girl?" the woman challenges. "After learning what we did from Sophie's autopsy, Lake's chance of success was—"

"We have to respect Sophie's decisions," the bearded man says. "She took her time finding this Candidate, and I have to believe they will merge. Need I remind you of what will happen to the girl if they don't?"

"We all understand the consequences of failure," the raven-haired man says.

The woman lifts a cloth handkerchief to her mouth and coughs. "Given the alternative, what harm is there if they meet once?"

"I concur. If there is any chance to save Sophie, we must allow it," the bearded man adds.

Lake

If I fail, who will take my place as the Nobel of Chemistry?

I was selected by the Darwinians to be one of the first six who shatter the fundamental belief that we only have one life. Each of us represents a Nobel Prize discipline: Chemistry, Physics, Physiology, Literature, Economics, and Peace. I've been so curious about the others in my inaugural class. Why did they choose to undergo the procedure? Which brilliant person was implanted into their brains? How are they going to change the world? They all must be impressive, but it's the Nobel for Peace who has me most intrigued. I've been picturing someone Gandhi-like. I'd planned to ask if they would teach me how to approach the world with more compassion.

My chest constricts and it becomes hard to breathe. If I get kicked out, the lost opportunities are unimaginable. Except, during my sleepless nights, that's all I've been imagining. And the losses aren't only mine. If we don't merge, Sophie loses her ability to experience aspects of a second life.

Deborah finally returns. "I want you to meet someone from the Program."

A Nobel? Then I recall the briefings. They said I wouldn't be fraternizing with Nobels until after Sophie and I merge. I suppose they don't want the washouts knowing the names of certain teenagers who suddenly display wisdom beyond their years.

A boy my age strides in with such an air of confidence, he must have already merged. He can tell me how he did it! Does this mean the Darwinians aren't giving up on me today? Hope tentatively emerges from its hiding place.

He nods a greeting when his near-black eyes land on me. I smile for the first time in a week.

He could be a movie star, or a model. Wavy, black hair; high cheekbones; and a dimpled, chiseled chin. He's basketball-player tall and wearing perfectly pressed, tan khakis and a perfectly pressed, blue Oxford shirt. I wouldn't be surprised if he went to one of those prep schools where the tuition costs more than Grandma Bee's house.

"Stryker, this is Lake," Deborah says. "We thought it would be helpful if our Candidates got to know each other."

Candidate? *Then he can't tell me what I'm doing wrong.* My renewed dream shatters like cold titanium.

Stryker's demeanor transforms from magnetic to haughty, and he looks at me as if I'm a foul-smelling beggar blocking the path to his Audi. "I came here to meet a *Nobel.*"

"I'm sure you two have a lot to talk about," Deborah says with a tight smile.

"This is a waste of time," Stryker says, turning his back on me.

"I'll return in an hour," Deborah announces.

An hour? With him? He's treating me like we're two protons, forever repelled by each other. And I haven't even uttered a word.

Stryker says, "Don't forget to lock the door." He heads to the bookcase and proceeds to ignore me.

Deborah's smile wavers, but she has no qualms about leaving us alone.

Two can play this game. I amble over to the other end of the bookcase, pull out the thickest book within reach, sit cross-legged on the couch, and draw the throw over my lap, as if settling in for a tranquil rainy afternoon. The only thing missing is a steaming mug of mint tea.

I see that I've chosen *Ulysses*, a book I've been meaning to read. I turn to the first page, and under hooded eyes watch Stryker circling the room while examining the ceiling. Apparently, he finds plaster more intriguing than me. Why do I care? I push down my irritation, lick the tip of my finger, and turn the unread page.

"So, it's Kate?" asks the most acrimonious guy I've ever met.

If he's a Nobel Candidate, his IQ is well into genius level. Yet he can't remember my name? "Lake. What's yours again?"

I think I see a flicker of admiration in his eyes. "Stryker."

He strolls the room, like he's perusing beach chairs, before choosing an uncomfortable, wooden chair over the option of sitting next to me. I have showered today. I even brushed my teeth.

"Have you completed the procedure?" He asks in a bored tone, as if our futures didn't hang on this monumental accomplishment.

I'd rather smell butyric acid than admit to him that I'm about to get kicked out of the Nobels Program. But this might be my only chance to compare experiences with another Candidate. Why else would Deborah bring us together?

Grandma Bee taught me the best way to deal with someone unpleasant is to kill them with kindness. "My final phase was a week ago," I answer, pleasantly.

"Aaah, hence the meeting."

Hence? Who talks like that? I force a smile. "Have you finished the final phase yet?"

Stryker examines his large, well-groomed hands as if he'd never noticed them before. "That's what they tell me."

It was a simple polar question. His apathetic response doesn't ring true. Could there be *two* of us who can't merge? "How long have you been trying to connect with your Mentor?" I test.

"A few weeks, maybe longer." His gaze flits around the room.

"Who can keep track when you're in lockdown?"

So I'm not the only one.

This news should make me feel better about my own failed attempts, except another significant mind might be lost. I take in the dark bags hanging from Stryker's eyes. If he wants this half as much as I do, then he has to be demoralized, too.

"I haven't been able to merge, either," I admit. "What if we work together to find the solution?" When he doesn't respond, I add, "Studies have confirmed that combined knowledge maximizes performance, but only when the participants are equally competent, and can discuss their disagreements."

He looks like he's contemplating it, until he shakes his head. Is the problem that he's not good with criticism, or that he doesn't consider me his equal?

"What's the alternative?" I snap. "Leave because you're too proud to admit you need help?"

Stryker looks into my eyes and I expect to see anger, but it's something else entirely. Fear?

He strides over to the door and starts pounding.

The last vestiges of hope vanish. And, he's not even willing to discuss it.

A guard opens the door. Deborah has asked me to stop calling the men dressed in black *guards*—despite the fact they resemble henchmen from a James Bond movie. She explained the Not-Guards are here for my protection.

"We want to take a walk outside," Stryker informs the man whose neck is thicker than my thigh.

News to me.

Lake

"We're not prisoners," Stryker counters after Not-A-Guard refuses to let us pass.

"I have my orders." He stands straighter, but he's only eye-level with Stryker's Adam's apple.

"I want to discuss this with the person who gave those orders." Stryker takes a step closer to the human barricade, and the room's barometric pressure plunges so quickly I brace myself for a migraine.

"Back off," Not-A-Guard says, an octave lower. "Now."

Stryker stands firm.

Deborah shows up then, breaking up the testosterone-fueled tension. I begin to breathe again. I can handle the sight of blood, but violence goes well beyond acceptable limits of reactants.

"Our protocol requires Nobel Candidates to remain within the complex," she says.

"Why is that again?" Stryker asks.

Deborah lets out a long sigh. "You agreed to these terms. Once you're a Nobel, you'll have free rein."

"You obviously brought us here because you hope we can help each other become Nobels." Stryker looks at me and raises one eyebrow. *An olive branch?* "Give us some space to build trust." He sounds so sincere, it's disconcerting that he was just acting as if he'd rather have direct contact with the Ebola virus than collaborate with me.

"It's raining," Deborah says.

Stryker turns to me and asks, "You don't mind a little weather, do you?"

"It would feel great to be outside," I admit. I haven't seen the sky in weeks, and I am curious to learn what Stryker is up to.

"Deb, we won't go far." Stryker flashes her a radiant smile, transforming his face into someone who appears almost likeable. "I'm sure you can find us a couple of umbrellas."

"All right," she finally agrees. "But someone needs to accompany you."

What does she think we'll do, escape? The only way I'm leaving here is with ripped fingernails after being pried from the door jamb.

Deborah unlocks the door and tells Not-A-Guard, "Find some umbrellas."

He returns with them in a surprisingly short amount of time. They've done an admirable job of anticipating our every need.

"Come on, Lake," Stryker commands, like I'm his faithful dog. At least he got my name right this time.

"Go with them," Deborah directs to the human tank.

I follow Stryker down the hallway and have to practically jog to keep up with his long strides. We enter an elevator and ascend in a silence so absolute it feels like we're in a vacuum. The doors slide open to a wall of windows, and I balk. A storm chaser would think twice before going out there.

"Don't tell me you're worried about your hair," Stryker says, dryly.

Why does the one person who may possess the knowledge I require have to be *him*? I mentally count to ten. "Let's do it."

After Not-A-Guard flashes his crystal keycard in front of the reader, Stryker pushes the exit door open. Within seconds, he's so far ahead, I can barely see him through the deluge.

"I thought we came out here to brainstorm," I yell.

He lopes back to me. "Sorry. I was going to lose it if I didn't get out of there."

I didn't expect an apology out of him.

He glances at our escort, who is standing within earshot, without an umbrella, as if trying to prove his heartiness to Stryker. "Let's go talk under that tree."

We dash to a towering oak. The umbrella did little to prevent me from getting saturated, but the dense canopy is at least sheltering us from the wind gusts. The humidity has transformed Stryker's hair into a helmet of ringlets. I'm sure mine looks like I'm touching a Van de Graaff generator.

"So, have you experienced any post-procedure dreams?" I ask.

"I need to frisk you for a wire first," Stryker says.

I step back. "Excuse me?"

"You're right, that might be awkward. Can you lift up your shirt enough so I can see your entire waist?"

"No!" I look over at our escort, and thankfully he's still not-guarding me.

Stryker slowly scans me from the crown of my head to my purple-painted toes. "It's probably not necessary. I doubt a wire would still function after getting as soaked as you are."

"Why would you think I'm wearing a wire?" I hold up my hands to ward off his answer. "Never mind. This is not worth it. I'll figure out how to merge by myself." I turn to leave.

"You do realize they were listening to us in the Sanctuary," Stryker says to my back.

My inquisitive nature gets the best of me. "What are you saying?"

"I didn't see any evidence of a bug in the ceiling. My guess is it's either in a light fixture or an electrical outlet."

Goosebumps sprout along my arms. "Did someone tell you we were being bugged?"

"No, but it's obvious. Deb showed up far too quickly."

"Or, she was walking by and heard you playing chicken with our friend over there."

Stryker looks at me as if I'd just told him matter is composed of air, water, earth, and fire. "Assume everything we say is being monitored."

I finally understand what Not-A-Guard could be protecting me from: the Nobel Candidate who outwardly looks like da Vinci's "David" but inwardly may be a conspiracy theorist. Which Nobel field requires paradoxical criterion like that?

"What's your discipline?" I ask.

"Peace."

My laugh catches in my throat when he doesn't smile. "You're joking, right?"

"Why is that so hard to believe?" His words leave ice crystals in the air. Either my perception of Gandhi is flawed, or I've been completely misjudging Stryker.

He looks away, but not before I see his face. I think I hurt his feelings, which only adds to my bewilderment. "I didn't mean to imply you wouldn't make a great Nobel for Peace," I say, even though that's exactly what I'm questioning.

"It doesn't matter anymore." He glances over my shoulder. "We need to get out of here."

"All indications point to our getting kicked out of the Program, so you'll soon get your wish."

"You don't understand," he says in an ominous whisper.

I cross my arms, then uncross them when I realize I might appear close-minded. "Then explain it to me."

"They're not going to let us walk away and return to our old lives."

A chill runs down my spine. "The documents clearly stated—"

"Think about it. They're conducting an experiment that involves ending the lives of some of the world's most influential people. They can't risk any loose ends."

"Stryker, *they're* the ones who created a cover story as a precaution if the transfer didn't work." Mine was that I'd been on a cruise with my aunt, and there was sketchy cell phone coverage, which was why none of my friends could reach me. I hoped to never need to use it.

"They had to create scenarios like that, so we'd agree to come here," he says.

"Our parents will call the police if they never hear from us again." *Dad would at least do that, wouldn't he?*

Stryker counts off on his fingers. "First, our parents signed Non-Disclosure Agreements with serious consequences for breaking them. Second, they don't know where we are. And third, you have no idea what they've been telling your parents since you got here."

Parent. Singular.

"And it's not only our parents they have to worry about," he continues. "Do you honestly think you could keep a secret this big to yourself? Even if you have the best of intentions, the odds are against them that something about this place is going to slip out at some point. They can't take that chance."

"You're forgetting, if we can't merge, they'll expunge our memories from the time we arrived."

"I'm not allowing them to electroshock my brain."

"That's old school. There are several drugs already created to overcome addiction by eliminating memories that occurred while on a stimulant, like meth. These drugs disrupt non-muscle myosin IIB, thus interrupting the unstable actin and erasing the memory of the high. It wouldn't take a huge leap to elevate that work and eliminate longer periods of time."

He looks at me with what might be an ounce of respect. "I take it you're the Nobel Candidate for Chemistry."

"And that's why I'm not leaving. I need to eliminate the word *Candidate.*"

"You'd better hope you do it before they *eliminate* you altogether."

The Darwinians want to preserve knowledge that would

otherwise be lost when someone dies. They're visionaries, not killers. Stryker has obviously spent too much time alone with his over-active imagination. A missing puzzle piece snaps into place.

"Stryker, are you willing to agree that there's no need to flee if you merge?"

"Sure, but—"

"I have a theory."

"Yeah, they screwed up when they implanted Bjorn into my brain."

"That's the issue. You no longer think Bjorn is viable. And you helped me understand that I've been doing the same. I've been so consumed with the state of Sophie's afterlife, I unintentionally dismissed the possibility that her consciousness is still alive."

"So, what are you suggesting?"

"I'm postulating that the solution to merging is to believe we still can."

Orfyn

Two days after *Take This Cup* and Rosa disappeared, I'm summoned to Sister Mo's office.

It's more crowded than I've ever seen it. The Bishop—*the Bishop!*—has commandeered her well-organized desk. I've endured more than one lengthy lecture from where he's seated. Father Burke, looking quite shoved aside, hovers behind him. Taking up the chairs against the wall are two men wearing stern expressions and even sterner suits. Not going-to-church suits. Power suits. One is in a charcoal hue, and the other is the color of cold, blue slate, like gathering storm clouds. The man in charcoal ruffles through his briefcase, and the other scrutinizes me as I stand in the doorway.

Sister Mo is in a chair normally reserved for us kids. The mismatched chair next to her waits expectantly.

A nun and an orphan in a room packed with men in suits and clerical collars. My heart starts racing.

Sister Mo stands as I enter, and when she does, the others jump to their feet. Even the Bishop. I know it's her way of exercising control. *Get your respect, you,* she always says.

"Please, make yourself comfortable, Kevin." The Bishop waves majestically toward the empty chair. It's startling to hear him say my name, and it's probably not a good thing that he knows it.

Only after Sister Mo lowers her imposing, six-foot-tall frame do I sit as directed, but I am far from feeling *comfortable*.

The Bishop clears his throat. "As I was saying, Sister, this is good news. A blessed success."

"We have procedures, Your Excellency." Sister Mo's tone is respectful, but it's clear she's not about to do whatever it is he wants her to do. Unwavering. "There is not even an application."

Application?

"We're approaching this particular case more pragmatically," the Bishop says.

"There are laws to protect a child. Don't you agree?" Her eyes shoot to Father Burke.

He becomes fascinated by a picture hanging on the wall. I painted it for Sister Mo when I was eight. He's seen that amateurish depiction of a Jamaican beach a hundred times, but it's as if he's stumbled into the Sistine Chapel, and no way and no how can he take his eyes off the ceiling.

The Bishop gestures to the man in charcoal. "Our attorney assures us this is legal, ethical, and without exposure."

The lawyer clears his throat and holds up a document. "Yes, Sister. Everything has been followed to the letter of the law."

The man in the gray-blue suit—the color of dusk and danger— says nothing. Does nothing. He's the only person I don't think anyone has looked at or spoken to. One thing for sure, he's no social worker.

What's going on?

Father Burke clears his throat. "The church encourages every adoption."

The Bishop nods sagely, as if Father Burke's words were scripture. "This is a gift from God." And then his eyes land on me.

Someone wants to adopt *me*? I'd given up on that hope years ago. All of us here at St. Catherine's have. We're the ones who failed to interest potential parents when we still had a chance as sweet-smelling babies.

Sister Mo rises and confronts the man in the gray-blue suit. "Finding the right home is essential." Her eyes bore into him. "I'm sure you can appreciate that."

My head is spinning. *Parents? A house? Maybe even a dog?*

"You need to gain his trust." Sister Mo's eyes grab hold of him. "And that takes time."

They remind me of two street dogs sparring to see which looks away first.

"Is *he* going to be my parent?" I ask.

"Oh, no, Kevin," the Bishop explains. "This gentleman only represents the adopting party."

Why is the Bishop even here? I can't believe he has the time to get involved in every adoption. Something is off—like, a painting-being-sandblasted-from-an-alley-wall off. Blues and yellows and reds wash over me. Confusing and exciting and scary, as if I'm about to meet the ghost of Rubens or something.

The Bishop steeples his fingers. "Sister, this boy has a chance for a real future. You're certainly not going to stand in his way." It isn't a question.

"We appreciate your diligence, Sister," the man in gray-blue adds. "But this meeting is merely a courtesy. The adoption has already been finalized." As easy as breathing, he reaches into his jacket, slides out an envelope from an inside pocket, and hands it to Sister Mo.

She makes no motion to accept it. "What is this?" All certainty has faded from her voice.

"A *court order.*"

"I've reviewed the document. It's all in order," the church's lawyer states.

"Who will be the mother? Who will be the father?" Sister Mo asks as her eyes challenge each one of them.

The lawyer leans forward. "I don't think that's the correct way to look at—"

"I don't see the harm," the man in gray-blue says. "The boy has been adopted," he extends his right palm, "by the Darwin Corporation."

"A corporation! That is … that is … inhuman!" Sister Mo sputters.

The man in gray-blue calmly answers, "The Darwin Corporation can provide Kevin with a wonderful home and amazing opportunities he would not otherwise have." His eyes hold less sincerity than someone selling sunglasses on the street—less sincerity than the word *corporation*.

Sister Mo's face fills with hurt. A revulsion to the thousands of wrongs done every day by men wearing suits and robes. This is not a typical adoption.

"Why me?" I ask.

"The Darwin Corporation's mission is to further young people's talents," answers the man in gray-blue. "You will be part of a very special mentoring program for the Arts."

I suddenly get the feeling he knows a lot more about my life than he should.

Father Burke adds, "Did we mention there will be a very generous honorarium, much of which will go to support St. Catherine's?"

Sister Mo's face takes on an ashen hue. "We do not *sell* our children."

The Bishop's eyes narrow. "You misunderstand, Sister. The Darwin Corporation is simply making a donation. It would be wise not to read anything more into it."

The lawyer speaks up. "Sister, it is important for you to understand that the Diocese and all its associates are bound by a Non-Disclosure Agreement. If you speak of this adoption to anyone, there will be serious repercussions for you and for the orphanage."

"Has anyone asked Kevin what *he* wants?" Sister Mo asks, finally looking in my direction.

Okay, I won't get parents, or a dog, but they're offering me a mentoring program. I'm being given the chance to evolve into a true artist, one whose work will last longer than a mayfly. I never dreamed that someone like me could ever have my paintings hanging in a gallery. But it could happen for real if I were mentored.

I want this chance.

And if the man in gray-blue had anything to do with erasing *Take This Cup*, then maybe he did it to save me from facing the consequences of my own stupidity. It really could be a coincidence that Rosa and her mom moved out that very same morning.

I study Sister Mo's eyes. The eyes always ready for battle. The eyes that make every one of us feel loved. The eyes that look more tired than I've ever seen them.

I put my hand on her arm. "It's all right, Sister. I want to do this."

"You will regret this." She glowers at the man in the gray-blue suit, but I have no doubt who she's really talking to.

The man in gray-blue stands and buttons his jacket. "Not likely, Sister."

Orfyn

"I'll visit soon," I tell Sister Mo as I'm escorted out of St. Catherine's by the man in gray-blue. "I promise."

"Don't make promises you can't keep, you." I almost don't survive her hug. She has the strength of God. She shuts the door, but not before I catch her wiping her eyes.

Unease ripples through me. I remind myself why I'm doing this, pull back my shoulders, and follow him to his car. If I don't like it there, I can always bolt.

He drives in silence, rhythmically tapping his fingers on the steering wheel to some song in his head. What kind of music sticks in the mind of a person like him? I decide on "Here Comes the Sun" by The Beatles, which cracks me up.

"I don't know your name," I say, turning in my seat to face him.

"It's unpronounceable."

"Then I'll call you Mr. Blue."

He almost smirks. "Sure, why not?"

I'd never been out of the City before. The tallest buildings in sight are silos. We pass endless rows of all shades of green and fields dotted with huge, black cows—real cows! Then woods with more trees than I've ever seen. There's no concrete anywhere. Even the sky is the wrong color. Robin's egg blue instead of grime gray.

After a few hours, we turn onto an unmarked road. We drive for a mile or two past freshly mowed grass and pull up to a massive, three-story, brick building that's being devoured by a tangle of ivy.

This can't be my new home.

"We're here," Mr. Blue says.

It looks a hundred years old, and it's surrounded by rolling hills and gardens. I've been to Central Park—every chance I get—but my new home feels like I'm in an English landscape. I can't wait to lie on the Kelly-green grass and breathe it in.

I get out of the car and can't stop gawking. It's got to be ten times bigger than St. Catherine's. Etched over the door is *The Flemming Academy* in fancy script so weathered, only the first few letters stand out. I don't know what I did to deserve this, but my guardian angel must've been working overtime.

I hear a familiar sound and turn to see a tall guy shooting hoops by himself while a buff man in a black uniform watches. This is getting better and better. I thought I'd be the only one here my age.

"Welcome to your new home, The Flem," Mr. Blue says.

"That's the name of this place?"

Mr. Blue's lips twitch. "It's what the kids call it."

There are more of us?

When we enter my new, super amazing home—The Flem—I'm greeted by wood-paneled walls, a black-and-white checkered marble floor, and a crystal chandelier overhead. There's a real suit of armor standing guard in the corner!

No such thing as a free lunch, you, I hear in my head in a Jamaican accent.

It's not free. I had to leave everyone and everything I know to be here. A ripple of unease rolls through me, which I shrug off. Sometimes good things *do* happen to good people. And I am a good person. When you're raised by Sister Mo, there is no alternative.

"Kevin, I'll bring you to your temporary room." Mr. Blue heads toward the wooden doors on the far wall.

What's on the other side, an indoor pool with a water slide?

He pulls out a clear keycard from his inside jacket pocket and swipes it in front of a small, black panel. The door slides into the wall.

I pass through the opening filled with anticipation, then my feet freeze in place. I'm faced with a long, white hallway lined with closed, white doors under a brightly-lit, white ceiling. It even smells like a hospital. Sweat pours from my pits, and my tongue suddenly gets stuck to the roof of my mouth.

Mr. Blue heads to an elevator leading to who-knows-where. He turns. "You need to come with me, Kevin."

"I don't think so."

"I know this may be a little overwhelming, but it will all be explained soon."

I look back at the front doors, picturing the hours of nature we drove past. I could run, but to where?

"We're in the middle of nowhere," Mr. Blue says, as if reading my mind. "Come with me. There's nothing to fear."

My pounding heart disagrees. I hear Sister Mo's voice in my head, reciting, *Yea, though I walk through the Valley of Death, I shall fear no evil, for the power of My Lord will eviscerate any demon, duppy, or dirtbag in this beautiful world.*

I reluctantly follow Mr. Blue into the elevator. He pushes the button with *-1* on it. The floor drops beneath my feet. We're going down. Down. My stomach plunges faster than the elevator.

"The laboratories and Candidates' quarters are on the lower level," he explains, as if it were all perfectly normal.

Laboratories? I study Mr. Blue out of the corner of my eye, suddenly wondering if he actually represents an underground organ-harvesting operation.

"Kevin, I know this may not be what you were expecting,

but we only have your best interest in mind. We're giving you the opportunity to enhance your life."

"Who's 'we'?"

"We're the good guys."

The elevator doors open, and we enter another long, white hallway. After we take a right and a left, Mr. Blue halts to unlock a door with the wave of his keycard.

"This is your room. For now."

The white room contains a single bed covered with a white blanket, black side table, black desk, and a matching black chair. Through a doorway, there's a white, tiled bathroom. I don't even know what it feels like not to share a toilet with eight other guys.

Mr. Blue eyes me. "It's been a long day. Get some rest. I'll come back in the morning." He points to a phone on the desk. "If you want anything, someone will take care of it. Anything at all." As he's shutting the door, he stops and turns. "You're going to like what I have to offer. Trust me."

When the door clicks shut, I try the handle and find it locked. No one knows where I am. I have two choices: I can freak myself out by imagining all the horrible things that might happen to me, or I can chill until morning.

Morning feels like a long way away.

I get bored within minutes. I pick up the phone and test what Mr. Blue told me about "anything at all." I ask for a dozen tubes of oil paint and different sized brushes. The guy tells me he's on it, even though there can't be an art supply store within fifty miles. So maybe Mr. Blue was being truthful about my getting mentored. My nerves rev down a notch, and my stomach grumbles. I call back and add a hamburger, fries, two Cokes, and a package of Oreos. It arrives fast. Even the Oreos. I take it as a good sign.

After wolfing down the food and way too many cookies—because I don't have to share—I grab my brushes and get to work. I paint cherubs on the wall over my bed, just in case the guy who said "Trust

41

me" can't be trusted. Then I dive into a seriously intimidating portrait of Saint Moses the Black, the saint Sister Mo named herself after. Stern and not-to-be-messed-with. He strides out of the painting, seething with attitude. Mr. Cool of the Fourth Century. And in the background, I paint the same stormy-blue sky and Kelly-green landscape that lies a floor above me.

After four or six hours—I have no sense of time when I'm painting—I lay on the bed, absorbing the colors and motion and story. It should take away the breath of everyone who enters, but the somber eyes of Saint Moses the Black make me miss Sister Mo. I picture her saying a prayer for me tonight—because I have no doubt she will—and then I say one of my own. It takes forever before I fall asleep.

The next morning, within minutes of finishing the stack of blueberry pancakes and bacon I'd ordered, Mr. Blue knocks and enters my room. He's wearing the same suit from yesterday, or one that looks exactly like it. Does he have one for every day of the week?

Mr. Blue lowers himself into the chair and places a thick, manila folder on his lap. I wait for him to comment on my evening's work, but he gives no indication of noticing the life-size black dude on the wall across from him.

I don't trust people who aren't moved by art.

"We have something unprecedented to propose to you."

"Okay," I say, wondering for the hundredth time how I got myself into this position.

"You're an exceptional painter, and you may even become a groundbreaking artist in ten or twenty years. But we can begin to make that happen in a week's time."

"How?"

"If you agree to our terms, you will transcend decades of study and practice." Mr. Blue hands me a stack of papers half-an-inch thick. "Take as much time as you need."

I flip through it and try to make sense of the legalese. I give up and set it aside. "Can you give me the highlights?"

"Certainly. We are an organization created to advance human accomplishment in a most dramatic way." His eyes catch the light, and they remind me of ice. "We have the ability to merge the consciousness of an exceptional Mentor with that of a very special sixteen-year-old."

"You mean, in here?" I point to my head.

He nods with the seriousness of a judge.

"I'm already using my brain," I say.

"Although we've debunked the myth that humans only use ten percent of their cerebral capacity, you've got the bandwidth. Trust me." He leans forward as if about to tell a secret. "What if I revealed that computer technology is advancing far faster than humans are evolving? Art will soon be produced by artificially intelligent machines—AI. They're already learning to mass reproduce art, music, and literature that is pleasing to humans based on trends in music downloads, social media postings, and online purchases. You're our chance to create a revolutionary artist who can maintain the humanity in our art."

"A computer doesn't have emotions. When I paint, I try to make people feel something."

Mr. Blue smirks. "But the problem is, nothing you paint lasts, Kevin. Or should I call you *Orfyn?*"

My skin crawls. *How long have they been watching me?*

"The Mentor we chose for you has one of the greatest creative minds of this generation."

"What's his name?" I ask.

"He's known as Bat."

It's a cool street name, though I doubt he ever needed to hide out in alleys to paint.

Mr. Blue points to the document. "Sign this and change your life. Or don't. It's up to you."

43

"What happens if I say no?"

"The Darwin Corporation will remain your legal guardian, but you'll lose the once-in-a-lifetime opportunity to become one of humanity's greatest hopes."

So basically, he's saying I'm stuck here either way. "Will I always be locked up?"

"That depends on your choices."

I wait for him to crack a smile. He doesn't.

I break eye contact and flip to the last page. There's one short paragraph stating that I've read the forty-one-page document (which I haven't), I understand the risks (which I don't), and I buy into the idea that two minds are better than one (or something like that). At the bottom, there's a line with my name printed below it.

"Is it dangerous?" I ask, really wishing my voice hadn't cracked.

Mr. Blue hesitates, and for a moment he almost appears human. "Every medical procedure has its risks, but the end result could change the world. And you'll be one of the few who have the ability to change it."

What if I could become the next Michelangelo? I've been given the chance to create art that makes a difference. For now, and even hundreds of years to come. "What else can you tell me about Bat?"

"He's very successful," Mr. Blue says, taking a pen from his suit pocket. "And he's dying."

"Can you give me a little more than that?"

"He specifically chose you."

Nobody has ever chosen *me*.

I grab Mr. Blue's pen and sign the document using the name I'm adopting. If I'm going to share my brain with someone and become a ground-breaking artist, I'm doing it as *Orfyn*.

Mr. Blue glances at my painting as he gets up. "Fourth century. The thief who changed the world." Then he looks back at me. "We'll begin the first phase in the morning." He smiles. Real and sincere. "You won't regret this. I promise."

The Darwinians

"I always knew Stryker would give us trouble," the woman says, shaking her head.

"His natural talents are too extraordinary to have passed him over," the raven-haired man answers. "As well as his *unique* background."

"You do realize what can happen if he isn't found?" the woman asks.

"I'm confident he's hiding within the complex."

"Stop posturing. You don't know that." The woman hungrily sucks on an inhaler. "If he escapes, the future of the Nobels Program is in jeopardy."

"Then, everyone better start praying Bjorn really is dead," the bearded man says.

"Aren't you an atheist?"

"You know what they say about desperate times."

"I'll make sure that kid doesn't have the opportunity to betray us," the raven-haired man says.

"Instruct them to keep searching," the bearded man orders. "In the meantime, we need to keep focusing on the Nobel of Chemistry. We can't let Sophie down."

Lake

"You're not supposed to be here until tomorrow," says the woman who answers my knock. She crosses her arms, making her canary-yellow suit's shoulder pads even more pronounced.

She looks to be in her late thirties. Sophie is—was—sixty-three, but Deborah explained that most Mentors choose to appear younger in the dreamspace.

"Sophie?" I confirm.

"I prefer that you call me Dr. Weiss." The bite in her tone is anything but welcoming. "Oh, well. What's done is done. Come on in." The wisp of smoke from her cigarette follows her like a chemtrail. No-smoking rules must not apply in her dream world.

"I'm sorry," I say. "I wasn't informed we were scheduled to meet on a specific day."

I've been conceptualizing our first meeting since I was accepted, placing Sophie in the role of a pseudo-grandmother. She'll patiently teach me everything she knows, and I'll patiently listen to her stories and keep her company, similar to my relationship with Grandma Bee. Not only have I somehow gotten off on the wrong foot, I need to reconsider our rapport. Sophie is closer to the age my mom would be today, if she were alive.

I blink away tears and search the room for a tissue. Is that a *typewriter* on the desk? Of course. According to Deborah, the Mentor is the one who creates our dreamspace, and they often select a favorite era. Given Sophie's—I mean, Dr. Weiss's—huge shoulder pads, bright make-up, and big hair, she's placed us in the 1980s. I then notice the lab equipment's knobs, dials, and rotary counters. Technology has significantly evolved since the eighties. Will we be able to accomplish what we need to with this antiquated equipment?

Sophie purses her fire-engine-red lips. "Someone needs to do something about the Placement Office."

The Darwinians didn't employ a placement office to recruit me. But more importantly, why isn't Sophie acting thrilled? The procedure was a success! I'm having a conversation with someone who physically died last week. Her terminal illness did not end her critical work. With her guidance, it will continue through me. Understandably, this experience is more than a little overwhelming. I'll overlook her odd reaction—because that's what colleagues who will be sharing a brain for the rest of their lives do.

I earnestly say, "I am honored to be your research partner for life."

"No need to be sarcastic. Working for me may feel like an eternity, but rest assured, your internship will only last four months."

What is she talking about?

Sophie stubs out her cigarette in an ashtray filled with lipstick-stained butts. She heads over to a counter with a black, laminate surface and shakes her head at the thirty-six petri dishes lined up in perfect rows of six. "First, I discover the post-mortem brain tissue samples didn't react to the octopus enzyme as I'd expected, and now I learn the University isn't managing our lab assistants as they should. It's enough to make me go back to teaching."

My scalp starts tingling. "Sophie—I mean, Dr. Weiss, don't you know who I am?"

She waves her hand dismissively. "They run so many of you through here, it's hard to keep track of all your names."

How can she not recognize me? Even though I've never met her, I'm quite aware she was behind the one-way glass during those grueling interviews. Maybe I appear different in the dreamspace, too. I look around but don't see anything reflective to confirm or deny my theory. "I'm Lake Summers."

I wait for the *aha* moment. Once she realizes her gaffe, I'll assure her it's an honest mistake. After all, the woman doesn't have a body anymore. Who wouldn't be out of sorts at first? I give her my best I'm-glad-you-chose-me smile as she scrutinizes my face. There's not a flicker of recognition.

"I hope you won't let writing your thesis interfere with your work here." Sophie returns her attention to the petri dishes, looking as displeased with them as she's been with me.

My stomach feels like I'm barreling down a rollercoaster. Except it's not thrill-seeking fear running through me; it's pure terror. She doesn't remember who I am.

"Dr. Weiss, I'm your—"

I'm wrenched from my dream by someone shaking me, and not gently. I take in the body towering over me—too massive to be Deborah's. The crack of light shining from under the door masks my intruder in shadow. Endorphins flush my brain and adrenaline flows to my heart. Within seconds, my heart rate is at its upper threshold.

A huge hand clamps over my mouth before I can scream. I violently shake my head, but he holds tight. There's a *click*, and the harsh light distorts his face's contours. Stryker's near-black eyes laser into mine, and my panic multiplies when he doesn't remove his hand. He leans in closer, and his breath rustles my hair.

"Don't scream," he whispers. He lifts his eyebrows questioningly.

I nod, at the ready to yell for help.

He studies me while lessening the pressure. "Please."

I hold still and try to appear docile. The second he releases me, I roll to the other side of the bed and scramble to my feet. "That was totally inappropriate. Leave! Now!"

He puts his finger to his lips and jerks his head toward the bathroom. It's the middle of the night, and after what he just pulled, he needs to have his cranium examined if he thinks I'm going in there with him. When I don't comply, he strides over with a determined look, and I back away until my shoulder blades dig into the wall.

He leans down, hovering his lips over my ear. "I'm sorry I scared you, but they can't know I'm here. I really need to talk to you. I've checked, and there are no bugs in the bathrooms."

He's not exactly building his case for me to trap myself in a tiny, windowless room with him. "You're delusional."

"Shhhhh!" He holds up his index finger, then heads to the other side of my room. He reaches up, removes the cover from the smoke detector, and points to a silver disc the size of a penny. From what I've seen in the movies, it appears to be exactly what I didn't expect to find in my room: a bug. My insides twist tight. Stryker has been, implausibly, correct.

I can comprehend needing precautionary measures for situations like a medical emergency, but why wouldn't Deborah have informed me?

Stryker gestures to the bathroom.

I warily follow him, and he closes the door behind us. I grab my hairbrush and hold it with the bristles out.

He eyes it. "Jeez, Lake. I'm not going to hurt you."

I cross my arms, primarily to cover up the fact that I'm not wearing a bra. "What do you want?"

"I'm breaking us out tonight."

"This isn't a jail." Then something occurs to me. "How did you get past your locked door?"

He points to the gaping hole in the ceiling. "Air ducts. Lake, I'm trying to save your life here." He entwines his fingers and cups his hands by my right knee. "I'll give you a boost."

Learning that I'm being bugged is unnerving, but accepting Stryker's story that they will literally kill me if I fail is simply insane. "Everything you believe about the Darwinians is speculative. I'm not going anywhere."

"I found proof while snooping around in one of the labs." He runs his fingers through his hair. "There was a stack of files on the desk, and they were all numbered. The one labeled *Candidate #23* is yours. My file is *Candidate #18*."

"So, there were others before us. Not everyone has the ability to merge."

"The last entry for Candidate #22 said she was *terminated*." He holds my eyes.

"Which would be the end result if she couldn't merge. They erased her memories about her time here, and she returned home to resume her life."

"Keep believing that if it makes you feel better, but I'm not sticking around to find out which of us is right. For your sake, I hope you figure out how to merge before it's too late."

I'd been so distracted with Stryker's unorthodox appearance, I haven't acknowledged my accomplishment. "I did it! I merged tonight. I was interacting with Sophie when you woke me." Not the time to get into how she mistook me for her new lab assistant. It was our first time, *and* Stryker interrupted us.

He doesn't quite meet my eyes. "Great. I hope it all works out for you. And here's a piece of advice: don't tell them you know about the bugs." He reaches for the bathroom's doorknob.

"Wait!" I grab his wrist. "Sophie wasn't expecting me until tomorrow. It could be the same with your Mentor. He's not connecting with you because it hasn't been the designated time."

"I've been trying to merge with Bjorn for nineteen nights. I think it's safe to say he's not showing."

"If I can do this, so can you."

Stryker looks like he's considering it, until his face fills with disdain. "I don't need your pedestrian motivational speeches."

It's his reaction that confirms my suspicion. He's not angry at me; he's angry at himself. He's probably never failed at anything, and he's using his unfounded fear to justify his decision to give up.

"Before you go, answer this. Are you certain Bjorn is dead?"

He doesn't say anything, but he also doesn't leave.

"You need to stop focusing the blame on the Darwinians and start believing Bjorn's consciousness has been successfully transferred."

"I tried. It didn't work." He shrugs as if the problem is out of his hands, but his eyes betray him. He wants this so badly.

"Trying isn't good enough. You have to *believe*." I reach up and place my hands on his shoulders. "You. Can. Do. This. And yes, that is a motivational speech, because you need to hear it."

His eyes meet mine. "If I don't merge tonight, I'm bolting."

"Fair enough." I self-consciously let go of his very broad shoulders.

It's not until after he hoists himself into the air duct that a twinge of doubt appears. I am correct about being allowed to return home, aren't I?

Orfyn

So I've agreed to merge with this great artist, and with his experience and my raw talent, we'll hold back the digital onslaught. I still find it hard to believe that a *machine* could ever create meaningful art. But I have the chance to merge with the artist who'll mentor me so I can become someone who makes a difference. Someone respected.

But I'm going bonkers.

They want me to have as little stimulation as possible to make my brain ultra-receptive. They made me change rooms during this Blanking Phase, so my cherubs and Saint Moses the Black don't invade my thoughts. They even took away my brushes and paints. It feels like I'm missing a limb.

After all the excitement of the last few days—*Take This Cup*'s disappearance, being adopted by the Darwin Corporation, learning my new home is actually a top-secret laboratory—you'd think some downtime would feel great. And it did. For about eleven minutes.

I expected my brain to calm down, but it sped up. Spinning. Making up crap. Pulling things from my past and monsterizing them. And I can't get Rosa out of my head. I want to believe the timing was one of those weird coincidences, and she's all right. Her mom got a day job, and they're now living in a safer place. Then the demons reappear, and I become convinced that something really bad happened to her—because of me.

It's the morning of my first session, and I'm pretty nervous. After today, nothing will ever be the same. Someone else will be sharing my brain. After putting on the white hospital gown that shows off my butt, I'm led into a white laboratory. In the center of the room are two long, white tubes big enough to hold a person each. They look harmless. Even comfortable. Not a terrible way to save a renowned artist—or hopefully become one.

Then I see them. His toes.

Plump, hairy, hobbit feet with too-long, cracked toenails sticking out of the tube. They look like they belong to a caveman recovered from a glacier.

"Hi, Bat!" I say to my Mentor's feet.

"He can't hear you while he's in there," the woman in a white lab coat says. "Only through this." She taps the tiny microphone clipped to her collar.

It hits me that I want to get to know Bat while he's still alive. And I want to see his hands to learn what the tools of a genuine Master artist look like. "Can I meet him after this?"

"It's against protocol," answers a male scientist with a British accent.

"I'm Deborah, by the way." Her friendly smile kind of makes up for his coldness.

"Time to get started," he says.

I lie on the stainless steel table, and Deborah straps down my head, then my wrists and ankles. A lightning bolt of fear strikes through my gut.

"Sorry about this," she says, "but we can't have you moving around while you're in there."

"Will it hurt?"

"You may feel a little dis—"

"Yes," the jerk-of-a-scientist says, not looking at all sorry.

53

"Are you going to give me something for the pain?" I ask, trying not to sound like a wimp.

"I'm sorry," Deborah says. "We can't. It would suppress your receptors. But afterward we'll give you a sedative, so you can sleep it off." She squeezes my shoulder. "They tell me it's not that bad. Here, hold this while you're in there." She hands me one of those rubber stress balls, which only stresses me out more.

I take slow, deep breaths as I enter the tube. The only thing I hear is my pounding heart.

"We'll start now," comes Deborah's voice out of a speaker above me.

The tube darkens, and a tiny light flashes. I feel a sharp prick in my head and then in my stomach, like when you get a shot, but using an elephant tranquilizer-sized needle. Then another prick in my head and one in my shoulder. Sharp and biting, and I tense when the next light flashes. Head and ankle this time. The flashes start coming quicker and it feels like my insides are on fire.

"Is it supposed to feel this bad?" I call out.

"Try to relax." Deborah's voice says through the speaker. "You're doing great."

I shut my eyes, grit my teeth, and squeeze and release the stress ball over and over. *I can endure this.* Before long, I'm revving. Every nerve is electrified. Flashes and pinpricks, flashes and pinpricks. Hot tears stream down my cheeks, but my bound hands keep me from wiping them away.

After only God knows how long, they slide me out. I'm covered in sweat and trembling all over. I look over at the other tube, but the feet are gone. The headache that had started in the back of my head has now spread to my temples.

"You'll probably be extra hungry this evening," Deborah says as she helps me sit up. "And you'll be tired, as well." She hands me two pills and a glass of water. "Take these. They'll help."

My shaking hands almost drop the glass. They put me in a

wheelchair, and by the time I'm back to my room, my head is throbbing so bad I'm seeing haloes around the lights. Deborah was dead-on. I'm exhausted, even though all I did was lie in a torture chamber and feel like a voodoo doll. Suddenly, I crave fried baloney and German potato salad and pickled beets, which is super strange because beets taste like dirt. I chow down on a bunch of food I've never eaten before, then crash under the white, white ceiling.

The next morning, I'm once again greeted by Bat's hobbit feet. "You doing okay in there?" I ask, even though I know he can't hear me. I walk up to my tube and my mouth goes dry. "Is it going to feel the same as yesterday?"

"The sensation will be deeper in your brain," my buddy, the British guy, answers.

"You'll do fine," Deborah says with an encouraging smile. "Are you ready?"

If I don't do this, my Mentor's consciousness will die, and I won't become the artist I could be. I can't let my fear stop me. I grit my teeth and climb onto the table. "I'm ready."

They strap me in and slide me into the tube, and once again my mind and body are hammered with pinpricks. Even more painful than yesterday. I begin pumping the stress ball to match my heartbeat.

I catch an image. I'm on the floor playing with a toy train, placing stuff on the track so it keeps derailing. I've never felt such loneliness. Then, out of nowhere, I'm being shoved to the ground. Fear grips me, then shame as I piss myself. I hear mocking laughter as a big kid starts kicking me in the ribs. Pain and humiliation overwhelm me. It's as if my life is flashing before my eyes, except it's not *my* life. I've never had a toy train, and I'm not the kind of guy who lets himself get beat up by bullies.

A gush of wetness slides over my upper lip. I lick at it and taste blood. It's not a memory. I can no longer breathe through my nose, and I start choking as blood runs down the back of my throat. I try to sit up, but the straps hold me down.

JIM AND STEPHANIE KROEPFL

"I need to get out of here!" I yell as panic claws at me.

"We can't stop mid-session," Dr. Sensitive says through the speaker.

"I'm bleeding from my nose!" My heart is racing so fast it feels like it's about to explode.

"Kevin, listen to me," Deborah says in a calm voice. "If we remove you now, it could irreparably damage both sets of memories. Can you hang in there a little longer?"

My body is screaming for me to say no, but I don't want to end up a drooling lump of flesh. I snort out my nose, blowing out a stream of warm blood. My throat clogs up, and I start coughing.

"Hold your head still!" he barks.

"I know you need to cough, but do it as gently as you can," Deborah directs.

I make myself cough in tiny bursts, and cautiously snort out the crap from my nose again and again until no longer feeling like I'm suffocating.

"How are you doing in there?" Deborah asks.

I'm covered in my own blood and snot and drool, but I say, "Better. I'm doing better." I want to get this over with and sleep for three days. "How much longer?"

"We're almost halfway there," Deborah answers.

That's all? I clench the stress ball so hard I expect it to deflate. I brace myself for more bad memories. Instead, in my mind's eye I'm watching as a landscape is painted from start to finish. It's gorgeous. I try holding onto the memory so I don't forget how the painter made it look like the water is shimmering, but then the scene vanishes, leaving me wanting for more. I lick my upper lip. No fresh blood.

I can endure this.

Each morning, I'm greeted by Bat's feet with toes like mushrooms. Even though I've never seen past his toenail fungus, in a way I've gotten to know Bat through his memories. He may be a great artist now, but he didn't have it easy growing up. There aren't any memories with friends. His mom is really nice, though.

Over the days, the images of the life that isn't mine get weaker. It feels as if the scientists are trying to hurry along the process, like Bat doesn't have much time left. A horrifying thought rips through me. What if he dies before we're done? Will I end up with a glitchy, half-a-dude in my brain? They ask if I can handle longer sessions. Despite the blinding headaches and the choking nosebleeds, I tell them I'll work twenty-four hours a day if I have to.

On the sixth day, we finish. God rested on the seventh, and I now understand why.

Orfyn

I'm standing in front of a nice-looking brick house along a quiet street lined with towering oaks, manicured lawns, and other nice-looking brick houses. Random cars slumber up the street while sprinklers spray lazy twists of water into the air. I look up, and the sun is directly overhead. It's the middle of the day. Where is everyone? And, where am I? Three black crows fly past, cawing to each other, and a fat squirrel dashes across the traffic-less street.

It finally hits me that I must be dreaming, but it feels more real than any dream I've ever had.

The front door opens, and a guy sticks out his head, cautiously looking up and down the street. He carefully edges his way on to the stoop. "You coming?"

He's all-over fat, and his scruffy beard looks more about being lazy than trendy. He's wearing stained slippers and a spotless Rangers jersey. It's his eyes that throw me. They contain the wits of ten men, the sereneness of five monks, and the detachment of an indie musician. I don't know how I'd begin to paint them. He stretches, exposing a furry Buddha belly, and smiles to himself. Then he goes back inside, leaving the door wide open.

Normally, I'd never consider following a stranger into his house, but this is a dream. Nothing can hurt me for real. I *think*. Besides, he is a Rangers fan. Then I recall his eyes. Somehow, I know that everything will be okay as long as I follow those white orbs that seem to hold the secrets of the universe.

I go in and enter a living room with a sagging, threadbare couch; a scarred, wooden china cabinet crammed with dusty knickknacks; and a rocking chair with a clean, white doily on the headrest. Rose-colored wallpaper with yellow and blue flowers covers all four walls, and on the floor is dirt-brown carpet that looks more dirt than brown.

The guy calls out from somewhere, "Want a grape soda?"

"Uhm, no. I'm good."

A cheesy photo of the guy when he was a chubby teenager hangs over the mantel. I always wanted to live in the kind of home where someone's proud to show off a cheesy photo of me. There's a framed photo on the fireplace mantle of a smiling woman. I've seen her before. Then it all snaps together.

"Bat?" I call out.

He rounds the corner. "Hey, Orfyn. Glad you made it." He jerks his head toward the back of the house. "I want to show you something." Bat lumbers down the dimly lit hall, opens a door, and disappears. When I finally get that he's not returning, I follow and descend burnt-orange, shag carpeted stairs into what I expect to be a moldy smelling basement.

Instead, I enter Oz.

It's awash with exploding colors and sharp-edged shapes. Dozens of paintings hang on the walls. Picasso, Ernst, and Klee. It feels like I'm seeing into multiple dimensions. I go over and take a closer look. They're not prints! And they're better lit than the ones in the Metropolitan Museum of Art.

Hidden in Bat's basement.

I start to feel spinny. "I need to sit down."

"Don't worry about it. Everything is chill in the Bat Cave."

He waves his hand to where two of the most comfortable-looking chairs I've ever seen wait in front of nine huge TV screens arranged in a square. He deflates himself into the left recliner. "Mozart, please." Classical music fills the room, and the screens light up to display paintings I recognize—Titian, Warhol, Rubens, Hopper—and others that are new to me.

"You look pale." Bat thrusts his can at me. "Here, have some grape soda."

I sip the too-sweet drink and start feeling better.

He kicks off his slippers and drops his feet—his hairy, hobbit feet—onto the footrest. "What do you wanna do today?"

Lake

I am a Nobel.

I keep repeating it to myself, trying to summon the excitement I should be experiencing, because it's a monumental achievement. I merged! When I told Deborah about late-thirties Sophie, the dated lab equipment, and how she was experimenting with octopus enzymes, the joy on Deborah's face helped some. But my accomplishment feels itchy around the edges, because I wasn't entirely honest. I fully planned to admit that Sophie thinks I'm her latest lab assistant, but as the words were forming on my lips, something stopped me.

I want to give Sophie time to realize she now only lives in my dreams. I owe it to her because she did, after all, allow her consciousness to be implanted into my brain. And that excuse is partly true. But there's more to it.

Sophie's and my situation is similar to strangers who have been shipwrecked on a deserted island. She's going to appear in my dreams for the rest of my life, and if we aren't compatible, not only will our interactions be miserable, the quality of our work will suffer. We need to build a relationship on our terms, not theirs. If I tell

Deborah, they're going to take control away from me. Sophie and I need to solve this issue ourselves. Because, of course, we will. We're very intelligent women.

As promised, they transferred me up to the Nobels wing, and I now have free reign of the unrestricted areas. And that's an aspect of my reasoning, too. If I told them the truth, I'm certain I'd still be locked in that depressing room while they try to determine why Sophie doesn't remember me. I beat the odds and merged, and now I'm going to help the person in my head understand what happened to her so we can discover the cure to Alzheimer's together.

I take a reassuring breath and pull open the door. Like the other areas in the complex, the Nobels' dining hall more resembles a hospital cafeteria than someplace inviting, unless one considers the red fire alarm on the wall as flair. The savory aroma, though, makes me realize how famished I am.

The room could hold fifty people, with tables arranged for twos, fours, and eights. I suppose they've planned for the future, when there will be more of us Nobels living here. Today, though, there are only two sitting at a corner table.

A petite girl with curled, long, blond hair and retro tortoise-shell glasses looks up from her sandwich. She gives me a huge, welcoming smile. The other Nobel, a boy with a bad case of acne, is shoveling food into his mouth. I'd swear he's thirteen years old, but every Nobel is sixteen.

Deborah explained that sixteen is the age when the brain has developed higher-order thinking skills based on learning taxonomies, but since the pre-frontal cortex won't be fully developed until we're twenty-four, it's still receptive to the infusion of a second consciousness. At our age, we aren't locked into a self-image of who we are and the person we'll evolve into.

I head over to them. "Hi. I'm Lake, the Nobel for Chemistry." It's exhilarating to say it to someone other than my mirror's reflection.

"I'm so glad you're *finally* on this floor," the girl says, gesturing to the seat next to her and moving aside a book. "My name is Juliette, but everyone calls me Jules. I'm Economics, and this is Marty. He's Literature. Join us."

"Thanks." I set down my tray while casting a sideways glance at Marty.

Jules explains, "He's not a big talker."

Marty continues to slurp up spaghetti, as if he's accustomed to being spoken about in the third person.

"Has Deborah showed you around The Flem?" she asks.

"The what?"

She wrinkles her nose. "I know it sounds gross. Alex started calling this place *The Flem*, and it caught on. I can't wait for you to meet him. He's so much fun."

I didn't have many friends in high school. I could never relate to what they found important. Excitement vibrates through me. Things may be different here.

"Wasn't meeting your Mentor the best ever?" Jules asks.

"It was extraordinary." To keep the full truth off my face, I select a French fry and chew it to mush. "What are you both working on—am I permitted to ask that?"

"Of course," Jules says. "We don't keep secrets here. I'll be working on a theory to fairly distribute wealth among the masses, but I won't start on it for a while. There's so much I first need to learn from my Mentor, Sarah. And Marty's novels will one day be heralded for creating a new social consciousness. Right, Marty?" She nudges him with her elbow.

"Uh-huh," he mumbles, without meeting my eyes.

"Your focus is on Alzheimer's, right?" Jules asks.

"How do you know that?"

"I pestered Deborah until she told me all about you." She giggles. "My mom is always accusing me of being such a busybody, but I can't help it. I find people so interesting. Don't you?"

I'm more fascinated with how chains of a molecule form the

backbone of the DNA of every creature on earth, but we all have our predilections. "Sure. Where are the other Nobels?"

"Probably sleeping." Jules shoves aside her barely eaten tuna sandwich. No wonder she's the size of an elf.

"It's past noon."

"Our sleep patterns are a little off," she explains.

"Off?" Marty says before stuffing an entire piece of garlic bread into his mouth.

"Some of us are sleeping more than others," Jules says. "But the longer we dream, the more we can accomplish with our Mentors, right?"

I need to determine what's considered the norm so the Darwinians don't label me as lackadaisical, which in my old life would have been laughable. After Mom got sick, Dad had to leave the tour to take care of us. When his ex-band won Best Jazz Album of the Year days after Mom died, he retreated into himself. He's never really reemerged. Since then, I've worked as many jobs as possible to help out.

"How many hours have you been sleeping?" I ask Jules.

"My Mentor is being totally fair."

"Thirteen hours today," Marty answers. "So far."

No wonder he's acting like a starving hyena. When Deborah suggested I get something to eat, I assumed it was because she wanted me to meet the others. Her true motivation may have been entirely different.

"Is there a particular reason you're sleeping that long?" I ask him.

Jules says, "Time in the dreamspace is ... Marty, you're better with words than me. How would you describe it?"

"Different."

I wait for him to expound, but he goes back to carb loading. I'd been led to believe this experience would be like going to school, but in reverse. At night, Sophie will instruct me on what I need to know. During the day, after I debrief with Deborah, I'll complete the homework Sophie assigns. Once my Mentor considers me sufficiently trained, I'll continue our experiments in the awake-world.

"Do you mind sleeping that much?" I ask Marty.

"It's fine," he says.

Is he avoiding my eyes because he's not being entirely truthful, or is he merely shy?

Jules says, "The whole purpose of our being here is to continue our Mentor's work. They aren't slave drivers. They just want to spend as much time as they can being conscious with us."

I hadn't considered that paradox. Every hour we're awake is an hour our Mentors don't, in essence, exist.

"Sarah has given me a ton of homework, and it's not going to get done by itself." Jules picks up her book, *Capitalism and Freedom.* "I'm *really* glad you're here."

I smile. "Me, too." It feels like I've already made a friend.

Jules flutters her fingertips as she leaves.

Marty stands. "Eat when you can." He grabs his notebook and follows Jules out the door.

I know I agreed to remain here until I'm twenty-one, but I didn't expect to sleep away the next five years. And what happens after I leave? The Darwinians said I could still have a career and a family, or do whatever I choose with my life. The significant difference for us Nobels, though, is we'll always have the advantage of a second intelligence when it comes to our careers.

But if I'm constantly sleeping, how can I lead a normal life?

Mental slap. Just because Marty's sleeping pattern is prolonged doesn't mean Sophie expects the same from me. Jules's Mentor sounds reasonable. Once we get past Sophie's misperception of my role in her life, these are the issues we'll figure out together. I'm certain tonight will be an entirely different experience. Why am I waiting? I can take a nap as soon as I finish eating.

To put me into a food coma, I abandon my burger and grab a turkey sandwich for the tryptophan and a cup of chamomile tea to calm me. No one else appears while I finish my lunch. No one, such as Stryker.

Was he able to merge last night? If I've been mistaken about the consequences of failure, then he—

I shove away my doubt and replace it with positive thinking: *Sophie will know who I am. Sophie will know who I am ...*

Lake

"I expected you this morning." Sophie's cigarette smoke writes exclamation marks in the air.

She's working on an ultra-thin laptop, which clashes with her eighties persona. Then, I notice the state-of-the-art lab equipment. Already, things are improving from our first dream session.

"Sorry. I was debriefing with Dr. Deborah Duvaney." She divulged that they'd been close. I look at Sophie expectantly, hoping her friend's name triggers her memories.

A line forms between Sophie's thick eyebrows.

I hold my breath in anticipation.

Sophie taps the cigarette over an ashtray. "I'd appreciate more consideration on her part. Please inform her I run on a strict schedule, and I need you here on time."

"Did I mention I'm from Pittsburgh? I won The American Chemistry Club's award twice, and—"

"I don't mean to sound rude, but your tardiness has already put us behind."

"Dr. Weiss, do I look at all familiar to you?"

"Why? Have we met before yesterday?"

"Not technically, but—"

"Then how would I know you?" She starts rubbing her temples, and beads of sweat form above her lip.

As much as I want to reveal the truth, all indications suggest Sophie isn't ready to accept the reality of our situation. For both of our sakes, I have to grant her the time she needs to come to terms with her new life. Otherwise, there's the possibility the woman living in my brain could become insane.

"Is there an extra laptop I can use to take notes?" I ask.

"What's a laptop?"

I turn to where hers had just been. In its place is a boxy, tan monitor with a green screen, which only confirms I need to take it slow. Patience, unfortunately, has never been one of my virtues. "I'll use this." I grab a pad of lined paper and a pen off her desk while furtively checking out what else she may have changed.

She reverted the lab equipment back to its archaic form, and a huge tank filled with live octopuses is on a counter. The cephalopods are different colors, and their arms move like fingers across the sand at the bottom. The items that were hanging on three of the walls appear the same, but there's a new picture on the fourth. It's of a tranquil lake with two white swans gliding across the water. I head over to take a closer look and read the poem.

Because I could not stop for Death –
He kindly stopped for me –
The carriage held but just ourselves –
And Immortality.

Not the inspiration one would expect to find in a neuroscientist's lab. But it wouldn't be out of place in a secret research complex whose mission is to curtail death. The Nobels Program is providing Sophie with a second life, and when my body wears out, it's feasible that her consciousness can be reinserted into another sixteen-year-old, mimicking immortality. Is she starting to remember?

"Dr. Weiss, what is this?"

She glances up with a perplexed look and comes over. "It's the first part of an Emily Dickenson poem. I wonder who put it there." She reaches into her lab coat's pocket, pulls out a pack of cigarettes, lights one, and draws in a deep breath. She studies the picture while polluting the air with bitter-smelling smoke. "I think I'll keep it here for the time being. Now, please prepare tissue samples from the specimens in the cooler."

I'm considering the presence of the poem as progress. It's only a matter of time before Sophie accepts that she's merged with me. I approach the cooler with a new bounce to my step, open the stainless steel door, and gasp. On the metal shelf are six gray, slimy brains. Human brains.

"If working with acute slices is going to be a problem, there's a long line of students who would be happy to take your place," Sophie says.

Her threat reminds me where I am. These are dream-brains. Once I get accustomed to doing it in our dream sessions, dissecting real human brains will be a cinch. "Sorry, Dr. Weiss. That was unprofessional. It won't happen again."

She appraises me until even I'm questioning if I deserve this fake position. She finally releases me from her scrutiny and takes a deep pull from her cigarette. Thankfully, I can't get lung cancer from second-hand dream-smoke.

"Brain slices maintain many aspects of *in vivo* biology, including functional synaptic circuitry," Sophie explains. "This makes them ideal platforms for dissection, letting us witness the development and degradation of the molecular pathways and real-time neuronal dysfunction."

"So, you're saying they're still alive outside of their body."

I wait for her to make the connection to her own existence.

"Not precisely, but brain slices do behave as if they are part of

69

a living organ for six to twelve hours post-removal. Three slides per sample." She starts heading back to her desk. "Please."

"Do you mind showing me how to prepare them?"

"I would expect a graduate student to understand basic research techniques." She leaves me and sits in front of what was considered a modern computer in the 1980s.

Until Sophie understands who I am, I can only do my best. Besides, I'm not going to ruin the integrity of her research. We're in a dream. I search through drawers and find a box of latex gloves and a scalpel. After gloving up, I gingerly pick up one of the brains, set it on the counter, and begin to mouth-breathe to overcome its dead organ smell.

I inspect the human brain to determine where to cut first, and …

I blink a few times, clearing the sleep from my eyes before turning to the clock on the night stand. It felt like we'd only been working three or four hours, but my "afternoon nap" lasted for seven, confirming that time is altered in the dreamstate. I stretch with pleasure. Facing the risks to become the Nobel for Chemistry was inconsequential compared to the benefits. People my age would never have the opportunity to learn how to prepare brain tissue samples from an esteemed neurologist. Admittedly, we had a slight issue when she noticed the scalpel in my hand. I'm not a grad student. How am I expected to know to use a microtone to slice brains?

I'm supposed to inform the Darwinians about everything that occurs in the dreamspace. I should probably tell them the truth about Sophie, but I'm observing moments when it appears she's figuring it out. And it's not preventing her from teaching me what I need to know to become an accomplished researcher. As long as we're progressing, I don't see the harm in giving her more time.

Lake

My second-story window looks onto The Flem's gardens, and I can picture what they must have looked like before they were overgrown with weeds. My room is sunny and efficient. I even have a separate living area and a kitchen, so I don't have to eat every meal in the dreary dining hall. I'm going to ask for a few items to make my place feel more like home, like a drawing of a DNA strand similar to the one I have in my bedroom.

A knock pulls me from my new view of The Flem. When I open the door, awaiting me is Stryker, looking even more gorgeous than I recall.

"You did it!" I throw my arms around his neck.

He holds his arms rigidly at his sides.

I let go, embarrassed. I'm not normally that expressive. Stryker's prediction of what would happen if he failed must have impacted me more than I thought. "Sorry. I'm just relieved you merged."

"You and me both. You really helped." He shoves his hands in his pockets, and I can't help thinking that he's worried I'll start kissing his fingertips or something.

I clear my throat. "Is Bjorn what you expected?"

Stryker's eyes flick to the ceiling, and he touches his ear. "Are you up for a walk?"

We're being monitored on this floor, too? I had assumed it was only while we were Candidates. Suddenly, it feels like I've been unwillingly cast in one of those reality shows where they put together the people most likely not to get along as roommates and then broadcast their terrible behavior.

"I was just thinking I'd like to take a closer look at the gardens." Did that sound contrived? And will I be scrutinizing everything I say for the next five years? "Give me a second. I need to grab a hat."

We head outside, no longer barred by locked doors. The Darwinians kept their word, as I expected. The air is deliciously warm, and the light breeze caresses my skin. Already, I feel lighter than helium. I steal a glance at Stryker's chiseled profile. If I'm going to live with strangers, I could do worse than him. And I suppose I'll get accustomed to being constantly monitored.

Eventually.

Hopefully.

"I want to thank you for what you did for me," Stryker says, shortening his stride to match mine.

"If you hadn't convinced them to let us take that walk, I would have never figured out what it was we were doing wrong."

Stryker nods. "We make a good team."

A flush blooms, which always makes my face look like a tomato. I duck my head until my cheeks cool. I'd suspected the Stryker I first encountered wasn't how he typically acts, but I didn't expect him to be this nice.

"You still haven't told me what you think about Bjorn," I ask.

"He's brilliant. Definitely intense. I'm pleased. He's going to be able to teach me the things I need to know."

I'd describe Sophie similarly, once she settles into her new life and realizes who I am. And as a bonus, we'll have a mother-daughter relationship, which is something I've been missing for years.

"What will you and Bjorn be working on?" I ask.

"We're going to end gun-related violence."

My eyebrows shoot up. His appearance suggests that his life has been consumed with sailing in New England and snowboarding in Aspen with friends named Chaz and Bronwyn, not hanging out in places with drive-by shootings.

"Why gun violence?" I ask in as neutral a tone as I can manage.

"It's a senseless crime." His voice crackles with anger.

I stop and place a hand on his arm. "Stryker, did something happen to you?"

He flinches, and I retract my hand. I attribute his reaction to my violation of his personal space—again—until I see his jaw clench and unclench.

After an awkwardly long time, he asks, "What's Sophie like?"

There's a story here, but I let it go because I haven't been forthcoming about my past, either. I also haven't been candid about Sophie's confusion. "Like Bjorn, she's definitely intense."

"And."

"And what?"

"What is it you're not telling me?"

How did he know? He could be testing me to see if I'm hiding anything, which I am. Although, it would be helpful to obtain a second perspective to determine if my logic is sound. I rub my finger against my thumb's scar. *Do I dare confide in him?*

"I'll make you a deal," Stryker says. "I'll tell you a secret about Bjorn so you'll have something on me, too."

The process of trying to achieve peace may be very different than what I'd imagined. "You go first."

"Bjorn changed his mind at the last minute, and they merged him anyway."

I gasp. "They killed him against his will?"

"He was weeks away from dying, so it was going to happen either way." Stryker runs his fingers through his hair. "Bjorn *says* he's come to terms with it, but there are moments when I'm not so sure."

So, Stryker has someone existing in his brain who may not want to be there, while my Mentor doesn't understand she only lives in my consciousness. I'm not sure which is worse.

"It appears we're both facing challenges we didn't anticipate." I let out a deep breath. "Sophie believes I'm her lab assistant." I proceed to tell him about my past two dream sessions.

Stryker kicks the dirt with his expensive-looking, leather shoe. "When I said we're a team, I didn't expect to be on the losing side."

"We're *not* going to lose. They'll both adjust. It might just take a little time, but thanks to us, they have another lifetime of time."

We silently wade through the thigh-high grasses and weeds, lost in our thoughts. Admittedly, my own doubts keep trying to sabotage my positive thinking, which I cannot allow to occur. *Sophie will figure it out. Sophie will figure it out. Sophie will—*

"Are you going to tell her the truth?" Stryker asks.

I explain my theory of how she needs to come to terms with it on her own.

"I think you should listen to your intuition on this one. Sophie could be subconsciously telling you what she needs."

I mull over his words as I head to the bench at the far end of the overgrown rose garden. I've always liked to believe that when an idea that's beyond my own knowledge and experience appears, it's coming from my mom. It's comforting to know that Sophie may be subconsciously guiding me, too.

Stryker lounges on the bench. His legs go on forever. He rests his arms across the back of the bench, grazing my shoulders. Was that intentional? He's never given any indication he wants to be more than friends, but we have been preoccupied with trying to keep our positions as Nobels. I've never had the time for a boyfriend. Stryker is brilliant, and we've already formed a bond. He's also hot. Maybe it's finally time.

My eyes land on the tangled mess of vegetation around us. This place must have been beautiful when it was a functioning boarding school. "My Grandma Bee grows roses. I created a natural fertilizer for her that's had amazing results." *Stimulating conversation, Lake. Next, why don't you tell him how the best fertilizer has the perfect balance of only three elements?*

"You should try it on these roses," he says.

I didn't expect him to care about something as trivial as flowers. I smile at the thought. "Maybe I will."

"Are you going to tell them about Sophie?" he asks, concluding my one minute of relaxation.

"Not unless I have to."

"Don't you think this is something they should be aware of?"

A river of guilt flows through me. "Why are you suddenly on their side?"

"Believe me, I'm not. But it's prudent to understand motivations. Tell me where you're going with this."

I kick off my flip-flops and run my purple-polished toes through the grass. "What's the harm if Sophie keeps thinking of me as her lab assistant? She's teaching me what I need to know. And even though she doesn't realize she's doing it in a dream, Deborah confirmed that Sophie is continuing the work she planned to explore with me, so it's not inhibiting our discovering the cure." When I say it out loud, it sounds justifiable. Stryker nods, which helps make me feel more confident in my decision.

"I see you've already identified the weakness in their controls: they can't ask the Mentors about what happens in our dreams." He closes his eyes and angles his face toward the sun. His skin is flawless, like he's been airbrushed for a Ralph Lauren ad.

I realize I'm gawking and avert my eyes. This garden could use some serious weeding.

"Have you considered what might happen if they find out you're not being entirely truthful?" Stryker brushes a mosquito off my arm, which feels intimate, especially after how he's reacted each time I've touched him.

"Lake?"

I clear my throat. "They won't know if I don't tell them."

He looks into my eyes, and I notice light brown flecks in his dark irises. "Do you play chess?" he asks.

Not quite what I expected him to say. "I was the Pittsburgh Chess League Champion in eighth grade."

"Then you understand the key to chess is to think ten moves ahead." He smiles conspiratorially. "I'm very good at chess."

"Why are you bringing this up now?"

"Don't tell any of the Nobels about Sophie."

"You don't trust our class?"

"One of them might be a spy for the Darwinians."

Despite the sun's warmth, I shiver. His imagination is working overtime again. Yet I find myself thinking about them, trying to fit each Nobel into that role. Could one of them really be spying for the Darwinians? I watch a bee visit one leggy plant after another until I'm ready to respond. "I'm not admitting you're right, but if there is a spy, who do you think it is?"

"I don't want to damn anyone until I've had more time to study them."

"I take it you don't have any facts to support your theory."

"True, but it's what I would do if I were them."

Is Stryker a chess master, or is he simply paranoid? It suddenly occurs to me that I didn't consider everyone. "How do I know *you're* not the spy?"

He leans down and whispers, "Now you get it. You don't."

If Stryker truly believes we shouldn't trust anyone, then I should be questioning his sudden friendship. "Why do you care about Sophie and me, anyway? What I do doesn't affect your work."

"It's in all our best interests to make sure there are no problems. If the Darwinians are satisfied with our results, they'll keep treating us as honored guests. If issues start to arise ... " Stryker shrugs. "Right now, there are only six of us to make disappear."

The Darwinians

"We have six functioning Nobels," the raven-haired man says, proudly.

"The Nobel for Art merged faster than all of the others." The woman releases a violent cough.

"Which means we now have to spread our resources even thinner," the bearded man says.

"Interestingly, Kevin is the only one able to maintain a normal sleep cycle."

The bearded man snorts. "That's because Bartholomew and he have nothing worthy to work on."

"He prefers to go by Bat," the woman says.

"Does it really matter? This is an exercise in futility. It dilutes our scientific mission."

"Let's remember, we needed his grant," the raven-haired man says.

"Which is the only reason I agreed to it. And if that gamer wants to spend the next sixty years trapped in the mind of a hoodlum, who am I to judge?"

"They're both a bit more than that," the woman says. "It may be time to establish measures of success for Art. I recommend we assign Deborah to him."

"No," the bearded man decides. "We need to keep her focused on our Nobel for Chemistry, and the other two Nobels. I won't approve shifting our people's time to debrief a vandal." He takes a sip of water from a crystal goblet. "We're on the verge of making monumental advances that will elevate the human condition. We're reaching for the stars, and we can't be distracted with these subjective pursuits. We owe it to the future. We owe it to Sophie."

The woman leans forward in her chair. "But what if we could transfer the ability to create the kind of art that alters the way society thinks. The implications would be—"

"It is not a practical science from which humanity can benefit," he declares.

The woman closes her eyes in exasperation. The raven-haired man sighs.

The woman puts on a tight smile. "You might remember, Reginald, that Alfred Nobel excluded Mathematics from the Nobel prizes because he didn't believe it was practical. Math!"

"Point noted, but I'm still against it."

The raven-haired man looks at the woman. "When do you want to schedule your procedure?"

"Not quite yet," she answers. "I won't put a member of my family at risk until I'm certain it's safe."

Orfyn

The Nobels' rec room is totally rigged out: ginormous TV, ping pong and pool tables, foosball, and all the latest video games. The kids at St. Catherine's would love a place like this. The only thing missing is the fun vibe. I don't get why whoever remodeled this old school made everything so *white*. This room should make them feel like they can kick back. I might have to do something about it.

Of the six of them, my eyes are drawn to the girl with long, red hair that reminds me of a New York sunset. But I'm not as ready to jump into their circle of brilliance as I first thought. They're all geniuses, and they've merged with someone equally as smart, if not more. I thought I'd end up with the same advantage, but I'm starting to have some serious doubts about the guy who's now living in my brain.

The girl I'd been eyeing notices me standing in the doorway. "Who are you?"

Everyone's heads turn, and their expressions make it obvious I wasn't expected.

"I'm new," is all I can muster.

"New?" a Hispanic-looking guy echoes.

The tall guy I saw shooting baskets when I first arrived rises from the couch and comes over with his hand extended. "I'm Stryker. What's your discipline?"

It takes me a second to figure out what he means. "Art," I answer, shaking his hand. "I'm a painter."

"That's not a Nobel field," says an Asian girl with heavily lined eyes, three piercings in her right eyebrow and dyed silver hair. Not silver-gray. Not silver-white. Silver. It gleams like newly polished metal.

I can't start off letting them think I'm cool with being the designated punching bag. "That's only because da Vinci isn't around to make it one. It's up to me."

A pimply-faced guy snorts in what sounds like appreciation, then jots something in his notebook.

"The Darwinians must have a good reason for adding a new field," says a tiny girl with glasses that make her look even smarter than she probably is.

"If Art is now included as part of this Program, then *Art* is welcome to join us," Stryker declares, making it clear his decision is final.

I can't tell if he's being friendly or dissing me, but I pull up a chair and maneuver it next to the girl with the sunset-red hair.

"Sorry, no one told us that another Nobel would be joining our class," the Hispanic guy explains.

"They needed a lucky number seven. My name is … Orfyn." It's the first time I've ever introduced myself using it. It feels right.

"Is that your *real* name?" The Asian girl makes it sound like a dare.

"It is now," I say with more defensiveness than I wanted to portray.

"Interesting." She looks at me in a way that makes me wonder if she knows who I am. "I'm Anna."

"Where are you from?" I ask her.

"The unshaven armpit of California. L.A."

She couldn't have heard of me. I'm not *that* famous.

"Anna is our Nobel for Physiology," Stryker explains.

"I'm Alex. Physics," says the Hispanic guy whose skin is darker than mine. His smile is wide and welcoming, and I know right away we'll be friends. When Alex stands to fist-bump me, I read his shirt. *Entropy isn't what it used to be.* That's supposed to be a joke—I think.

"Don't let Alex demonstrate what he calls his Wile E. Coyote Theory of Gravity on you," Stryker says to me.

I fake chuckle along with the rest of them. I am so out of my league.

Stryker points to the girl with the glasses who's been so nice. "This is Jules. She's Economics." Then he jerks his head at the guy whose nose is buried in his notebook. "And that's Marty, our very own Word Man."

"Hey," Marty says without looking up. He has a major case of bedhead that I'm pretty sure wasn't styled to look that way, and he looks younger than the others. Maybe fourteen.

Stryker finally gets to the person I've been eyeing this whole time. "And last, but not least, is Lake, our Nobel for Chemistry."

Her eyes remind me of a clear mountain lake, but there's a sadness in them. I hold out my hand. After a long moment, Lake takes it. I swear a rush of energy surges between us. Did she feel it, too? I may not know how to perform brain surgery—like they all probably do— but I know one thing: this is a girl I'm going to paint.

"Who are you merged with?" Anna asks me.

"Bat ..." I realize too late that I never learned his last name. "Just Bat. You know, like Rihanna or Bono." I *think* I pulled it off.

"Never heard of him, but I'm sure he's somebody amazing if they merged him with you," she says, then turns to say something to Lake.

Now that I think about it, Bat's house is filled with masterpieces, but I've never seen *his* work.

"Where did you study?" Jules asks me.

"Under a bridge." It's the truth. Long story.

Stryker asks, "The Ponte Vecchio?"

"Uhm, no." So what if I didn't go to some fancy art school? I don't have anything to be ashamed of. People get into my work. "I'm a street artist."

"Good one," Alex says. "Like they'd ever select a vandal for this Program."

"Some of that stuff is pretty cool," Anna says.

"I hate how those people destroy the beauty of our cities," Lake says.

"I know!" Jules seconds. "It's so disrespectful."

My shaky confidence plunges even further. I'd always kept what I did a secret to protect St. Catherine's, and, yeah, to keep me out of jail, but I never thought I'd need to keep it a secret here. I'm not disrespecting. I'm turning ugly places into something beautiful.

"When did you get here, Orfyn?" Alex asks.

By now, I'm almost afraid to answer. "A week ago."

"And you've already merged?" Lake asks.

"Yeah," I answer, trying not to make it sound like a question. Maybe *merged* means something different to them.

Stryker looks at me oddly. "Art would certainly use different parts of the brain than our disciplines."

Another strike. I've been trying to tell them the truth, and they laughed. Even worse, they looked down on me. If I'm going to live with these people for the next five years, I will not be that guy—the freak, the outcast, the loner. A Bible verse Sister Mo loves to repeat pops into my head: *Even a foofool, when he keeps silent, is considered wise.* I don't even care about the wise part, but to survive here, I need to keep my past a secret.

"I called this meeting because it's important that the *seven*—" Stryker winks at me, making me wonder if he knew all along I'd show up today "—of us help each other navigate through this unique experience."

"I think that's a *wonderful* idea, Stryker," Jules says, looking like she's already planning their wedding.

"Thanks, Jules. Actually, Lake is the one who showed me how important it is to work together." He smiles at her a bit too long.

"I propose we meet in the dining hall at noon on Mondays," Alex says. "That way, we can eat lunch at lunchtime."

Is that a joke?

Anna's expression makes it obvious she thinks his suggestion is the stupidest ever. "It'll never happen. I slept through my alarm and barely got here on time."

"Good work, Anna. You've identified our first group assignment," Stryker says, and I have to hold in my grin. "We each need to work with our Guardian to figure out how to wake up when *we* choose."

Do I have a Guardian? No one said anything about that.

"I vote for no hand over the mouth," Lake says to Stryker, and they share a look.

My stomach lurches. Do they have something going on?

Stryker turns his eyes away from Lake, though I can't seem to. "The first item we need to discuss," he says, "is whether everyone is having abnormally long sleep cycles."

That hasn't been happening to me. Do I dare admit it?

Everyone else nods, except for Marty, who's absorbed in his notebook. Stryker looks at me questioningly.

"I've only dreamed twice, so I'm not sure yet," I hedge.

Jules says, "We're here to change the world. Who cares if we're sleeping a little more?"

"I agree," Anna says. "The longer we work, the sooner my Mentor and I will figure out how to deactivate the trigger for autoimmune diseases."

And I thought I was intimidated before.

I look at Lake under hooded eyes. What amazing thing is she working on? Suddenly, keeping the humanity in Art doesn't sound all that earth-shattering. And when are Bat and I going to get started?

"I'm all for a good snooze," Alex says. "But I haven't played my guitar in weeks."

"For real?" Anna asks. "Why would you want to waste time on *music* instead of discovering a renewable energy source?"

Alex must understand, but do the others feel the same way about the arts? Why did they add Art if it isn't a Nobel field?

"Everyone should sleep for as long as their Mentor deems is necessary," Jules says.

"Within reason," Lake adds.

"Let's not forget that our Mentors are only conscious when we're interacting with them in our dreams," Stryker adds.

Jules looks at Stryker like he's surprised her with an engagement ring. "Exactly. It's not like they can watch TV or work out while they're waiting for us to fall asleep. We need to respect their needs, too."

Until now, I've never thought about what Bat did when I'm awake. Nothing, which isn't all that different from what he does when we're together.

The others start debating about the optimum sleep versus awake time. I zone out and spend my time stealing glances at Lake, who is spending more time observing than participating.

When Alex holds up a finger in the air, I'm expecting to hear something brilliant. "Let's throw a party!"

"We shouldn't waste time on trivial things like that," Anna says.

"We all defied the risks to become the first Nobels," Alex says. "In my culture, we celebrate our triumphs."

"And now we've got the new guy to pull it together," Stryker says. "All in favor?" He holds up his right hand, and everyone else does the same.

"Uhm ... " I want to protest, but I can't think of a good reason why I can't do it. Now that I've merged, I've actually got a lot of time on my hands. But I have the feeling Stryker's reason for picking me isn't to raise my status.

I'm about to tell them how I'm too busy when Lake looks at me. "I know this sounds implausible, but I've never been to a party. I mean, with people our age."

"You've got to be kidding," Anna says snarkily.

"I've always had more important things to do," Lake says, looking hurt.

"Then it's about time, Lake," I say. "I'll throw you a killer party." *Game on, Stryker.*

When everyone is heading out, Lake comes over to me. "Thanks for volunteering," she says with a smirk, since we both know I was sabotaged. "And don't let them get to you. We're all out of our element."

Orfyn

All great parties have a theme. The only one I could think of comes from the creepy stories Sister Mo told us about Jamaica: full-moon parties, duppies, and voodoo. She always spoke in this apocalyptic lilt, and when a nun tells you that you really do need to watch out for zombies, you'd better believe her.

I knew just the place to hold ours. The Darwinians set up a studio for me in the school's old art classroom, and they filled it with all the supplies I could ever wish for: oils, brushes, pencils, canvases, easels, spotlights. I prefer walls instead of canvas, so I've never painted there. Until now.

The music will be reggae, of course, but instead of the expected Bob Marley, I chose stuff they've probably never heard of, like The Abyssinians and Toots & the Maytals. The cooks got into it and agreed to make jerk chicken, fried plantains, and coconut tarts.

I'm headed to the kitchen to check on things when I spot Jules in the dining hall. She must have just gotten here, since she's only taken one bite out of her burger.

She smiles and pats the seat next to her. "Keep me company while I'm eating."

Jules has never made me feel like I don't belong here—other than telling everyone she hates street art. But I don't think she believed me, so we've been getting along.

"How's the party planning going?" she asks.

"Great. It's going to rock."

"I knew Stryker chose the right person. Anything I can do to help?"

This is the first time anyone's offered, which I guess is okay. They're all really busy. "I'm still trying to figure out the drinks. I want to make something special."

"Let me take care of it."

I notice the book lying next to her: *Capitalism and Freedom.* "It'll get in the way of your work."

"Sarah has given me a ton of stuff to learn, but they always say, 'If you want something done, ask a busy person to do it.'"

"Thanks. That's really nice of you." I mean it; she is nice. And she's cute, if you like the kind of girl you see cheerleading at football games. I reach over and touch her arm, like I'm thanking her. And … nothing. The electricity between us is about the same level as when I open a refrigerator, unlike what I felt with Lake.

"The theme is Jamaican Beach Party," I explain.

Jules claps excitedly. "I love it! I have the perfect outfit."

"I hadn't thought about having everyone dress up. Great idea. I'll let the others know." I'm really glad I ran into Jules.

"So how's everything going with your Mentor? Bat, is it?" She leans forward, and I get the feeling she's not just being polite. She really cares.

"Everything's good." I still haven't seen Bat's work, because we keep getting distracted with his stories behind the masterpieces on his wall. The guy knows more about art than I knew there was to know.

"Is he what you expected?"

I have to laugh. "Not exactly. But he's okay."

"What are you working on?"

Good question. We haven't done anything but hang out and talk. When are we going to get started? I don't want Jules to think I'm a slacker. "We're brainstorming right now."

"Measure twice, cut once, right?" She chuckles.

I don't have a clue what she means. "Yeah, right."

"I can't wait to hear about the great work you're going to create. Keep me updated, okay?"

I will, once I know what Bat and I are up to. "Sure. I still have a lot to do to get ready for the party. I'd better get going."

"Me, too." She picks up her plate. "See you at the party."

"Hey, I feel bad. We were talking so much you never got the chance to eat."

"It's okay. I wasn't that hungry."

I watch as she dumps the burger in the trash. Sister Mo would have had a thing or two to say about that.

Anna shows up fifteen minutes before the party is supposed to start, which is hilarious since she'd dissed it.

"Hey," she says, without a smile. Her interpretation of beach-party-wear is skin-tight leather pants and a black T-shirt with a skull that has blood dripping out of its eye sockets. She actually looks pretty cool.

"You're early. I'm still finishing up."

"Pretend I'm invisible. Everybody does."

I chuckle, even though I'm not sure she meant to be funny. I set a blank canvas on an easel so anyone who wants to can try painting. To get things started, I sketch a stick figure holding a brush with the words "Paint Me." No need to show off.

Anna strolls the room, inspecting my work. On three of the

walls, I painted a dense jungle. The trick is to have the light hit all of the leaves from the same direction, or no one will buy the illusion, as Bat told me. My final touch was to point a couple of spotlights at the walls, making the room feel hot and tropical.

Anna brushes her fingertips against the fourth wall where I'd painted a beach with ultramarine-blue surf. I added a few palm trees and beachgoers, including Sister Mo in her nun's habit looking for shells. "Who's this?"

"Don't! It's not dry."

"Sorrrrrry." She breaks into a grin that gives me the creeps. "I know you're the famous street artist. Is Bat one, too?"

I'm not admitting anything to her, and I'm not really sure what kind of stuff Bat paints. "You said you're from California."

"I spent last spring break with my grandparents. They live in The Bronx. Can you believe it?"

I've always thought The Bronx would be a nice place to grow up, but I've only painted there three, maybe four times. What are the chances?

She raises her multi-perforated eyebrow. "I saw how you were looking at Lake. I wonder what she'd think of your secret."

"It's not a secret," I say, as if I could care less that I'll be the outcast if the others find out.

"Nice try. What's it worth for me to keep my mouth shut?"

"I grew up in an orphanage. I don't own anything."

"Then you'll owe me."

"Owe you what?" I say through clenched teeth.

"I'll let you know when the right opportunity comes along."

That's when the others show up for the party. I check out their faces, but no one is acting like they overheard Anna blackmailing me.

My attention zooms to Lake. The light blue shirt tied at her waist makes her eyes pop. My heart does a backflip.

"It feels like I'm at the beach!" she says with a huge smile.

Mission accomplished.

"Isn't Orfyn's style *unique?*" Anna's eyes send the message loud and clear that she wants me to squirm. I can either let her ruin my party, or I can ignore her. Not a tough choice.

"Nice job, Art." Stryker is wearing a suit the exact same shade as Mr. Blue's, which is the best outfit here. I'd bet Mr. Blue would wear a suit even on the beach.

Marty—who I wasn't sure would come—is wearing this hilarious shirt with monkeys swinging from palm tree to palm tree. "I love Jamaica," he says.

"Never been."

"Great jerk chicken."

"We have some over there."

He smiles for the first time since I've met him. "Cool."

Jules looks great. She's wearing a Hawaiian print dress and a crimson flower in her hair that looks real. How did she get something like that here?

Jules says, "I made a special drink for everyone. They're over here, labeled with your names, but I made enough so you can try the others, too." She invented some great ones, like a *Black Hole* for Physics—a mix of all the sodas she could find—and a *Starry Night* for me—grape soda, vanilla ice cream and pop rocks.

"This is *almost* perfect," Stryker says while turning a three-sixty. I brace myself for what he thinks *isn't* perfect.

"Alex, care to do the honors?"

Alex has on a black hoodie that's got to be hot. He pulls a small metal box from his hoodie's pocket and walks around the room, watching the gadget. He points to the smoke detector on the ceiling. Then he hands Stryker a coil of wire. Stryker easily reaches the ceiling and winds the wire around the detector.

"That's the dummy," Alex tells us in a whisper. "It's a guitar string." He reaches in his hoodie's pocket again, pulls out a larger metal box, and gives it to Stryker. Stryker pushes up one of the ceiling tiles, slides the box on top of the tile, then eases it back into place. Alex holds up the first box and pushes the orange button, which lights up. "We are now in stealth mode, people."

Stryker fist-bumps him. "My man."

"What is that thing?" I ask.

"It's a soundwave-canceling re-transmitter. It's a great example of destructive interference."

I look at him blankly.

"It messes with their bug."

"Someone bugged my studio?"

"Assume that any place we have access to is being monitored," Stryker says. "Except your bathroom." He gives Lake a knowing look and she nods.

Anna places her hands on her hips. "Why didn't anyone tell me?"

"You're so easy to approach," Marty answers. He laughs, and Anna slugs him in the arm.

Marty knew about it, too? I know I'm the new guy, but it would've been nice if one of them had clued me in.

"Alex, where did you get the parts?" Jules asks.

I'd been wondering the same thing. Art supplies are one thing, but it's not like we can just have anti-listening-device equipment delivered to our fake boarding school.

Alex shrugs. "I'm pretty good at repurposing household electronics."

"Q." Marty nods in approval.

"You're all so immature," Anna says. "This is a party. They don't care."

"It would be nice if you were right," Stryker says, then turns to me. "Art, what exciting things do you have planned for us?"

"Thanks for asking, *Peace*. I set up this easel so everyone can take a turn at painting."

"Talk about a wild time," Stryker says, dryly.

"I've never painted on canvas before." Lake goes over and starts examining the different brushes.

Sorry, Stryker. Point: Orfyn.

Lake is soon absorbed in swirling all shades of colors onto the canvas. I never imagined her as an abstract girl. She sets down the brush and touches her fingers to the wet paint. Within seconds, she's using her entire hand. My jaw literally drops. Then, she touches the canvas with both hands! I think I'm in love.

"I have a better idea," Anna says, breaking me out of my Lake trance. "How about we play One True Thing? Let's start with Orfyn."

Orfyn

"I don't have a One True Thing," I lie.

"Why don't you tell them how you got your name?" Anna says.

I shrug, as if it's no big deal my parents didn't want me. "I'm an orphan."

"That's not the entire reason, is it?" Anna asks.

I want to give her a *Shut up!* look, but everyone's eyes are on me.

"Come on, spill it," Stryker says. "What's said in the jungle stays in the jungle—thanks to Alex."

"Yeah, what's up with your name?" Alex, unlike Anna, looks genuinely curious.

"I needed something unique … for when I'm famous." It hurts that I can't admit I already am.

Anna crosses her arms. "But there's more to it."

"He's already told us his One True Thing," Lake says from across the room. "He's an orphan."

"That's too innocent for a One True Thing," Anna says.

"It's true, that's what counts." Lake holds her eyes, and Anna is the first to look away.

The door opens, and a man in tan overalls strolls into the room, carrying a toolbox. "Sorry. I didn't realize anyone was in here. I'm inspecting smoke detectors. You kids don't mind if I do a quick check, do you?"

Marty catches my eye, confirming there's something strange going on.

Stryker answers, "No problem, sir. Do whatever you need."

The *maintenance man* double-takes Stryker in his gray-blue suit. "Ah, there it is." He makes a big deal about pointing at the plastic circle on the ceiling.

Alex sticks his hands into his hoodie pocket.

"Hey, what's that?" The man pulls over a chair, climbs up, and grabs at the guitar string. After he uncoils it, he places the guitar string into a plastic bag that he just happens to have on him. He points an electronic device at the smoke detector, checks the reading, and nods.

As soon as he leaves, Alex pulls out his gadget and turns it back on. "Still think it's all fun and games, Anna?" Stryker asks.

She glares at him, as if it's his fault we're being spied on.

All we wanted was a few hours alone. But they wouldn't let us have even that. I thought I didn't have any privacy living at St. Catherine's, but this is different. They're listening to everything we say. Always. It suddenly feels like a ghost has walked into the room, stealing all the warmth.

"Hey guys, I have a One True Thing," Alex says, and we all look at him. If anyone can add a laugh when we need it, it's Alex.

Jules gives him an encouraging smile. "Tell us."

"My dad is the top oil producer in West Texas."

"But you're working on alternative energy," Anna counters.

"Now you get my One True Thing. My dad says he'll disown me if I succeed, but that didn't stop him from taking their payoff."

I may be an orphan, but Sister Mo never made me feel bad about doing what I love.

"It's not a payoff," Jules says. "It's their way of thanking our parents for giving us up to science."

"Ha!" comes from Marty, who's got the eraser end of a pencil in his mouth and his eyes focused on his notebook.

Lake says, "That money will improve their lives. At least, it has for my family."

It will for St. Catherine's, too—as long as the Bishop sticks to his word.

I go to the food table. "Let's eat. This is jerk chicken, which I just learned is one of Marty's favorite foods. If you've never had it before, then you're going to be thanking me big time." I wave toward the chips. "This is the island version of French fries. And this—" A *crash* cuts off my words.

I turn to see Alex on the floor, gasping for air.

Before any of us can react, Lake is on her knees next to him, propping up his head, smearing paint every place she touches.

"What's wrong with him?" Jules's face is filled with horror.

"This happened to a guy at my orphanage when he ate peanuts," I say.

"Alex didn't eat anything," Marty says.

"His airway isn't blocked," Lake says with her fingers down his throat. She tilts his head back, takes a deep breath, wraps her lips around his and breathes air into his lungs. After a couple of times, she turns to Stryker. "Get help!"

Stryker removes the box from Alex's hoodie, points it at the ceiling, and pushes the orange button. Then he yells, "We need medical attention in the art classroom. Now!"

Even though I now know about the bugs, it's still a shock when two men in white lab coats arrive within a minute.

"He's having difficulty breathing," Lake informs them.

They hurry over to Alex. Lake moves aside. One of the men flashes a light into Alex's eyes, and the other checks his vitals. They cover Alex's face with an oxygen mask and lift him onto a gurney.

Then they wheel Alex out of the party that was his idea in the first place.

Stryker's eyes land on Lake. "You may have saved Alex's life."

A flush colors her cheeks. "A few years ago, I got certified in CPR for my babysitting certificate."

The rest of us didn't think to give Alex mouth-to-mouth. And Lake stayed so calm. I thought she was amazing *before.*

"I need to get back to work," Anna says, as if nothing terrifying had just happened. As she passes me, she whispers, "I was once the very first person to discover an Orfyn." Then she strolls out the door without a backward glance.

I check out the others, but no one is acting like they heard her.

"Nice party. Seriously," Marty says as he heads out, clutching his notebook.

Within minutes, everyone else follows, leaving me alone with trays of untouched food and glasses of barely drunk drinks. I lower myself to the floor, bummed. I'd like to say it's only because of Alex, but I'd be lying to myself. I wanted to give Lake an amazing party, and I didn't deliver.

My eyes land on her abstract painting. She has a great sense of balance, and I love her color choices: yellows and purples and all different greens. The party wasn't a total failure. Lake got to paint a picture for the first time—using her hands, which gives me an idea.

I grab what I need and head to her place. Nothing hangs from her door. They all put something on their handle as a signal to let each other know when they're working and don't want to be disturbed. I haven't bothered, since I'm always awake during the day. I should probably talk to Bat about that. We actually have a lot to talk about in our next dream session.

I knock on Lake's door.

When she opens it, confusion fills her face. "Hi?"

I hold up the can. "I thought you could use this. It's walnut oil. It works as good as turpentine, but smells a whole lot better." Bat told me it's what the Renaissance painters used to use.

She shows me her rainbow-colored hands. "Thanks. I've been trying to remove this."

"It's oil paint. Soap and water doesn't cut it."

She takes the can, then looks at me expectantly while I wait for her to invite me in.

"Once your painting dries, I'll hang it up for you," I offer.

"It's not worthy to be displayed."

"You're wrong. It has a great feel."

Lake looks pleased, but she doesn't invite me in. Probably not comfortable being alone with a guy in her room.

I lean against the door jamb to let her know I'm fine with talking in the hallway. "Have you heard anything about Alex?"

"I presume they're running some tests. It'll probably take some time."

"Right. That makes sense." I need to think before shooting off my mouth around Lake. "It's weird how it came on so fast."

"I've been thinking about that, too. His lungs were inflating and deflating, but there didn't seem to be any gas exchange. It's as if his body decided not to turn oxygen into carbon dioxide, which of course is impossible."

Yeah, my thoughts exactly.

She gives me a strained smile. "Is there anything else?"

"Want to grab something to eat?"

She looks down at her hands. "Sorry, but I need to take care of this."

"Sure, I understand. It's getting late." It's not even eight o'clock, but it has been a crazy night.

"Thanks for the walnut oil." She sort of slams the door in my face, but it could've been because of her oily fingers.

That went well.

I think.

The Darwinians

"Kids get sick," the raven-haired man says. "That's why we have an infirmary."

"This isn't exactly the common cold," the woman says.

"We're asking one brain to handle two consciousnesses. We can't expect everything to go according to plan. Consider the advances we're already seeing."

"But Alex's situation is unexplainable. His lungs are operating as if he's been smoking for fifty years."

"It's psychosomatic," explains the white-bearded man. "His brain only *thinks* he has emphysema. There is no physical degeneration."

"He can barely breathe." She turns away and coughs.

"We are not shutting down this Program because one kid is having a temporary health issue," the raven-haired man says.

"If his life is at stake, we should consider—"

"Out of the question," the bearded man says.

"I suggest we cut back on his dream sessions for the time being," the woman says. "We can medicate him to limit his REM cycles." She places her trembling hands on the mahogany conference table. "He needs rest."

"Not possible," the raven-haired man says. "We need all of them working as much as they can to make a major advance and prove the Program's success. Then, there is no limit to where we can go. Rest can wait."

"I agree," says the bearded man. "Continue as planned."

"How is our Nobel for Literature?" the woman asks in between coughs.

"Cecil isn't concerned," the raven-haired man says, dismissively.

"Are you sure he's paying attention to the right things?"

"This is about accelerating the future. It's never easy, and it's never without cost."

"Certainly. But let's keep them alive, shall we?" the woman says.

"Of course," the bearded man answers, looking up at the portrait of the woman with curly, salt-and-pepper hair. "But let's also remember who we're committed to keep alive when you say *them.*"

Orfyn

In the last week of dreams, I've been in Bat's basement—technically, his dead mother's basement—and done nothing but hang out in the world's most comfortable recliners, listening to cool music and talking about paintings. It would be great if this were my old life. But he's supposed to be mentoring me in … something.

Lately, he's been asking me these bizarre questions like: Why do you think Picasso was so obsessed with fawns? and Don't you think Andy Warhol was a big phony? and Isn't it time to bring nudes back into mainstream art? And the whole time we're together, Bat plays this video game. His avatar, who looks like a troll version of himself, walks through a garden. That's it. No sword fights or car chases or snipers. Just walking. It's weird.

"You know, the other Nobels are trying to change the world," I say.

Bat stares at me blankly, which is pretty much his normal expression.

"You're my Mentor. We're supposed to be advancing the state of art."

"What do you mean?"

"You know, we were brought together to beat the machines and keep humanity in art." Saying it out loud makes it sound like I've lost my mind. But I'm saying this in a dream created by Bat after his brain patterns were implanted into my head. Reality isn't in play anymore.

"Is that what they told you?" he says with the concern of someone selecting socks.

"That's why we're here!"

"If you say so." He directs his avatar to circle a tree. "Is that really what you want to do?"

"No," I admit. "I came here because I want to learn from you."

"What do you want to learn?"

He's got to be messing with me. "Bat, you do realize you're my Mentor, right?"

He shrugs with the innocence of a little kid. "I don't always grok everything that's going on, but I know this isn't the only world. Sometimes it takes me a while to remember there's another one. I know the important things, though. I know you painted this." He nods to the screens, and a new image appears: Christ, his Disciples, and the Stanley Cup.

Take This Cup.

"How ... how do you have my painting?" I manage to ask.

"Didn't you give it to me?"

"Noooo."

"You must've been thinking about it."

Prickles run down my spine. "You know what I'm thinking?"

"Didn't think so." Bat studies my painting. "I think it's my favorite. Really. Of all time."

If this whole situation isn't strange enough, he's telling me he likes my painting over a basement full of true masterpieces. "I painted it on a brick wall in Brooklyn. It was gone that same day."

His mouth turns down, and he shakes his head. "What a loss. Hey, want a grape soda?"

JIM AND STEPHANIE KROEPFL

"No, I don't want a grape soda. I want you to teach me how to be a great artist."

"No one can teach you to be great. You're going to be great, or you're not." Bat takes a long swig of soda, burps loudly, and starts typing.

As I watch his fingers race across the keyboard, a terrible thought hits me. "What did you do for a living? I mean, before."

"Pretty sure it was games."

"You got paid to play games?"

"I created them."

I suddenly want to barf. "Bat, aren't you a painter?"

He takes a moment to look around and nods in satisfaction. "I think I painted this basement."

I want to strangle him—except his body is already dead. "During the procedure, I saw an artist painting a picture. Wasn't that you?"

"Me? No." He scratches at his stubble. "Maybe I commissioned it for you. You know, as a gift. Did it seem like Rauschenberg? I bet I chose Rauschenberg."

My dream-self takes a deep breath to keep from screaming in frustration. "So, are you or are you not an artist?"

"I've always considered myself to be an electronic artist."

"What does that even mean?!" I get up and wave my hand at the screens. "All you've done since we've merged is waste time playing this stupid video game. You're supposed to be a Master and teach me how to become one."

"My game isn't stupid. Did you notice all the greens?"

The screens display the garden from his game, but now the view has expanded to include a forest that goes on forever. The electronic sunlight filtering through the electronic leaves highlights what has to be a hundred shades of green. It almost feels like I could walk right into it. It's impressive, but it's still just a game.

"A painter can play with perspective," Bat says. "But can you shift the scene one hundred and eighty degrees?" His chubby fingers hit a half a dozen keys, and suddenly I'm looking at the back of the same trees. "Can you alter the light to reflect the time of day?" The sun slides lower on the horizon, casting long shadows. "How about make a plant grow?" I watch as a dandelion rapidly goes through its life cycle, ending with its seeds drifting in the wind.

It finally dawns on me that Bat created this game. "It's cool, it really is, but no one would consider it art."

"A lot of people don't call what you do art, either. But I always did."

Okay, now I feel like a total jerk. "I'm sorry, Bat. I really am. It's just that you're supposed to be my Mentor. We're here to do something important."

Bat pulls himself out of the recliner, heads over to the screens, and stares into the forest behind the screen. "Let me ask you this. Why did you paint what you did?"

"I wanted to blow people's minds."

"Then my advice as your Mentor is: go paint something that blows someone's mind."

When I wake up, my first thought is that Mr. Blue had to have known the truth. Why did the Darwinians choose Bat? Everyone else has a Mentor who's trying to make the world better. Then I get it. Gaming programmers make a ton of money. My pride at being chosen withers and dies faster than Bat's dandelion. The Darwinians never wanted me. They only needed a sixteen-year-old, and it was a whole lot simpler if that body belonged to an orphan.

If all this is true—which I'm pretty sure it is—the Darwinians sold out, Mr. Blue lied about why I'm here, and Bat bought my body. I'm nothing like the others.

I can never let them know.

Lake

Another marathon dream session.

Even though I lost the entire morning, it was worth it. I'd been working on something that, for once, didn't require mouth-breathing. Sophie had me testing our octopuses' intelligence by timing how long they took to escape from various containers. An octopus can thread itself through a hole not much larger than the diameter of its eyeball. George, my favorite, won hands down. They're fascinating creatures. They have three hearts, and their blood uses copper rather than an iron-based carrier for oxygen. Sophie warns me not to become attached because they're purpose isn't for companionship. But how can I not? They're surprisingly affectionate.

Sophie still hasn't figured out she only lives in my dreams, but we're getting along fairly well. She only pursed her lips twice today—a new record. And Deborah is impressed with my progress. Luckily, she attributes it to my scientific proclivity and not to the fact that Sophie still believes she has the power to flunk me.

I nuke a bowl of oatmeal in my microwave and savor the gristy aroma that reminds me of home. Grandma Bee has eaten it every morning for as long as I can remember. I hope every once in a while

Dad gets up in time to chat with her over coffee. She likes that.

I grab my hat and book, planning to read under the shade of the immense oak tree. When I open my door, I discover someone on his knees. My heart rate doubles.

"Careful," Orfyn warns. "This side is wet."

My optical nerves are hit with an explosion of colors. The outside of my door now has a painting of downtown Pittsburgh on it, even though I don't recall ever telling him where I'm from. On the floor lies a photo of the skyline, which he's perfectly captured. Except instead of the city's true grays and browns and tans, he's painted it in vibrant blues and oranges and purples.

Orfyn looks up with a smile. Until now, I hadn't noticed how his golden-green eyes glow against his light brown skin. "Marty seems homesick, so I'm painting everyone's hometown on their door."

As soon as I learned about his discipline, I made a promise to myself not to fall for him. "That's very thoughtful," I say, making sure to sound polite, not flirty.

"One of Sister Mo's favorite verses is, 'The generous man will be prosperous, and he who waters will himself be watered.' It took me years to figure out it's about a lot more than just money."

"Who's Sister Mo?" I ask.

"She runs the orphanage where I grew up. Her full name is Sister Moses the Black."

"Is Moses the Black a saint?" I sound like I find him fascinating, which is giving the wrong impression. I need to be acting aloof and disinterested.

"He was an awesome saint. There are so many great stories about his life," he says, stealing my chance at a quick getaway. "He was this huge black dude who lived in the fourth century in Egypt. Moses started out as a robber and ended up a monk and a priest. I guess you never know how life is going to turn out. Look at us!"

I chuckle along with him and find myself sitting on the floor, crossing my legs to match his. How did that just occur?

"Mind if I fix this bridge while we talk? The perspective is a little off." He grabs a rag, pours some walnut oil on it, and erases the bridge I thought looked perfect.

This is the time to leave, except I'm transfixed. His long fingers barely move, yet the brush dances across my door as he recreates the Fort Duquesne Bridge in bright pink. Orfyn has me entranced as he tells me story after story about Moses the Black. He accomplished so many wonderful things, I can't believe I've never heard of him.

"How did you become such a skilled storyteller?" I ask.

"I was one of the older kids at the orphanage. It was my job to get the little ones to sleep. You can only read *Goodnight Moon* so many times."

"It sounds like you miss Sister Mo and those kids."

"It's hard sometimes. They were the only family I ever had." He starts dotting the river with yellow specs, making it appear to sparkle.

"Do you miss your parents?"

I use my standard line, which cuts off having to get into the painful parts. "My grandmother raised me."

"What happened to your mom and dad?"

I start to examine the hem of my jeans.

"Sorry," he says. "You don't have to answer that."

I'd normally joke to deflect the pain, or ignore the question, but he's not like anyone I've ever met. He carries himself differently than the guys I know, as if he can't wait to discover what's around the next corner. And he doesn't act cool; he just is. He also happens to be cute, none of which is helping me keep my promise to myself. But he seems genuinely curious about my life. We are going to be here for years, and it would be strange not to know anything about each other.

"My mom died of cancer when I was seven. My dad ... he spends his time with his regrets."

"What happened, if you don't mind my asking?"

"My dad was a professional musician, but he had to quit the band when my mom got sick. I once asked him why he didn't join another one. He said you only get one shot and he'd had his, but life got in the way." I don't agree with his excuse, but one day, because of us and future Nobels, everyone might get their second shot.

"It's great that you have your grandmother," Orfyn says, oblivious that talking about Grandma Bee is what causes me the most distress.

How much time do we have before she stops remembering who I am? That was the most difficult part about deciding to come here. I'll probably never see her alive again. Even though she was aware of that fact, Grandma Bee insisted I accept their offer to become a Nobel Candidate. She didn't want me to lose this amazing opportunity because of her illness. I duck my head and blink away tears.

Orfyn gently touches my arm. "Hey, what's your favorite color?"

Shivers run through me. What is wrong with me? I've been doing the opposite of what I promised myself, and now my body is betraying me, too. I grew up with an artist, and I will not bind my emotions to another. I have firsthand experience of what life is like when their dreams don't pan out.

Dad would constantly boast about his trumpet playing. And then he'd become severely depressed because he wasn't as successful as the people he believed weren't as accomplished as him. During those times, Mom couldn't do anything right. I used to hide in my closet so I couldn't hear her cry. The only happy times for me were when he was on tour.

He grew worse after she died.

"I need to get going," I say.

"I'm almost done. I just need to know your favorite color."

"Green." It's red. Why did I say green?

"Tell me which shade you like best." He mixes together blue, yellow, and white paint on his palette, then does it a second time. But the two greens appear completely different. "The left one is the color of spring leaves in the sunshine," he says. "And the right one is how Central Park's grass looks after it's been mowed. Which do you like better?"

I can practically feel the sun's warmth on my cheeks, and I could swear I smell freshly mown grass. I never realized color triggers one's senses. I need to explore this concept further. I point to my choice.

He paints *Lake* in spring-leaf green at the top of my door. "Now I won't have any problem finding you." When his golden-green eyes grab hold of mine, my breath catches, and my skin feels effervescent.

Warning bells clang in my head.

Artists are dreamers, and one thing I've learned from my dad—and it could be the only thing—is you can't rely on them when things get tough. I am not falling for a guy who probably thinks responsibility means selecting the appropriate shade of green.

Down the hall, Anna emerges from her room.

"Hi, Anna," I greet, silently thanking her for the interruption.

She passes by as if we're invisible.

I shake my head. "I've tried to be friendly, but she doesn't seem to like me."

"Her loss. I think you're great."

No! No! No! I hurriedly get to my feet. "I'm sure you want to get started on someone else's door."

He stands, thankfully taking my hint. "I'm in no rush. I like watching paint dry with you." His adorable smile is precisely why I need him to leave. "Want to get some ice cream?"

A chocolate-dipped soft serve sounds heavenly, but this conversation has proven I need to keep my distance from Orfyn. "I can't right now. Thank you for my door. It's beautiful," I say, trying to sound grateful but not interested. I'm fairly confident my delivery is closer to schizophrenic.

I tear myself away and dash down the hall, sensing his hurt eyes following me.

Stryker

Her head is down as she comes barreling down the hallway. I thrust out my hands to keep Lake from taking us both down. She smells sweet, like sun-warmed strawberries. My heart rate starts working double-time.

"Sorry," Lake yelps. "I was, uhm, lost in thought."

I make myself let go of her. "Anything you want to talk about?" My eyes shoot to the ceiling as a reminder to keep her response neutral.

Her eyes go wide. "No!"

Interesting. What secret is she withholding? Lake hasn't told me anything about her life. But if I ask, then she'll expect me to answer those same questions. I came here to escape my past.

And to prevent it from happening again.

"I mean, no, everything is fine," she says, which is obviously a lie.

I can't begin to describe the color of her hair. Every time she moves, it reminds me of staring into a midnight bonfire on my family's beach, which only resurfaces the memories I've been trying to suppress. Alicia loved that beach.

I make myself look away. "I should get going."

"Have you eaten yet?"

"Just finished," I lie.

"Want to keep me company?"

I do, which is the problem. "Bjorn and I were in the middle of something, and I want to get back to it."

Her smile fades. "I understand."

I should leave, but it's as if her eyes have a magnetic power and I can't pull away. "What were you working on last night?"

Her face lights up as she tells me about George and the other octopuses, growing more animated when she shifts into the consistency of dead human brains.

"What does Bjorn have you working on?" she asks.

Lake thinks past herself. Alicia was like that, too. A shiver runs through me when I picture her face.

Lake is looking at me expectantly.

"We're studying the *Art of War* by Sun Tzu. Bjorn has a brilliant take on it." I'm not saying it for the benefit of those listening. He knows about my past, and he's trying to make sure I don't make the same mistakes again.

Lake's smile warms away my shivers. "This is an amazing experience, isn't it?"

"Sure is." No need to scare her any worse until I know what's going on.

Before they sealed my air duct, I discovered there's a second team of scientists, and they've taken a lot of precautions to isolate us from them. Since Bjorn has no way of letting them know what I know, I asked him about them. For the first time, he wasn't forthcoming, saying that it has nothing to do with our work. That worries me.

As Bjorn has been teaching me, I need to question everyone's underlying motive. What's the purpose of keeping them from us? I don't want to alarm the others until I learn what they're up to.

"You sure you don't want to hang out for a bit?" she asks.

"Can't right now. See you later," I say to urge her along.

"Another time then." She takes a few steps, then stops and turns to me. "Stryker, I'm glad we're here together."

My guts twist. I cannot allow myself to have feelings for Lake. My natural inclination is to push her away by acting like a jerk, but I can't make myself hurt her like that. She deserves better. I have to cram what I'm feeling down deep, where I've buried everything else.

I force myself to smile. "Me, too. You're a good friend."

Five years is a long time to pretend you don't care.

Lake

I'm riding the subway.

The three girls across from me have their noses buried in their phones, so in this dream we're not in the eighties, which is a first. I scan the faces. Sophie isn't on the train. When we pull into the station, *Grand Central* is written in tile on the wall.

What is happening?

A rush of people scramble to board, but my Mentor isn't one of them. Where is she? The doors slide open and close at each stop as we swiftly travel beneath New York City, but Sophie doesn't appear. Did she decide to fire me? I thought our dream session went well last night.

"Lake!"

My anxiety dissipates, and I turn around. Instead of Sophie, a guy with a fade haircut and a wide smile is heading toward me. I'm doubly surprised when Orfyn leans down and gives me a quick kiss on the lips, as if it's perfectly natural. Why does he think he has the right to kiss me? He slides in next to me and throws his arm around my shoulders.

I remove it and place it in his lap, then press myself into the wall.

"What are you doing here?"

"I thought the plan was to picnic in Central Park."

"Picnic?"

He holds up a take-out bag. "Paninis and coleslaw. Great, you brought chips."

I follow his eyes and see barbeque kettle chips in a plastic bag on my lap that wasn't there before. Of course. Orfyn's strange behavior so flustered me, I forgot this is a dream. But that realization only adds to my confusion.

"Orfyn, why are you in Sophie's dreamspace?"

He moves closer and winds a lock of my hair around his finger. "Who's Sophie?"

"Stop it!" I tug my hair from his grasp. Why is he acting this way? "She's my Mentor. And right now, I should be working with her in our lab. You know all this."

"The next stop is ours," he says.

We don't have a stop because there is no *us*. I sit up straighter, and my eyes scan the newest passengers, but Sophie isn't one of them.

"Call in sick," he says, with a mischievous smile.

I'll get right on that.

He stands as the train slows. "You're coming, right?"

I can't blow off my Mentor to picnic, especially with the person I don't dare spend time with.

"Come on, Lake. You deserve a break. You work too hard." His golden-green eyes hold promises of fun.

I have been putting in the hours, and I've never been to Central Park. Am I actually considering it?

Orfyn holds out his hand. "It's a beautiful day, and I promise to get you back in an hour. Two, tops."

I suppose one hour won't interfere with my work, especially since Sophie is still missing for some reason.

I tentatively place my hand in his, and Orfyn pulls me up.

"This isn't a date," I clarify. "We're simply eating together."

He chuckles. "Yeah, right." He wraps his other arm around me. "You look beautiful today." He leans down and presses his lips against mine—and this time it's not quick.

My mind is telling me to stop, but my body disobeys as it intensifies into a we're-the-only-people-in-the-world kiss. His cinnamon-walnut oil scent envelops me as I lean into him, losing myself to the sensation. His lips make my body feel like it's filled with twinkling lightning bugs. I've never been kissed like this before.

I jerk away. Orfyn is *not* my boyfriend.

And he shouldn't be in this dream.

"This is wrong." I dash through the subway's closing doors.

I wake with a start. Moonlight shines through my window, and I check the time. I've only been asleep for an hour. I touch my lips, but they're not swollen from Orfyn's kisses. Because none of it was real.

I take a long, hot shower, attempting to wash away the memory of him. What just happened? How could Orfyn appear in my dream? And where was Sophie?

I return to bed, but each time I close my eyes, I picture Orfyn kissing me. Why was I dreaming about him? It should've been Stryker on that train. He's the more logical choice. Except, I shouldn't be dreaming about either one of them. My purpose is to work with Sophie, not play hooky in New York City with a boy.

After reciting the elements of the Periodic Table too many times to count, I finally drift off to sleep. I wake after seven hours. Normally, I'd be thrilled, but I'm not. I'm terrified.

Lake

I need Stryker's advice.

I knock. Unlike everyone else's door, his is still white. Was it Orfyn or Stryker who chose not to embellish it with Stryker's hometown? Now that I think about it, Stryker has never mentioned where he's from, or anything else about his life. I make a mental note to have that conversation.

Just when I'm about to leave, Stryker opens his door. His damp curls glisten, and a towel is wrapped around his toned waist. It takes longer than it should to drag my eyes back up to his face.

"Are you up for a walk?" I flick my eyes upward.

"It's not a good time."

"This is important."

He hesitates and finally answers, "Give me a minute to get dressed."

He shuts the door, allowing my blood pressure to return to normal. I mentally recite the Arrhenius equation to regain my composure. Losing control of my emotions is most likely what caused this issue.

Once we're outside, Stryker veers left. "Let's go to the creek."

"What creek?"

"It's past those trees." He points to the rise beyond the weedy meadow that was once the athletic field. The two rusty goal posts resemble long-forgotten sentries.

"We were instructed not to leave campus." I know I sound straight-laced, but I don't need to compound my problems.

"This place is bigger than you realize. And stop looking like you're about to divulge the date the earth will be destroyed. They're probably watching us."

I re-adjust my face, despite the fact Sophie's world may have already ended. Wasn't I going to ask him about something? It had to do with … It must not have been important.

"I know you instructed me not to trust anyone—including you—but I have a situation," I say.

He stops and turns to me. "I shouldn't have said that. I was only trying to get my point across. If it weren't for you, I wouldn't be here. I'm the one person you *can* trust."

I choose not to believe that. I trust Deborah. And even though I don't know him well, I consider Orfyn trustworthy. Same with Marty, Alex, and Jules. The only person I don't entirely trust is Anna, but only because she's never allowed me to get to know her. I don't express my thoughts, though. Stryker's ability to trust others isn't going to be altered through a debate.

"What's going on?" he asks.

"It started two nights ago," I say with a shaky voice.

His eyebrows furrow. "Why don't you hold off until we get there?"

We walk in silence while I press my lips tight, containing the news that makes me quake. I run my index finger against the scar on my thumb, but its usual soothing comfort fails me.

We reach a strand of weeping willows lining a creek bank. Their branches touch, forming a sun-dappled canopy, and I easily spot a crayfish darting beneath a rock in the clear water. It's the ideal place for a picnic. Nix that. Contemplating a picnic is most likely what created my dilemma.

Stryker lowers himself to the ground, and I join him. Sweet-smelling oxygen rushes in, replacing The Flem's stale, recirculated air in my lungs.

"I almost forgot what it feels like to have some privacy," I say.

"That's why I like coming here." He pulls off his shoes, rolls up his pants legs, and dangles his canoe-sized feet in the water.

I kick off my flip-flops, wiggle my purple-polished toes in the cool water, and relish in the current tickling my ankles. This would be the perfect place to meditate—if I could forget about my last two dream sessions.

"Tell me what's going on, Lake."

I watch a robin gobble up bright red berries from a flourishing bush, and hold my gaze on the peaceful scene as I ask, "Have you ever had a dream session that Bjorn wasn't in?" I dare a glance at his face.

His surprised expression provides me with the answer. "I take it this isn't a hypothetical question."

"I wish. Two nights ago, when I appeared in Sophie's lab, I assumed she finally acknowledged my hints and was outside taking a smoking break. I began working, expecting her any minute. But after she didn't appear, I went to look for her."

By now, my heart feels like I'm running a six-minute mile.

"I opened the door, and there was nothing on the other side," I explain. "Literally nothing. Absolute blackness. I didn't know what else to do, so I took refuge in our lab until I woke up. The same thing occurred last night."

He looks at me in disbelief.

I take a deep breath. And then another.

"Do they know?" he asks.

"No. I reported to Deborah that we've been repeating tests to validate our results." It wasn't an outright lie. It's what Sophie and I had planned to work on, except with her there.

"Good thinking. You don't know what they'll do to you if they think she's not coming back."

I hate when he says things like that.

"Any idea what caused it?" he asks.

I nod, then sketchily describe the subway scene, glossing over the kiss. And failing to mention whom I'd been kissing.

"I think you're right," Stryker says. "The timing was too close."

I didn't intend to dream about Orfyn. And because of it, I've somehow broken my link with my Mentor. This is another example of why I need to avoid Orfyn's company.

"There's the possibility Sophie went on vacation and forgot to tell me." I force on a wobbly smile.

"Did she tell you she planned to go somewhere?"

In addition to losing Sophie, it seems that I've lost my ability to be funny, too. "I'm joking, Stryker."

"I am astute enough to realize that, but it would be a game changer if you weren't."

"What are you implying?"

"Bjorn and I have been testing our limits, and we've confirmed he can't put us into a location he's never been. He also can't create a dreamspace he's not in. He's tried to place me in various locations alone, but he always ends up there with me."

"Sophie and I've never explored how our dreamspace works, since she'd first have to realize she only lives in my brain." I pluck a piece of quartz from the water and examine it. I've been telling myself it doesn't matter if she's confused about our roles, but I didn't consider how much of the experience I've been missing.

"Lake, you're not getting it. You're able to do something that I haven't been able to achieve. At least, not yet."

I snort, which is so attractive. "It's not an achievement, believe me."

And why is he making it seem like a contest? We're all trying to accomplish different things. But I suppose one of us will be heralded as the first to help our Mentor achieve their life's purpose. I'll be terminated if I can't find Sophie. A prick of unease pierces me. They would let me go home, even after all this time.

Wouldn't they?

Stryker cuts through my thoughts. "Bjorn and I realized that since our Mentors create our dreamspaces, they'll never get to experience anything new. For example, they can't go to Paris if they've never been, even if we go there in the future. And they'll never be able to meet anyone new. We've been concerned that this lack of stimulation could impact their mental health. But if Sophie is having her own experiences ... What you're doing is amazing." He's staring into my eyes with an intensity that catches me by surprise. "*You're* amazing."

My cheeks flush while my mind scrambles to catch up. He's acting as if he likes me. Or am I assessing the situation completely wrong? He's never treated me as more than a friend. After these last two horrible nights, I don't dare trust my instincts. I settle on the premise that he was only being encouraging.

"I appreciate that," I say. "But at this moment I don't feel amazing. I have no purpose for being here if Sophie doesn't reappear."

He moves closer, then ever so gently pulls me into his arms, as if I'm a fragile piece of glass. "I'm sorry you've been going through this," he says into my hair.

Once I get over the shock, I tentatively lean into his chest. He holds me tighter, and I breathe in his clean soap scent. When I wrap my arms around his neck, he pulls back his head so we're cheek-to-cheek. A random thought occurs: the kisspeptin hormone isn't elevating my heartbeat as it should. Then Stryker leans back and looks at me in that way where I know I'm about to be kissed. I want him to. I think.

He suddenly releases me. "We should go." He rolls down his pants legs and rises to his feet.

"Is something wrong?" He may have noticed my limiting reagent.

"No." His sharp tone says otherwise.

He's regretting what almost happened, but he was the one who initiated it. I stand and step into my flip-flops, trying to act as if nothing about his behavior is odd, hoping we haven't destroyed our friendship.

119

JIM AND STEPHANIE KROEPFL

We head back to The Flem, and after not speaking for an awkwardly long time, Stryker grabs my hand and gives it a quick squeeze.

"Sorry about that back there," he says. "I still have some things to deal with."

"Do you want to talk about it?"

"Is it okay if we don't?"

I hope one day he trusts me enough to share whatever happened to him. I study Stryker out of the corner of my eye. He's the type of guy girls dream of. Brilliant. Practical. Dependable. Not to mention gorgeous. I could like him, perhaps even love him one day. But the lack of adrenaline and cortisol in my blood stream while we hugged is something I need to consider.

Maybe Stryker isn't the only one who has issues.

"I've been wondering if that dream hurt Sophie's feelings," Stryker says, not-so-subtly changing the subject.

Finding Sophie is the reason I sought him out in the first place. And if I can determine how to get her back, Stryker and I'll have the plenty of time to figure out our relationship. I return my attention to what's most important right now.

"Sophie wasn't on the subway," I say. "She shouldn't have been aware I was with ... someone else." I need to obliterate that kiss from my thoughts.

"She could have some level of awareness beyond your dreamspace."

Unease ripples through me. "Are you suggesting Sophie is aware of what I'm thinking?"

"It's one theory. Have you ever attempted to communicate with her while you're awake?" Stryker asks, adding to my discomfort.

"Our Mentors are not supposed to be conscious when we're awake."

"The Darwinians may have underestimated the impact of combining two minds."

Lake

If Stryker's hypothesis is correct, Sophie's feelings were hurt when I had a dream without her. I feel terrible if I caused her to believe I don't enjoy working with her, because I do. Almost always. Though I do get uneasy when considering she may be aware of my every thought.

But that concern is moot if we never re-merge. Even though it's early, I change into my PJs and crawl into bed. I force myself to focus on the positive. Sophie has already taught me so many invaluable skills. I love the work we're doing, and she obviously loves it, too, or she wouldn't have wanted to extend her life by merging with me. I can understand why she sometimes gets impatient, but my competence has been improving. We're going to be an outstanding team in a year or two. I couldn't have asked for a better Mentor. And, I'm certain, together, we'll find the cure for Alzheimer's.

I close my eyes and begin talking to her in my mind. "Sophie, I'm sorry if I made you believe I'd rather dream my own dreams than be with you. I didn't invite Orfyn into our dreamspace, and he shouldn't have been there. I want to continue our work. Together. Please come back to me."

I drift off to sleep and find myself in a noisy cafeteria filled with people in white lab coats.

Sophie sits across from me, angrily spearing a cucumber with her fork. "I didn't think you were coming back."

Is it a coincidence she returned after I just apologized?

She sighs dramatically. "Because of your stunt with that boy, we're now weeks behind schedule."

Boy? As in Orfyn? But my dream—that was wrong on so many levels—only occurred two nights ago. "How long have I been gone?"

"Twelve days, not that I'm counting."

Until now, Sophie and I have always picked up from where we left off the previous night. Somehow, Sophie's concept of time has become nonlinear.

"What's done is done." Sophie's tone conveys that she's not yet forgiven me. "I can only hope you didn't neglect your other obligations. I'd hate to see you receiving a semester of Incompletes." She lights a cigarette—in the cafeteria where everyone is eating—and takes a long drag.

"I'll work hard to catch up," I answer, because what else can I say?

I need to tell Stryker so he can get Bjorn's input. A part of me wishes I can admit to Deborah about how Stryker's Mentor will be helping mine adjust to her new life. It is significant. But I'm not ready to admit things aren't going as well as I've led her to believe.

"I'm going to need longer hours from you to make up for the lost time," Sophie says.

I stare blindly into my chicken noodle soup that wasn't there seconds before, trying to fight off my panic. I want a life, too. One that she's not constantly in. I recall what Stryker said about how the Mentors won't be stimulated because of their lack of new experiences. "Did you go anywhere while I was gone?"

"How could I? Someone had to feed the octopuses." Her bright red lips mash together. "I'm sorry. I didn't mean it to sound that way. I don't know what's been wrong with me lately."

"Neither of us have been ourselves." It would be funny, if it wasn't. "May I ask you a personal question?"

"That depends on what it is."

"Are you happy?"

She blows smoke out through her nostrils. "Happiness is a state of mind."

Exactly. But she no longer has a brain. "What did … what *do* you like to do for fun?"

She looks at me oddly.

"If we're going to spend even more time together, it would be nice to know each other better."

She takes a few puffs, then finally nods. "I love to travel to new cities and explore their art museums." Her face softens, and her eyes take on a wistful look.

My heart breaks for her. According to Bjorn and Stryker, she'll never be able to experience that again. Did she truly comprehend what she'd have to give up to live this way?

I take a moment to mentally navigate this landmine of a conversation by stirring my steaming soup. If Orfyn appeared in my dream, then Sophie may have conjured someone else in our dreamspace. "Did you spend time with anyone while I was gone?"

"Just me, all by myself for weeks. Everyone must have decided to take a vacation at the same time."

If she experienced time as she remembers, she had to have been confused when everyone she knows wasn't around. And lonely. "I'm truly sorry I was gone for so long, Sophie. I won't let it happen again."

"I may have been pushing you too hard," she says. "We need to get back to work, but how about we take it easy today?"

"That sounds wonderful."

We smile at each other, and it feels like we've made a leap in our relationship. She doesn't realize she's intruding on my life, and once she understands I'm her Nobel, I'm sure she'll respect my privacy.

True to Sophie's word, I wake a mere seven hours later, feeling refreshed. I stretch, and my thoughts for some reason drift to Stryker.

When considering all the factors, we would make the ideal couple. We really need to spend more time together and get to know each other better. I don't even know where he's from. There's a tickling sensation at the edge of my mind. Lately, it hasn't been as sharp as usual. It's even been getting difficult to recall what Sophie and I worked on. I don't think Deborah has picked up on it, but I have to concentrate to remember the particulars so I can give her a detailed debrief.

The long hours in our dream sessions must be wearing me out. I wish I could tell Sophie I'll be more productive if we cut back on our work schedule, but for now that's still impossible. Until then, I need some way to capture my thoughts.

I rummage through my desk and grab the journal I brought from home. I'd thought it would be interesting to document my time here, but I'd forgotten about it until now. Given all that occurs while I'm at work, it would be prudent to start writing down the important things as soon as I wake. I turn to the first page and shut my eyes, trying to piece together my dream.

We started off in a cafeteria. Sophie was angry at me for being with Orfyn. There was something about an art museum. I remember feeling good at the end because we'd crossed a hurdle. And then we went to the lab. What were we working on? I wince. I had to kill and dissect Ramona, the sweetest of all the octopuses, which helps explain why I'm having problems remembering my dreams. We've gone through octopus after octopus, trying to understand their nervous system, of which only a part is localized in their brain. Their arms contain most of their neurons, which gives them exquisite sensitivity. Their severed limbs show a variety of complex reflex actions with no input from their brains. And, octopuses can grow back lost arms, which could help us determine how to regenerate nerves or organ segments.

The key is to keep reminding myself they're not alive for real.

I clutch the journal to my chest. It's already helped. A fleeting thought appears, then disperses too fast to grab hold of. Was I supposed to tell something to Stryker?

Orfyn

Something is going on, and I need to find out what it is.

As an orphan living on the charity of others, I've spent my life around those who believe they're better than me. I know the way their eyes look through me. I know how their voices sound when they talk at me. And I know how they act while congratulating themselves on how decently they treat me. That superiority isn't in Lake's eyes or her voice or her actions. But she's been avoiding me big time.

A hair thingee is wrapped around her door handle, so I'm waiting it out. She'll have to come out at some point. Until then, I'm an expert at entertaining myself when there's a white wall begging to be beautified. Like the white wall across from her room.

I'm soon lost in the details: the folds of the white dress, the multi-colored tapestry, the long, red hair that I perfectly match to Lake's.

After a couple of hours, Lake emerges and sees my half-finished painting. "That's beautiful."

I watch for her realization that the girl's face is a perfect likeness of her own.

"Why did you make her so forlorn?" she asks.

Does she seriously not recognize herself? Or is she messing with my head? Again.

I dab my brush on the palette and add a burnt-orange streak to the girl's hair, hoping it draws Lake's attention to the face. "That's how Waterhouse painted her. Want to hear the story? It's like a fairytale."

Lake bites her lip. It's almost as if she's afraid to hang out with me.

Fine. I'm not going to beg her to stay. "Don't worry about it."

The plan had been that she'd be so thrilled—flattered—whatever, she'd let down her guard, and I'd learn if I have any hope with her, because she's been all about the mixed signals.

"I can't stay long." She sits on the floor with a good couple of feet between us.

I *think* this is progress. "I'll tell you the condensed version, then. There's a curse on this beautiful girl." I point to her face and pause, glancing at Lake. No recognition whatsoever. "Her name is the Lady of Shalott. I can't remember why she was cursed, but if she looks toward Camelot, she'll die. She can only see the outside through a mirror as she weaves." I grab a different brush and begin working on the reeds in the water. "One day, she sees Lancelot ride by on his horse—*the* Lancelot. He's literally a knight in shining armor. The Lady of Shalott thinks about how bored she's been, stuck in the castle for her whole life, never doing anything fun. She defies her fate and turns around, and when she looks at Lancelot, the mirror cracks, unleashing the curse. The Lady leaves the castle for the first time, writes her name on the boat, and gets in. She floats down the river, knowing she's going to die." I pause to draw out the ending, and Lake leans in closer. "When the Lady of Shalott floats by Camelot, she's already dead, and Lancelot mourns that he never got to kiss this beautiful girl."

I'm feeling pretty good about my plan—until Lake says, "And that's what happens when you allow your heart to rule your head."

Okay, maybe I should've chosen a picture where the girl didn't die in the end. "You're missing the point. She was willing to take a chance to live a more exciting life."

Lake shakes her head, making her long hair ripple. "The Lady of Shalott threw her life away. For a guy."

This is *not* going how I'd imagined. "She wanted to know what it felt like to fall in love."

"Life is filtered ... *filled* with disappointment when you choose someone who's not good for you."

I don't think we're only talking about the picture anymore. I started this, and there's no going back now. "Why do you think he's not good for her?"

"He's a knight! He'll never be there when she needs him. When he is home, he'll be miserable, dreaming about his next adventure. Then he'll blame her for holding him back, and she'll regret ever falling in love with him."

"Lake, not everyone is like that." I hold her eyes with mine. "I'm not like that."

"What are you guys doing?"

I turn to see Stryker striding toward us. Could his timing suck any worse?

Lake looks like she's been caught doing something wrong. "We're discussing the Lady of Shalott."

Stryker glances at my work. "In the original, she doesn't look that much like Lake."

She gasps. "Is that supposed to be me?"

Thanks a lot, Stryker. I shrug self-consciously. "I wanted to make you smile."

"I'm grabbing some pizza," Stryker butts in. "Want to join me, Lake?"

She looks from him to me, then back to him. "Thanks, but I'm going to stay here a little longer."

It takes superhuman strength to hold in my grin.

"No prob," he says, smooth as a canvas. He stuffs his hands in his pockets and saunters away.

"He's been sleeping so much lately," Lake says as she watches him turn a corner. "This is the first time I've seen him in three days."

I caught him pacing our hall last night. When I asked him if everything was okay, he gave me the finger and went back into his room, slamming the door. It caught me by surprise because he's not normally that guy.

Lake frowns. "Maybe I should go see if he's okay."

"Whatever you want to do," I force myself to say. I start working on the trees in the background as if I could care less what she decides.

After an epically long minute, she says, "I'll look for him later."

Out of the corner of my eye, I watch as Lake picks up a tube of oil paint and reads the color's name, puts it down, picks up another and then another.

"What's your favorite painting?" Her voice sounds different, as if her vocal cords are finally allowed to release her words. And the tension in her face is gone. Even her lips look fuller.

I want to go back to the conversation we were having before, but at least we're still talking. "It's an almost-finished copy of *The Birth of Venus*."

"I've always liked that painting," she says. "But I thought it was finished."

"That's the original. The one I'm talking about was on the underside of a bridge."

"You mentioned that when I first met you," she says. "I thought you were joking."

Crap. I've painted myself into a corner. "Artists learn from everything we see." Will she make the leap that I also wasn't joking about being a street artist? But I want her to know about that painting because it's important to me.

I reach behind me and add more paint to my brush as an excuse to glimpse at her. She looks more curious than anything else, so I continue. "I hung out under that bridge for a week, studying the technique. I liked that nobody owned it, except maybe the New York Transportation Department. They demolished the bridge last year, but that unfinished painting had to be worth more than the bridge itself. And nobody knew about it. That's the painting that made me realize what I wanted to do."

Lake draws her strawberry-blond eyebrows together. "Do you know who painted it?"

"I asked around, but I never found anyone who knew, so I always picture a homeless guy," I say. "I even made up a story about his life. In my mind, his paintings hang in museums all over the world, but he was mugged while at a show in New York, and he got amnesia. He ended up living on the streets, not remembering he was once a respected artist, but he never lost his passion to paint." I let out a laugh. "That sounds kinda dumb, doesn't it?"

"No, it's imaginative. It's fascinating how differently our minds work."

"What would your story about him be?"

Lake's forehead crinkles. "I have no idea, which is my point. Now, if you asked me to tell you what elements need to be in play to make a steel bridge decompose, I'm your girl."

I laugh along with her. "You are a romantic."

"I prefer your story to the ... *fairytale*," Lake says.

"Bad choice. I'll cover this one over and paint you something else."

"No, please don't. I like it." While staring at my painting of her, she says, "My Grandma Bee has Alzheimer's. I have to believe Sophie and I can find the cure in time to help her." Her face is as determined as Sister Mo during Lent.

"I'm sorry. I didn't know."

"The cruelest aspect of that disease is you not only forget everyone you've ever loved, you don't remember your own life. All those experiences. Gone. It's almost as if you never existed."

What I don't tell her is that I couldn't have chosen a better subject. At this moment, Lake's flushed cheeks and sad-looking eyes perfectly match the girl's in *The Lady of Shalott*.

"Do you believe we can make a difference?" she asks.

"If anyone can, it's you guys."

"Why aren't you including yourself?"

I touch up the water as a stall tactic until coming to the decision to stop dodging the truth. "You were all chosen for a reason. I was just a body available for purchase."

She tilts her head. "Is the money the reason you agreed to come here?"

"I don't even know much they gave the church."

"Then, why are you selling yourself short?"

When Lake inches closer, I feel bolder. "I didn't know what they were going to do to me until I got here."

"Then you're more courageous than me. I had two weeks to decide if I was going to accept their offer."

"I did it to become a famous artist, but you're trying to end Alzheimer's."

Lake smirks. "I'm not here for entirely altruistic reasons. I want to be recognized for my achievements, just like you." She points to my painting. "The real difference between us is you're already using your enhanced knowledge outside of the dreamstate."

"I never thought of it that way." The pride I've always felt after finishing a painting returns for the first time since I got here. Thanks to Lake.

"Do you think we'll be able to experience a normal life after leaving here?" she asks.

"I've always thought being normal is overrated."

She looks at me with a funny smile.

"What?" I ask. "Do I have paint on my face?"

"You're ... *different* than I thought you'd be."

I lean in closer and whisper mysteriously, "Is that a good or bad thing?"

Lake gives me a sad little smile. I could never recreate the way her eyes look at this moment. "Both." She looks away, breaking the spell. She rises and brushes off the back of her jeans. "I should find Stryker."

What? Now?

"Thank you for painting me, but I don't look like that."

"Don't you know how beautiful you are?"

She bites her lip. "I really need to go."

What just happened?

Stryker

I storm away from Orfyn and Lake. Does she realize no one else's wall is adorned with a forged painting?

I don't care if they're spending time together on that grubby floor.

I don't even care that they're discussing his all-too-obvious, ultra-romantic version of *Lady of Shalott*, with Lake in the starring role.

It's okay if she ends up with him. It's better that way. I can't let myself get distracted by her.

But if I know there's something special between us, can I let it go? I must.

I've talked to Bjorn about this. He tells me one thing over and over. *Be bound to the purpose.*

And I am.

Bound and chained. I'm ready to make the biggest difference I possibly can. Dedicated to fulfilling the greatest purpose I will ever have. Then why do I want to put my fist through a wall?

I slap my hand across Jules's door. Orfyn's smelly paint isn't quite dry, and my hand swipes through the farm scene, slashing through the corn fields and farmhouse. Scratching up the undercoat and ruining Orfyn's painting of Jules's home.

I've destroyed something.

A mixture of shock and shame and adrenaline surges through me. Anger has gotten the best of me, again, and I've ruined something special. All the hidden, raw feelings come rushing back. The memories of what happened in Boston. Painful images of Alicia's smile. The blame I can't escape.

I crack my knuckles. I won't let it happen again. Lake deserves to be the most she can be. She's special. Not only smart and driven. Lake has forgiveness in her eyes.

Forgiveness.

This world needs Lake.

I'm not here to fall in love. I'm here to succeed. Ensure something like Boston never happens again. Help the world find peace.

I stare at the ruined picture of Jules's home.

No. I will not let it happen again.

I will not lose anyone else.

Orfyn

I'm in the Bat Cave for five minutes before realizing something is wrong. He isn't here. I mean, where else could he be? "Bat?"

The screens flicker to life, and my New York Rangerized version of *The Last Supper* fills the wall. Christ. His twelve disciples. And Bat.

He's in an electronic version of my oil painting. Wearing a pink bathrobe over a faded Metallica T-shirt. Standing behind Jesus Christ.

"Is that really you?" I ask.

He looks himself up and down. "Yeah."

"Uhm, do you realize you're *in* the painting?"

He scans the scene da Vinci painted five hundred years ago and smiles. "Yep."

It looks like he's inside the room. Not a painting of a room, and not a two-dimensional room like on TV. A real life room. If I didn't know better, I'd think I was actually sitting across from the disciples and watching Bat hang out at Christ's last supper.

"How did you get in there?" I ask.

"You tell me. It's your dream."

"I thought you controlled the dreams."

Bat shrugs, then picks up a piece of bread and takes a bite.

This is now beyond weird. "Is that real? I mean, does it taste like bread?"

"As close to bread as you painted it."

Bat walks around the electronic painting, and as he moves, the scene shifts with him. "It's awkward that they're all sitting on the same side of the table, but that's da Vinci." He gets up and puts his hand on Christ's shoulder.

Bat is literally touching Jesus Christ!

Bat looks out at me and wrinkles his nose. "Man, this place even smells like the Renaissance."

"There are smells in there?"

He nods, as if all videos games have a scratch-and-sniff feature.

"What's it smell like?"

He waves his hand in front of his face. "Like the fifteenth century, and it's not as enlightened as you'd think."

I can't take my eyes off Bat acting like this thing he's doing is perfectly normal. "Is this the first time you've done this?"

"Done what?"

Sometimes it takes the patience of a saint to talk to him. "Gone into my painting. Do you do this when I'm not here?"

He frowns. "I don't know what happens to me. I think I go back to being nothing."

I knew that, but I kind of forgot. I've been too hung up on trying to get Lake to like me. A lifetime of lessons about helping thy neighbor prod at me. If someone living in your brain isn't considered a neighbor, who is?

"Bat, is this life okay? I mean, should I be sleeping more?"

"Are you tired?"

I can't help but smile. "No, Bat. I feel fine."

"Then it's all chill."

He moves to the back of the room and looks out the window. "Madison Square Garden. Nice add, Orfyn."

"Thanks."

"I think I owned it." He leans out the window and teeters on his dirty, bare feet. He regains his balance and shuffles to the front of the painting. "Don't you think da Vinci could've done a better job in the original making the landscape look like Jerusalem?"

And, now we're back to his useless questions. "I don't care! There's nothing we can do about it."

He drops his head. "Just asking."

I take in a deep breath and slowly let it out. "Bat, I didn't mean to yell. But everyone else is working on really important things. I don't want to spend the rest of my life doing nothing. I want a purpose."

"Okay," he says, as if I'd told him it's time for lunch. He licks his index finger, dabs up crumbs off the tablecloth, and sticks his finger in his mouth.

He *touched* the crumbs. He *tasted* the bread. He *smelled* the stink. He *hears* me talk. And he's able to *see* my painting from a completely different viewpoint—inside.

"What if we can do it?" I ask.

"Do what?"

"Create a new form of Art. We could combine what you know about writing video games and what I know about painting so someone can experience a painting like you are right now."

He nods his head energetically, which is probably the most athletic thing I've seen him do. "I think that's why I chose you."

The dark weight of bitterness pushes hard against my chest. "The Darwinians picked me because I was disposable."

"They didn't choose you. I did. They were going to make you an example."

"The Darwinians?"

"No, the Anti-Graffiti Task Force. You were days away from getting arrested. I didn't want you to have to stop painting."

Orfyn

I hang tarps to keep my surprise from the others.

I can't give them more than one sense—yet. But I can make them feel like they're inside a painting. I start at one end of the dining hall and paint water and flowers on each white wall, converting the dining hall into Monet's *Water Lilies*. His original is twelve separate paintings, and he meant them to be laid out side by side and displayed in a specially made oval room to create an endless whole. I'd never known that story; Bat told it to me.

I finish just in time for our noon meeting. Lake's delight is my reward. I even get a smile out of Marty, and I haven't seen one on him for a while.

Stryker pulls out the chair next to him. "Lake, sit by me. I haven't seen you in days."

She does as he asked. "I've been meaning to come by, but time has gotten away from me."

He nods knowingly. "I've been putting in the hours, too."

So she didn't leave me to be with Stryker. We were getting along great until I told her she's beautiful, which obviously backfired. I go over and sit in the chair on the other side of her.

She smiles at me.

Between Lake's reaction and their praises about my Monet reproduction, this is the best I've felt since I got here.

Then Anna drops her tray on the table and plops down next to me. "We need to talk."

When it comes to Anna, I've been using my own share of avoidance tactics. "Why?"

"Do I need a reason to talk to my notorious artist friend?" Her heavily lined eyes offer a challenge.

I don't have a thing going on, but I'm not going to let her stomp her black army boots all over my good mood. "I'm busy."

I can almost see a thundercloud forming over her head. "How exactly did an orphan capture the attention of the Darwinians?"

Stryker's head whips around.

I shrug. "Just lucky, I guess."

Stryker studies me for a few more ticks of the clock, then turns to the others. "Let's get this meeting started. First on the agenda, has anyone heard how Alex is doing?"

"His breathing is much better," Jules relays while re-arranging vegetables in her salad.

"Are you sure?" Lake says. "I visited Alex last night and he said his symptoms haven't improved. And he doesn't know when he's being released from … that place. The *infirmary*."

"I meant, he isn't getting any worse," Jules explains.

"Isn't this his third time in there?" Anna asks.

"Fourth," Marty answers without looking up from his notebook.

"Have they figured out what's wrong with him?" I ask.

No one offers up an explanation.

"Lungs don't just give out." Anna says. She slams down her pop can with enough force to make the brown liquid shoot up from the hole in the top. Her nails are chewed down to the quick, which looks painful. I don't remember them being that way before.

"Environmental?" Marty says.

"This is an old building," Lake says. "There could be mold, or ..."

"Asbestos?" I guess.

She nods with a frown.

"Is anyone else having problems breathing?" Stryker asks.

Headshakes all around.

"How about any other symptoms, like headaches or nausea?" he asks.

More nos.

"They'd never allow us to live in a sick building," Jules says. "Our health and safety is their top priority."

Lake rolls up a napkin and holds it like a cigarette, which is strange because I've never seen her smoke.

I catch Stryker noticing it, too. "I'll ask them to test our air quality," he says.

"You've been sleeping so much lately." Jules all but flutters her eyelashes at him. "I'll ask them to do it."

Lake leans over and whispers to me, "Who is the girl in the boat?"

Lake must not have been as into my story as I thought. "The Lady of Shalott."

"Of course." Lake looks at the napkin cigarette and wads it up, looking confused. "Why is she sad again?"

My heart plummets into my stomach. She's playing some kind of twisted mind game with me. I'd hoped we were past that. "Quit messing with me, Lake. You know about the curse."

"That's right," she says quickly. Her eyes don't meet mine.

We had a great talk because of that story. Did it mean nothing to her?

A guttural sound cuts through the air. All eyes turn to Marty as he rips a few pages from his notebook, crumples them into a ball, and whips it across the room. Probably the best throw of his life. He dashes out of my water lily covered dining hall.

"Marty, wait!" Jules calls as she goes after him.

I get up and grab Marty's crumpled ball of papers. I'd love to read it, but whatever is on those pages is between Marty and his Mentor, Angus. I'll give them back to Marty later. I stuff them into my front pocket and sit back down next to Lake. Her attention is focused on unwrapping a piece of gum.

I've been so psyched about my *Water Lilies* reproduction, I didn't notice the dark bags under Lake's eyes, or that her skin is paler than usual. I can see blue blood vessels at her temples. She looks exhausted. I guess she could've forgotten about our conversation.

The pressure of trying to change the world is starting to get to all of them. I don't have that kind of stress, but Bat is my Mentor. I thought I got shafted when I learned the truth about him, but I may have won the jackpot.

"Does anyone have anything else we need to cover?" Stryker asks.

"I'd like to thank Orfyn for painting this room." Anna makes a big point of scanning the entire length of my painting. "Your style is so urban chic."

"It's called Impressionism," I say through gritted teeth.

When everyone gets up to leave, I ask Lake, "Do you have a minute?"

"You coming, Orfyn?" Anna demands.

"I need to talk to Lake first."

Anna clamps down on her jaw so hard, I'm afraid she's going to crack a molar. "Be sure to come by my place when you're done."

I wait until Anna leaves. "Lake, are you feeling okay?"

"Never better." She doesn't quite meet my eyes.

"I'm worried about you. I think you forgot the Lady of Shalott's story. It's pretty memorable, and I did paint her to look like you."

"Everything isn't always about you." Her glare feels like it could burn off a few layers of my skin. "Thanks for reminding me who you *really* are." Her hair bounces with each angry step as she heads to the door.

I've never seen Lake blow up like that. And what she said doesn't even make sense.

"Lake, you okay?" Stryker asks as she rushes past him.

On the other side of the door, I hear, "Why does everyone keep ... keep ... *asking* me that?"

Stryker comes over, grabs me by the arm, and pretty much drags me out the door. Once we're outside, he demands, "What was that about?"

"Lake's not thinking clearly."

He starts grinning. "If she blew you off, then she's finally coming to her senses."

"I'm not kidding. Something might be wrong with her memory." I tell him what just happened.

Stryker's smile drops, and he finally looks like he's taking me seriously. "I'll go talk to her."

"I'll come with you."

He shakes his head. "She trusts me. She'll tell me if something is wrong."

"Are you saying she doesn't trust me?"

"If she did, she'd still be talking to you. Leave it up to me."

I want to keep fighting him, but he's right. Lake wouldn't admit to me that she didn't remember. I come back inside, reach Anna's room, and keep walking. I can't deal with her now. Minutes later, someone starts pounding on my door. I turn on music and crank up the volume to drown out Anna's demands.

I'm hurt and angry and sad all at the same time. My insides are buzzing so bad I feel electrified. Lake doesn't trust me. And even worse than that, she trusts Stryker. Are they together? Is that why she's been acting so distant? Then why didn't one of them tell me?

The music starts grating on my nerves, and I turn it off. I open the fridge, but nothing looks good. I grab a brush and some paints. Sitting cross-legged in front of my wall, I wait for inspiration to hit. All I can see in my mind is Lake's angry face, and all I can think about is how she wouldn't confide in me. I should go to sleep and forget about this day, but I'm too worked up.

I touch my brush to the black paint on the palette and, despite everything, soon lose myself. A few hours later, I lean back and inspect my work. I didn't plan it, but I've painted rolling purple and gray clouds, and a churning white-capped sea. Turquoise waves crash on shore, pounding the sand like fists. I don't know where this scene came from, because I've never been to a beach like this.

I stand and stretch my arms over my head. The tightness in my chest is gone, and my nerves aren't so jangly. I'm calm enough to admit that my pride got in the way. I cared more about how Lake trusts Stryker, and not me, than I did about Lake's forgetting.

I'm going to tell Bat what's going on. We've never talked about my awake-life because there's not much he can do about it, but he's the closest friend I have.

A twinge of guilt zings me. Anna wanted to talk to me, and I blew her off. I'll stop by tomorrow.

Orfyn

B at is in a painting, but I don't recognize it.

He's on a cold-looking beach. There are some differences, but it looks a lot like the one I painted. Strange coincidence? Bat isn't sure, either.

He's part of a crowd looking at an enormous beached whale. Bat told me it's called *View of Scheveningen Sands,* and it's famous because when they cleaned the painting, the whale was uncovered. Years after it was completed, some idiot painted over the whale, erasing van Anthonissen's depiction of a once-in-a-lifetime event. Who'd be that arrogant? That's even worse than getting my work tagged over, because I never expected mine to last.

Bat waves his hands, and the whale vanishes.

"Hey! Put that back!"

Bat claps his hands twice and the dead, gray whale reappears. "What's up with you today?"

"Sorry. I've been worried about Lake."

He waddles to the front of the painting. "What's wrong with her?"

"She forgot an entire conversation."

"Is she the only one?"

"I don't think the others are forgetting stuff, but Alex can barely breathe, Marty is a wreck, and even Stryker, who usually shows less emotion than my dirty socks, is losing his cool."

Bat frowns, which transforms his face into a person I barely recognize. "Are the doctors doing anything about it?"

"I'm not sure."

He leans in closer and studies my face. "Anything wrong with you?"

"Do you mean, aside from an annoying craving for grape soda?" I joke, hoping I'm not getting his meaning.

He doesn't chuckle, like I expect. "Let me know if you start feeling strange, okay?"

I've felt strange since the moment I passed through The Flem's wooden doors, but I don't think that's what he means. "I'm good."

"The thing with health is, you never really know," Bat says.

A single thread of uncertainty wraps itself around my confidence and binds itself with a sturdy knot.

Bat picks up a stone and attempts to skip it. It warbles through the air, making it six feet from shore, then plunges into the ocean skip-free. The water splashes, and the cold light shimmers through the water drops. "I found a live starfish!" He picks it up and trudges to the edge of the shore, places the starfish in the surf, and lets the waves return it to its undersea life. "This is the first time I've been to the beach in years." He falls backward and his butt dents the sand.

"Because you were sick?"

He shakes his head. "That happened later. I couldn't leave the house. Whenever I went past my stoop I'd start shaking and couldn't breathe."

I look around his basement with fresh eyes. "Was it always like that, Bat?"

He sweeps his legs like a windshield wiper. "It wasn't so bad before my mom died."

"How long ago was that?"

"What's the date?"

I tell him.

"Eight years, two months, and six days."

He was basically a prisoner. "That's why you're creating your program."

He nods. "Now I can go wherever I want."

And Bat doesn't have to be the only one. If we create this game for real, everyone could experience a world beyond their four walls—a world as painted by centuries of artists. That's not a fake goal like saving the humanity in Art. It's something that would truly change people's lives. Everyone could travel everywhere. Go back in time. See anything. *That's* a real purpose.

Bat pulls the pink robe's edges over his belly. "It's getting cold. I'm coming back." Within a blink, he's in his recliner.

He had to have been so lonely all those years. Even worse than how it feels to paint in an alley in the middle of the night. Now, neither of us will ever be that alone again. I wish Sister Mo could've met Bat; she would've liked him.

"It's time for you to go," he says.

Sometimes you've got to ask, just to make sure you're wrong. "I don't need to be worried about the others, right?"

"Who knows what's going to happen the longer we're here."

My stomach flutters. "Do you know something you're not telling me?"

"It's simple probability. You never get it perfect the first time. Sometimes it takes a second or third or fiftieth attempt."

Stryker

I turn the corner, dreading to see the painting I damaged. I'm going to need to own up to it, admit I lost control.

Orfyn hasn't said a word.

I do a double-take when I reach Jules's door.

There's now a new painting of a landscape with a pond, and a farmhouse with a dog out front. It's beautiful.

Who wouldn't seek out the person who destroyed his work? Who wouldn't get angry? Want to retaliate? Orfyn just fixed it.

He's a really good guy, and he's right. Something is off with Lake. She's been struggling to find the right words. Not all the time, but it's been happening enough to be noticeable. I would have asked her about it earlier, but I barely have time to eat. It's a pathetic excuse. I should have checked in with Lake sooner, but it takes so much energy to maintain the wall blocking out my feelings for her.

Which is worse, caring too much or not caring enough? Bjorn, I know, would love to weigh in.

I've been a pitiful friend by pretending nothing is wrong with her, just because I'm afraid I can't control my emotions. I put on a mask of indifference and head to her room. There isn't a scrunchie around Lake's handle. I knock, but she doesn't answer. We don't have locks—they'd be redundant with Big Brother—but we do have an unspoken code where you don't barge in on someone. I ease open her door. "Lake? Are you in there?"

When she doesn't answer, I peek in. She's stretched out on the couch with an arm thrown across her eyes.

"Go away, Orfyn."

My insides twist. Does he come here that often? Not that I care. "It's Stryker. How about a walk?"

Lake doesn't move. "Not now."

"It's been a while since we've caught up."

She sighs dramatically, gets to her feet, and takes her own sweet time reaching the door.

"Don't forget your hat," I say.

"I didn't forget," she snaps. She turns around and snatches her hat off the counter.

When we get outside, I say, "Let's go to the rose garden. I know you like it there."

She robotically walks beside me. I gesture to the bench, and she obediently sits. As I'm trying to figure out a way to start this not-so-easy conversation, I notice that the closest bush has huge yellow roses. The other roses look healthy, too, and all the weeds are gone.

"Did you do this?" I gesture to the garden.

"Deborah found me the supplies I needed to make my fertilizer."

"These roses look great."

"Thanks." She almost smiles.

I mean it, but I also need her to be less defensive, or we'll get nowhere. I take her hand as reassurance. When she intertwines her fingers with mine, my heart rate soars. Her skin is so soft, and it's as white as marble.

I should not be holding her hand.

I force myself to keep clasping it. "Still Sophie's lab assistant?"

She nods. "Does Bjorn still have second thoughts about being merged?"

JIM AND STEPHANIE KROEPFL

Unease runs through me. "He says he's fine with it. What does she have you working on these days?"

She grimaces. "Dissecting."

"The octopi?"

"Sophie and I prefer to use octopuses as the plural." She drops her head and mumbles, "They're not real."

"But it feels like they are when you're in the dreamspace."

"Sophie assures me I'll get novel ... I mean, *numb* to it. Eventually."

Her stumble makes me wince. "You've been doing that more and more."

"Doing what?"

"Mixing up words."

She yanks her hand out of mine. "I apologize if I'm not communicating properly, but you'd have difficulty too if you had to kill your pets day after day."

I retrieve her hand and hold it in both of mine. It's so small. I feel like I need to hold it as gently as a Fabergé egg. "Lake, don't be angry. I'm worried about you."

"I'm just tired."

"It could be more than that," I push.

Her eyes pull away from mine. "I'm fine."

"Will you talk to Deborah about it?"

She turns to me, and her eyes are flashing with anger. "Aren't you the one who's constantly lecturing me not to provide them a reason to be concerned?"

I chuckle. "Touché. This is what happens when you like the smart girl."

Lake cocks her head. "Did you just admit to liking me?"

I never make that kind of mistake. Never. I've been telling myself I only think of Lake as a friend, but you can only fool yourself for so long. The truth is, I do like her. A lot. And that's the problem. I can't.

"Of course I like you," I say. "We're friends."

"Stryker, friends don't usually hold hands." Her eyes gesture down to my hands, which still haven't released hers.

I carefully set her hands on her lap. "Interactions are different here." So much for my keen ability to think on my feet. I'm only glad Bjorn didn't witness my barely believable explanation.

"So … are you telling me you don't want to be more than friends?"

Somehow, I've lost control of this conversation. We're here to talk about her memory issue, not us. "We can't get involved."

"There was nothing in the Agreement forbidding Nobels from being in a relationship."

I run my fingers through my hair. "It would be a distraction from our work." Even I don't believe myself.

"You're wrong. It's counter-productive to work like we are. We need to add an element of fun to our awake-lives. If we don't, the stove … the *stress* only compounds. And don't look at me like that. I realize I stammered, which is my point."

Despite the fact that I agree with everything she said, I say, "Lake, I don't want to ruin what we have."

"I concur."

"You do?"

Lake gets up, not looking at all upset. "I needed to understand where we stand. Now I know."

Is she for real, or is she that much better than me at hiding her feelings? "Then, we're good?"

"We're great. And thanks for making me come out here. I'm feeling calmer."

I watch as she stops to smell a rose. She smiles to herself, then heads back to The Flem. Is she really fine with us being friends? Because I'm not sure I am. I want to take it back. Tell her how I really feel. Hold her in my arms and kiss her.

But that can never happen.

When I joined the Program, I made a promise to myself: I will never put someone in harm's way again. Bjorn's and my mission will anger some people, and I know only too well what can happen. I can't let anyone get close to me. It won't make up for what I did, but it'll stop another person I love from getting hurt.

I should've told Lake the truth, but it's still too hard to talk about. I also should've made Lake promise she'll talk to Deborah. I should've done a lot of things differently.

The guilt that never goes away feels like it's burying me alive.

Lake

While Stryker was striving to convince me we should only be friends, I realized he was right. When he was holding my hand, I felt nothing. No spark. No rush of heat. One force that causes attraction is magnetic force, which is electrical currents. Magnetic attraction is what causes opposites to attract. Stryker and I may be too similar. Orfyn on the other hand …

I'm not sure what to do about him. My head wants to shield me while my heart is threatening to break my promise to myself.

I pass Marty's door and take a moment to appreciate the Space Needle that appears to be bursting out from it. Orfyn painted it from a bird's eye view, complete with hilariously dressed tourists on the platform. Far below, ferries cross the Puget Sound, leaving tiny white wakes. It doesn't take much imagination to feel the wind tangling my hair as I hover above Seattle with the other seagulls. Orfyn is truly talented.

Marty's door is ajar. We're not close. In fact, I'm not sure if we've ever had an actual conversation, but he was obviously upset the other day. We all need to identify ways to de-stress, and I plan to create a list of ways we can have more fun and share it with everyone at the next meeting. I chuckle at the thought of Anna taking up knitting.

"Are you in there, Marty?" I call out.

When he doesn't appear, I peek in. It's a disaster. The towers of books stacked on the floor compete with the plates of pizza bones and discarded clothes, which helps explain the funky smell. A walk outside would do Marty good—and air him out.

Cecil is headed my way and acting as if he hasn't noticed me, even though we're the only ones in the hallway.

"Have you seen Marty?" I ask.

He stops and regards me in his usual annoyed manner. "He's in the library, I think."

The *I think* was a nice touch, but I wouldn't be surprised if they can pinpoint our location at all times. "I'm glad. He needs a break."

"I'm not sure if he's eaten. Do me a favor and get him a snack from the dining hall."

Marty hasn't eaten? That's always the first thing he does after a dream session. "I'm happy to."

When I get to the end of the hall, I look right, left, then right again. "Cecil?" I yell as he's rounding the corner.

"What is it now?"

"Which way is the dining hall?"

He looks at me oddly, then returns.

"All these hallways look the same and it's easy to get lost," I explain, then realize it's true. Yesterday, I couldn't find Deborah's office, which I visit daily.

"It can be confusing," Cecil says without a trace of sarcasm, confirming my observation. "Turn right, and then take a left."

"Thanks."

He doesn't move to leave. "How are you feeling?"

"Fine."

He stares down at me skeptically.

I clear my throat. "I'm a little tired. I've been putting in a lot of hours."

"Tell Deborah if something like this happens again."

"Sure." My disorientation is only a side effect of my exhaustion. Taking a break with Marty is exactly what we *both* need.

I make my way to The Flem's expansive library without a problem. Wooden tables with green-hooded reading lamps are arranged in the center of the room, and tucked away in the corners are upholstered chairs. There are an impressive number of periodicals for each of our disciplines, along with a large fiction selection, not that I've had much time to read. I smile while recalling my favorite Gandhi quote: *Be the change you wish to see in the world.* I grab an interesting-looking book and ruffle the pages under my nose, inhaling one of my favorite smells. I've missed reading for pleasure.

I tuck the book under my arm and search each aisle until I reach the end without seeing anyone. I yell, "Marty?" feeling like I'm breaking a sacred rule, even though there isn't a librarian around to shush me.

Then I hear something. A low moaning, like the sound of an injured animal. Goosebumps sprout along my arms. I follow the sound and spot something behind one of the chairs. My breath catches when I push it aside.

"Marty?"

He's rocking back and forth, making a keening sound.

I kneel across from him. "Marty, tell me what's wrong." He doesn't look at me or speak. I inspect his huddled body. No blood or torn clothing, but I can't see his face. "Marty, please look at me." When he doesn't react, I gently touch his chin and lift his head. His face is tear-streaked, and snot dribbles over his quivering lips.

"Did someone hurt you?"

He doesn't meet my eyes, but he stops making that awful noise.

"I'm going to get help."

"Leave me alone." His voice reminds me of a wounded bird's.

"Did something happen with … " I can't seem to remember the name of the famous writer implanted in him. "Your Mentor?"

When he lifts his head, his eyes are as lifeless as a doll's. "Don't have it."

"Did you lose something?"

"Never had it."

"What?"

"Talent." Fresh tears slide down his cheeks.

"Marty, you're being too hard on yourself. You were picked as the Nobel for … for *Literature* for a reason."

"Disappointing everyone."

"No, you're not. You've been working more hours than any of us."

Marty drops his head into his arms, and I can barely hear him. "Not enough."

He's spinning. I need to help him regain perspective. "There's a pretty place outside I want to show you. That's why I came to get you."

"Can't," he says.

"The creek isn't far. Come on. You'll feel better after a walk."

"You don't get it." His eyes grasp onto mine. They're filled with desperation.

"Marty, I'm trying. Help me understand."

He takes a deep breath, as if speaking requires more energy than he has. "It's not right."

"Your novel?"

"No!"

It feels as if I've lost my grip on his lifeline. "Please, Marty. Tell me what's not right."

"The first paragraph," he whispers, as if betraying a life-or-death secret.

"But you've written other parts you like, right?"

He shakes his head.

"You've only been working on the first paragraph?"

He nods while running his sleeve across his nose, leaving a trail of snot.

I want to confront Marty's Mentor—whatever his name is, and if he had a body—to make him realize he's pushing Marty past his limits. And what about his Guardian? Cecil has to realize how distressed Marty is.

"What if you took a break from writing and—"

Marty's shrill laugh causes the rest of my suggestion to scurry into hiding. He pulls himself up like he's not used to carrying his own weight. His waist is at my eye level, and I notice the series of holes punched into his belt. He's withering away.

I didn't stop by the dining hall. How could I have forgotten? "How about we get something to eat?"

"Not hungry."

He's always hungry. "What about a *Big Bang Theory* rerun? We both could use a good laugh."

"Can't. It's not perfect." He moves down the aisle of books like it takes monumental effort to place one foot in front of the other.

I feel useless as I watch Marty leave. No! I can help him. I march to the wing that contains our Guardians' offices, needing to retrace my steps, and knock.

"What?"

I take it as an invitation to enter.

"You need to do something about … *Marty's Mentor*," I tell Cecil, making sure it sounds like a demand and not a request. It's unnerving that I can't remember his Mentor's name. I read one of his books in ninth grade.

Cecil raises his eyes from his computer screen. "Did we have an appointment?"

"You need to have Marty talk to his Mentor about shortening his dream sessions."

"I'm sorry, but I think you're mistaken about our roles here. I don't report to you."

I clench my toes to stand my ground. "I'm worried about Marty. He's acting as if he's having a nervous breakdown."

"So now you're an expert on mental health?"

"He has to have lost twenty pounds."

"I've been monitoring his weight, and it's within the acceptable standards."

"Cecil, I found him crying in the lipstick … I mean, *library*."

"It's healthy to let off a little steam. He'll be fine by morning." Cecil waves his hand to dismiss me. "Shut the door."

"It's not only his weight. He's—"

"Fine. I'll run a few more tests. Now let me get back to work."

I knock on Deborah's office door, but she doesn't answer. I try the handle and find it locked. I'll talk to her about Marty first thing in the morning to make her aware of my concerns.

When I pass his door, there's a wrinkled T-shirt hanging from the handle and turbulent snores coming from behind the painting of the Space Needle. He's already back at work.

The Darwinians

"We may have another problem," the raven-haired man states. The man with the beard sighs. "What is it now?"

"The Nobel for Chemistry is exhibiting strange behavior."

"Define *strange.*"

"Deborah and Cecil have observed signs of memory loss," the raven-haired man says. "I told you I thought something like this might happen."

"That's what my father would call closing the barn door after the horse got out," the woman says.

"Might I warn you both against making unfounded speculations," the bearded man says.

The woman pointedly looks at him. "You didn't know about her pre-existing condition, did you?"

"That's preposterous!"

"I believe you, sir," the raven-haired man says. "However, it may be wise to shorten our test phase for Procedure Omega-Sixteen."

"Are you implying what I think you are?"

"I'm merely ensuring our team is adequately prepared, should the need arise."

"And what happens to our colleagues then?" the bearded man asks.

"Exactly," the woman says. "Besides, I can't sign off on potentially inflicting the same outcome on another child. When I think about what happened to those other children—"

"They signed the Agreement," the raven-haired man cuts in.

The woman's breathing is wet and labored. "This isn't about hiding behind our legal rights. We need to protect them. It's our moral obligation."

"If you believe that, I don't know how you can justify what you plan to do."

"*That* is entirely different."

Lake

I wake with the feeling that I'm supposed to do something. But what?

I grab my journal from the night stand and record the events from last night's dream session. Whatever I need to do remains elusive.

God, I could use a cigarette.

My head snaps up. I don't smoke. Never have. But that same bizarre thought has been in my mind for days. I grab a piece of gum and chew until the disgusting craving lessens. Why would I want a cigarette? The smell makes me gag.

It's time for my daily debrief. I focus on the route and reach Deborah's office without a misstep. I stand outside her door, basking in the accomplishment I wouldn't have thought twice about last week. Should I listen to Stryker and tell her what I've been experiencing? A wave of relief washes through me. *That's* what I couldn't remember. Stryker said he needed to have more fun, and we were going to create a list, or was I supposed to do that? I wish I had my journal to jog my memory. From now on, I'll keep it with me.

Deborah looks up from her computer with a smile. "Come on in, Lake."

I grab a pen off her desk and scribble on my hand *List of fun*.

"What are you doing?" she asks with a tight smile.

"Reminding myself of something."

The telltale worry line between her eyebrows appears. "Are you having problems remembering things?"

"It only happens when I'm tired, which shouldn't be an issue considering how much I've been sleeping."

"I suspect the two internal biological mechanisms that regulate your awake and sleep, circadian rhythm and sleep/wake homeostasis, are being disrupted because your body isn't naturally waking on its own. I'll prescribe something that might help." She types something into the computer.

I should've brought it up sooner. I'll be feeling better in no time.

Deborah refocuses on me. "I've also been noticing small changes in your speech pattern."

My stomach clenches. I didn't think it was obvious. "It started a few days ago, but every once in a while it's been … *challenging* to find the right word."

I study her face for a reaction, but there is none. A good sign.

"Have you noticed anything else?" she asks, apparently unconcerned.

I could lie, but I've always tried to be honest in my debriefs—except about Sophie's continued belief that she'll be rid of me after the semester ends. "I got lost on the way to your office, but that only happened once. Twice. But everyone gets turned around sometimes."

She nods again. "Cecil mentioned that to me."

Glad I told the truth.

Deborah's theory is since my thoughts are co-mingled with Sophie's, my brain is still learning how to extract information when I'm awake. She assures me my glutamate and gamma-aminobutyric acid transmitters are at acceptable levels so my excitation and inhibition—my E/I balance—is properly controlling my flexible behavior and cognition. It's a relief my brain activity is functioning properly, but no one else seems to be having memory issues. Or they could be and aren't admitting to it.

Deborah has always been honest with me, and I want to believe her when she tells me not to be concerned. But I did forget parts of Orfyn's story. It was disconcerting because I've always had a great memory, tired or not. I was embarrassed, and maybe a little worried. I should apologize to Orfyn for getting angry.

When I'm back in my room, I transfer the reminder about my fun list onto a fresh page in my journal. Then I sketch out a map of The Flem, which is pointless since I've lived here for almost a month, but I do it anyway. As long as I have my journal, I won't get lost. Feeling more in control, I head to the dining hall, journal in hand.

I take a moment to admire Orfyn's water lilies. He transformed the dining hall into a place I now enjoy spending time. Jules is at a table, her ever-present copy of *Capitalism and Freedom* lying next to her barely eaten chicken nuggets. The rest of us eat like marathoners. I don't know how she hasn't withered away. A twinge of a memory surfaces, then flees too quickly to grab hold of. Was it about runners? Chicken?

"Alex was released from the infirmary today," says the girl who's always in the know.

"Have they determined why he can't ... *breathe?*"

"They think he contracted a parasite while visiting relatives in Mexico. He went before he came here, which is why at first they thought it was caused by the procedure."

"It had crossed my mind that whatever is happening to him might start affecting the rest of us," I admit.

"You can take that worry out of your head. Merging is perfectly safe."

Between Deborah's and Jules's assurances, I'm feeling more carefree. I start eating my embarrassingly large slab of meatloaf. "Has Stryker been here today?"

"No, I've only seen Anna when she grabbed something to eat

between dream sessions. She was barely awake and didn't have a lot to say, which wasn't such a tragedy."

I smirk conspiratorially. "I think Marty's the only one she talks to anymore."

Marty!

The image of him huddled in the library comes rushing back. I was going to ask Deborah to check on him. And I didn't. How could I have forgotten something so important? Fear grabs hold of me like a magnet.

"Have you seen Marty today?" *Please, please, please let him be okay.*

"First thing this morning. He said he'd finished writing a new chapter." Jules's eyes shift to study Orfyn's painting.

I let out the breath I didn't realize I was holding. He's fine. But this memory lapse was far more serious than forgetting a word. I slide my journal under the table and write, `Tell Deborah I forgot about Marty.`

He wouldn't want everyone to know how he was acting in the library, especially the Gossip Girl. "Did he seem all right to you?"

Her perkiness plunges a few notches. "It won't be a secret for long. He's being moved to the Darwinians' wing for observation." She leans in closer. "He agreed to undergo treatment for depression, which I find so admirable. I mean, there's nothing to be ashamed of. It's a disease."

If Marty had done something to hurt himself—I shove away the thought. My failing wasn't as disastrous as I feared.

Jules pats her flat stomach. "I'm stuffed. I'll be right back. I'm in serious need of caffeine." She picks up her barely eaten lunch and heads to the kitchen.

I hurriedly eat my meatloaf before she returns, feeling like I'm doing something wrong by consuming calories. A drip of gravy flies off my fork and lands on the worn cover of Jules's book. I carefully wipe off the gravy with a napkin, and luckily it doesn't leave a grease stain. What is so fascinating about this particular book?

I flip open the cover. Glued to the inside is a manila pocket that once held a log of borrowers and due dates. Stamped in red on the pocket is *The Flemming Academy Library*. It was here long before this building was remodeled into the Darwinians' secret laboratory. I notice a slight impression in the pocket and pull out a crystal rectangle. Why would Jules have a keycard when the rest of us don't?

Something occurs to me that should have occurred to me sooner. How does Jules know Marty is being treated for depression? I just finished debriefing with Deborah, and she didn't mention it. Or tell me about Alex's diagnosis. I can't see Cecil being so cavalier with my classmates' medical information.

According to Jules, she'd seen Marty this morning, and he told her he'd finished a new chapter. But he was distraught because he couldn't get the first paragraph perfect. How did I not catch that earlier? And what else has Jules been lying about?

Out of nowhere, I get this feeling that something is wrong with Marty, more than just him being depressed. I have no logical reason to believe it, but even though I keep reminding myself that a competent researcher relies on facts, I can't shake the feeling. Is it Mom or Sophie warning me?

I see Jules returning and grab her keycard, slipping it into my back pocket.

"Back to slicing dead human brains." I stand to leave.

"Gross!" Jules squeals.

As soon as I'm out of her sight, I write in my journal, `Verify that Marty is okay.`

Lake

I don't know why Jules lied about Marty's writing. But considering how he was acting in the library, there is the possibility he's clinically depressed. Jules didn't lie about that part, so she may be telling the truth about him being moved to the Darwinians' wing. In a restricted area.

When I first arrived, Deborah had explained that certain areas are restricted because it's where the Darwinians live. She'd chuckled and admitted it's the only place they can get away from us. I'm not sure how many restricted areas there are since I've never had a reason to test which doors are locked. I wouldn't be surprised if Stryker knows. I should get him, but I may not have long before Jules discovers I swiped the keycard.

My heart is pounding in my ears. Why am I so nervous? I'm not planning to steal their secrets and open my own you-too-can-live-in-someone-else's-brain business. But I will be where I'm not supposed to be.

I open my journal and review my sketch of The Flem. I turn down what I think is the right hall and come upon the person I've been avoiding. Before I can back away, Orfyn looks up and smiles.

My carefully-thought-out apology vanishes as my eyes glom onto the wall covered in gruesome, devilish creatures. One is hacking at a human as others watch in glee, and another is vomiting up smaller monsters. It's truly disturbing.

"Is there a reason you're painting this?" I ask, wondering if I've been intuitive about avoiding him.

"A lot of Catholic churches have paintings of demons to show the congregation that their actions have consequences. I thought the Darwinians could use a reminder."

"Orfyn, why do they need a reminder?"

The mischief in his eyes evaporates. "It's complicated."

I edge closer and whisper in his ear, "Are we in danger?"

"No, it's nothing like that."

Why do I continue to allow Stryker's distrust to influence me? For all I know, Orfyn is retaliating because they forgot to order his art supplies.

"What are you doing here?" he asks.

I tighten my grip on the stolen keycard. I've seen Orfyn paint often enough to know he's not leaving until his work is finished. I could abandon my plan, but I owe this to Marty. The problem is, there's not a semi-believable lie to explain how I got the key, and why I need to sneak into the restricted area.

I open my hand. "I'm looking for Marty," I mouth, then shoot my eyes to the Darwinians' wing.

Orfyn's brows meet. He leans down and whispers, "What's he doing in there?" His breath tickles my neck, sending shivers down my spine.

"I'll explain later," I whisper back.

He points to his chest, then to the doors.

I can either lose precious minutes whispering protests, or give in. Honestly, it would be a relief to have someone come with me. If only Orfyn didn't look so cute with that streak of yellow paint on his forehead.

I wave the keycard over the panel and hear a click. I'd been hoping I was wrong about what Jules's key unlocks. I open my journal and add, `Jules's key unlocks the Darwinians' wing.`

Orfyn looks at me curiously.

I just confirmed to him that I can't trust my own memory. I'll have to deal with that later.

After the door closes behind us, Orfyn says at a normal volume, "I doubt they have bugs in their own wing."

"Good point. If we see anyone, we'll tell them the door was left ajar."

He nods. "We need a reason for being here."

"We'll say we heard someone crying out in ... in *pain* and we were concerned."

"Works for me."

I finally notice my surroundings. I expected the Darwinians' wing to resemble the Sanctuary's décor, but it's the standard white walls, white tile floors and no embellishments. Our wing is vibrant now, thanks to Orfyn's paintings.

"Tell me what's going on with Marty," he says.

"Jules told me he's being treated for depression and he was moved to the Darwinian's wing. I saw him last night, and I can believe that part. But she lied to me about his writing, and then I found this kite, I mean, *key* in her book. So now I'm questioning everything she's told me."

"Why would Jules lie?"

"I don't know. That's why we're here."

If I tell him about forgetting to ask Deborah to talk to Cecil about Marty, Orfyn's going to lose any respect he may have had for me. I opt for a different truth. "I have this feeling I can't shake. I think something is wrong with Marty."

Instead of questioning my sanity, Orfyn simply says, "Let's go look for him."

We make our way down the hall, reading the name plates as we pass. There's actually quite a few Darwinians I don't know. It's the afternoon, and they all must be working. Even though I've devoted three minutes of thought to my plan, the timing couldn't be better.

It feels as if there's a liter of adrenaline running through my veins. I make myself say, "What are those double doors near the end of the hall?"

As we get closer, we hear muffled voices coming from behind the plaque labeled *Conference Room.*

"We sure could use an invisibility cloak," Orfyn whispers.

"If only I brought propylene and triethylene glycol."

He gives me a quizzical look.

"It creates an instant dense fog." For the thousandth time, I wonder if *chemistry joke* is an oxymoron.

The conference room doorknob turns, and the door opens a crack. We press ourselves against the wall, which doesn't do much to conceal us. I suddenly really do wish I had my chemistry kit on me.

"I have to say it again," we hear from the room. "It's not the results we anticipated, but it's a true game changer." I don't recognize the man's voice.

"As you both suggest, I'll give some more thought to my decision," says a woman who begins to cough violently.

I point to an elevator at the end of the hall, and we rush past the conference room. Orfyn pushes the button, the elevator doors slide open, and we step in without being seen. My heart is beating as fast as a hummingbird's.

The elevator buttons are labelled *-1, 1, 2,* and *3.* "The elevator in our wing doesn't have a button for the third floor."

"Nope. There also aren't any stairs that lead up to it." Orfyn hovers his finger over the *3* and looks at me questioningly. "If we go up there, our excuse that we heard something isn't going to cut it."

"Then let's not get caught." I push the button labeled *3,* hoping this isn't one of those times when bravado is synonymous with stupidity.

The elevator doesn't ascend.

"Try the keycard," Orfyn suggests.

I pass it in front of the black panel above the buttons, then press 3 again. I hear a sound behind me. We turn to see the rear wall sliding open, exposing a stone staircase.

"That's not what I was expecting." My voice sounds like I inhaled helium.

Orfyn stands straighter. "We're doing this, right?"

I give him the nod. I have to see this through for Marty. My eyes follow the worn stairs leading up. The walls are covered in dark wood paneling, and it's well-lit by a large hanging lamp with six round globes. Why is this place designed so we have no access to the third floor?

As we make our way up the steps, Orfyn says, "Why didn't they keep the rest of the The Flem looking like this?"

That's what he's thinking right now? I'm trying not to pee my pants.

"Look at this." Orfyn points to the banister. Carved into the wood is: *Ashley Chambers 1916, Lest We Forget.* "World War I." Orfyn runs his fingertips across the hundred-year-old tribute. "They called it the 'war to end all wars.'"

"Wouldn't it be wonderful if Stryker and ... *Bjorn* can create a more peaceful world?"

A look of annoyance flashes across Orfyn's face, and then it's gone. "We've got to believe they can."

We reach the top step and are met by a hallway going off in opposite directions. The same globe lamps extend down the ceiling, casting a soft, yellow glow. This floor hasn't changed since the last class let out who knows how many years ago. I'd expect it to be musty, but it has a sharp disinfectant smell.

When a phone rings, my heart skips a beat. We're not alone. After a few seconds, a woman's voice says, "I'll be right there."

Orfyn opens the nearest door and pulls me in. The room

contains whirring and beeping mainframe computers, which is an anachronism next to the blackboard that still has chalk smudges on it. The woman's shoes *click-clack* on the tile floor in the hallway. The sound grows closer, passes us, and then fades as she descends the stairs.

Orfyn looks at me questioningly.

"The cleaning ladies I know don't wear high heels." I take a bracing breath. "We need to see what's down there."

Orfyn takes my hand, and it feels like I'm touching a bare electrical wire. I know I should let go, but it's giving me the courage to do this. As we creep down the hall, I hear the sound of squishes doing a body's breathing, and blips monitoring a beating heart.

Please, let me be wrong.

I peer into the last room. A row of hospital beds line the far wall. My stomach drops when I recognize the face nearest the door.

It's Marty.

Plastic tubes snake out of his nose and arms, electrodes are attached to his shaven head, and he's hooked up to a number of machines. As he lies unconscious, he barely looks ten years old.

"This isn't how they treat depression," I whisper.

Orfyn touches Marty's shoulder and shakes it, but he doesn't wake up.

"He has a … a *feeding* tube," I say with a shaky voice. "They must think he's going to be here for a while."

The memory of Marty's keening rings in my head. He was sleeping when I returned from Cecil's. What happened to him?

Orfyn gestures to the other six kids. "Who are they?"

Lake

One of the machines begins beeping rapidly.

Orfyn says, "We need to get out of here."

I gaze at the unconscious kids as frustration replaces my shock. I need to help them. But how? Oryfyn is right, though. Putting our positions as Nobels at stake will only prevent us from being able to figure out what's going on.

We sprint down the stairs and enter the bizarre elevator. After the doors on the other side open, Orfyn peeks down the hall. "We're in the clear."

We fast-walk it until reaching the conference room, where we begin to tiptoe, but no voices come from behind the double doors. I don't breathe until we reach the door leading to safety. Orfyn pulls it open a crack, peeks through, and waves for me to follow. Seconds after the door shuts behind us, a man with black, glistening hair rounds the corner from the unrestricted area.

"What are you two doing here?" His eyes shoot to the wall of ghastly creatures. "And what the hell is that?"

"It's a classic theme," Orfyn says with a straight face.

"I don't want to see that dreck every day. Get rid of it. Now."

"I don't keep that much white paint in my bag," Orfyn says with a shrug.

I keep my mouth shut since he's handling the situation far better than I ever would.

The Darwinian studies Orfyn as if he's a parasite. "I'll get Maintenance to take care of it. Both of you, get out of here."

Orfyn methodically packs up his supplies while the Darwinian glares at him, then slings the canvas bag over his shoulder. He puts a lot of thought into what he paints. I still want to understand why the Darwinians need to consider the consequences of their actions. And I have to remember it until I have the opportunity to write myself a note.

The Darwinian says, "You'd better believe I'll discuss this incident with your Guardian."

"I don't have one," Orfyn says.

I ask, "Why not?"

"Good question," Orfyn says.

I'd just assumed Cecil was Orfyn's Mentor since I know Deborah oversees Alex, Anna and me.

The Darwinian points. "Go. Now."

We reach the exit door and simultaneously press the bar that releases us to the outside. Fake schoolyard air never smelled so restorative.

"Let's go over to that tree to talk," Orfyn says.

Before finding Marty, I would've rejected his suggestion because I do my best thinking alone. And Orfyn is far too distracting. But discovering a row of unconscious kids with shaved heads changes one's perspective.

We head over to the same tree that Stryker and I had huddled under in the rainstorm. Orfyn grabs a branch, pulls himself up, and settles on a thick limb four feet off the ground. "Want some help up?"

"I can do it, but first I need a minute."

I open my journal and document, `Elevator. 3rd floor. Marty unconscious. Shaved head. Feeding tube.` The thought of that room makes me shudder. I add, `Six others.`

I glance up at Orfyn, who's intently watching me create reminders. I'm glad he came with me, but I need to ask him to keep the news about my journaling to himself. I don't want the others to start questioning my competence.

I stare at the page. There's something else I was going to document, but now I can't recall what it is. Deborah believes my memory glitches are temporary, but it's happening more frequently. A flutter of fear ripples through me, and I try to dismiss it. I'll be better as soon as the pills Deborah prescribed me start taking effect.

I prop my journal against the trunk and attempt to lift myself into the tree. I end up looking like I'm having a seizure. Orfyn grabs my arms and easily hoists me up. His touch sends sparks through me. I scooch down the branch to create space between us so I can think more clearly.

He leans his head back. "Aren't clouds amazing?"

After what we just discovered, he wants to discuss condensation? "Can we focus on—"

"See that one?" He points to the left. "It looks like a dog. What do you think?"

I glance up to appease him. "It's a cow." The cloud shifts in the air currents. "Now it's a ... a *horse*."

"How about that one?" He points a few inches to the right.

I spend some time studying it. When I think I have it, the cloud transforms into something entirely different.

"I used to spend hours watching them on the orphanage's rooftop," Orfyn says. "It's not only about the shapes. Clouds reflect every color there is. When it's storming, they're on one side of the color wheel, violets and purples and blues. But at sunrise and sunset their colors are on the other side, reds and oranges and yellows. I don't know anything else that changes like that."

"A chameleon?"

He laughs. "You got me there." His smile drops. "I think those kids are Candidates, but something went wrong."

"I knew the procedure has risks, but there are so many of them." I recall the numbered files Stryker found. "And there may have been even more who didn't make it." I rub my finger along the scar on my thumb, but cloud-watching feels more soothing.

"But what happened to Marty? If it was an accident, he'd be in the infirmary, not hidden away on a floor we can't get to."

"For some reason, they don't want us to be aware of his condition," I say.

Marty wasn't rational in the library. Was he despondent enough to try to commit suicide? If I'd remembered to talk to Deborah, could I have prevented it? I watch the racing clouds, blinking back tears.

Orfyn starts moving closer, looking concerned.

I hold up my hand. "Can you stay there? Please."

He, thankfully, does as I ask. I can't handle what I saw in that room and Orfyn's close proximity simultaneously. I spot a cloud in the shape of an angel. Unlike the others that are shifting in the winds, it holds firm. I take a deep breath and slowly let it out. I made a mistake, and now I need to move past it so I can focus on learning the truth.

"We need to determine if Marty's condition is associated with his merging." I say.

Orfyn nods. "How hard do you think it would be to break into Cecil's office?"

"Cecil, I need you," Orfyn says.

"Excuse me?"

I'm hiding around the corner and can hear Cecil's words spewing like venom from his snake lips.

"There's this guy—I think he's a Darwinian, but I've never seen him before. He wants to destroy my painting."

"And?"

"I need you to stop him."

"Kevin, I'm extremely—"

"It's Orfyn."

"I don't have time for this."

"I was trying to do something nice for you guys. You know, restore the old charm to this building. He called my painting dreck—I don't even know what that means, but it doesn't sound like a compliment." Orfyn's performance is Oscar-worthy. Hurt, a little pleading, and a touch of defiance.

"What do you expect me to do?" Cecil asks.

"Come and take a look. If you hate my painting, then I'll cover it over. But beauty is in the eye of the beholder, and I don't want one guy's bias to overrule everyone else's appreciation for fine art."

I cover my mouth so I don't laugh out loud.

"It won't take long," Orfyn says. "Come on, help me out here. I don't have a Guardian on my side."

I forgot about that. Who's been conducting his daily debriefs? I make a note in my journal to ask him later.

When Cecil says, "Where is it?" I want to shout in triumph.

As orchestrated, Orfyn follows Cecil so he can drop a tube of paint to prevent the door from fully closing. Orfyn talks non-stop, holding Cecil's attention as they head down the hallway.

I'd labeled Orfyn as irresponsible, but he was willing to put his position at risk by coming with me into the restricted area. It feels as if he's watching out for me. And now he's doing this. Am I accurate or prejudiced about those who are dominant on the right hemisphere of their brain?

Orfyn pulled off his part. Now it's my turn.

His paint tube stopped the door, but it got crushed in the process, oozing chromium oxide green onto the white tile floor. Will

Cecil believe it fell out of Orfyn's bag and just happened to land in the perfect spot to prop open his office door? I can't risk it. I search Cecil's office but can't find a box of tissues. I end up losing precious time wiping up the oil paint with the bottom of my shirt, ruining it.

I sit in front of Cecil's computer. On his desk is a photo of a little girl who resembles him. Cecil lives here full-time, so she's growing up without a dad. Actually, not having him in her life may save her from years of psychotherapy.

I wasn't sure if I could access our computer files, but I luck out. Cecil had been in the midst of making notes in Marty's record. I start skimming the information and feel burning bile rising up my esophagus. I clasp my pen tighter and jot down key phrases from Cecil's notes into my journal without allowing myself to process the horrifying implications.

Mental breakdown exacerbated by continued pressure to reach standards that may or may not be achievable.

Subject's brain patterns indicate high dreamstate activity. Unknown at this time if subject is an active participant.

Mentor's consciousness appears to have superseded the subject's. Unknown at this time if situation is permanent.

Possible loss of subject's self-awareness.

Currently unable to determine whose identity will be dominant should the subject regain consciousness.

If situation continues, recommend we

Whatever-His-Name-Is is trying to hijack Marty's mind! But the even more frightening realization is: what can the Darwinians do to stop him? They can't expel Marty's Mentor, or sentence him to jail, or even hold an intervention. Contrary to everyone who is alive, there are no consequences for his actions—unless he ends up destroying his own consciousness by killing Marty.

My body starts to tremble, but I can't let fury consume me. There's something else I need to do.

We'd timed how long it takes to travel from Cecil's office to Orfyn's painting and back, which gave me seven minutes max. I have one minute left, thanks to the sacrificial paint tube. I click on my file and am barred by a black screen demanding a password. It's useless to believe I can crack his password and have to give up on that part of my plan. I write down what I'd hoped to learn instead. Is Deborah telling me the truth about my memory? Then something occurs to me. Cecil isn't my Guardian, but he is Stryker's.

His file opens with a click, and I see *Subject's Name: Stryker Paix, alias.* Why would he be using a false name? I jot down, Stryker. Alias? I read about how a previous incident has made Stryker question his judgment. What happened to him? He always appears confident. Is it all an act?

As much as I want to keep delving in Stryker's file, I'm out of time. I click back to Marty's file and make sure it's as Cecil left it. I stare in frustration at his unfinished thought. What is Cecil's recommendation?

Within seconds of ducking around the corner, I hear Orfyn. "I get that not everyone appreciates medieval-style demons, but I was trying to express an updated theme that depicts the challenges modern man faces."

"I want it gone before tomorrow," Cecil says.

When we reach my room, I gesture for Orfyn to come in and glance at the ceiling as a warning. I open my journal to the page where I'd copied Cecil's notes, and hand it to Orfyn. Shock fills his face as he reads. When Orfyn looks back at me, his golden-green eyes are glistening.

Before I can stop him, he pulls me into his arms and holds me close. I know I shouldn't let him, but it's been a *really* disturbing day. I lean my head against his shoulder, breathe in his cinnamon-walnut oil scent, feel his warmth against my cheek, and hear his heartbeat pumping against mine. I finally pull away. "I need to sail ... I mean, *sort* out my thoughts. Alone, if you don't mind."

Orfyn looks down at his paint-drip-covered shoes, then back up at me. "Are you sure?"

No, which is why I need him to leave. I have so many conflicting thoughts, it feels as if I'm at war with myself. Where's the Nobel for Peace when I need him? I then realize that not once had I wished it were Stryker with me today. Despite everything I believe to be true about artists, I fear I'm falling for the wrong boy.

I nod, because I don't trust that I won't ask him to stay.

"What about the others? Should we tell them about," he glances at the ceiling, "that surprise birthday party you're planning for Anna?"

That's what he came up with? Despite everything, I choke back a laugh. "Her birthday is coming up soon. We'd better hold a special meeting today." I notice how long his eyelashes are. "I just need a little time to create a lion ... I mean, a *list* of tasks. Then we'll wake everybody up."

He leans down, and his lips graze my cheek. A rush of heat flows through me. Once Orfyn leaves, I look down, fully expecting to see the floor scorched. I am in so much trouble.

I collapse onto my couch. Even though I've only been awake for five hours, my body feels as if I haven't slept in a week, but I don't dare dream. Enough traumatic things have happened today; I can't handle topping it off by slaying another one of my octopus friends.

My hand touches the spot where Orfyn's lips kissed me. I can't keep pretending I don't like him. But liking someone and doing something about it are two entirely different things.

I shake my head to dislodge my fixation on Orfyn and open my journal. I re-read my notes and write, Why does Jules have a key? I'm actually surprised no one is pounding on my door, demanding me to forfeit it. My mind grasps onto a hypothesis, but Sherlock Holmes warned that one shouldn't theorize before reviewing all the evidence. I start a list of possible reasons.

(1) She found it and was planning to return it. Except her book now seems more like a hiding place than homework.

(2) Cecil asked Jules to fetch something from his living quarters and gave her the key. He would have made Jules return it. I can't see him allowing her to frequent a restricted area, which triggers another thought. How does Jules have so much time to socialize?

(3) Jules stole it. She loves being the first in the know, but would she trespass in their offices to search for gossip? I can't see it.

(4) What I first suspected, but didn't want to believe.

Orfyn

I want to punch my fist through every white wall I pass. But if I break my right hand, I can't paint. If I'm not a painter, I'm nothing.

My skin stings, and I'm grinding my teeth into gravel. What's happening in Marty's mind? Does he understand his Mentor is battling him for control? Was it Angus's intention all along, or did he only discover after merging that he couldn't handle living without a body?

Ever since I got here, Marty has been slaving away, working a hell of a lot longer than I've been. What was the big rush? He and Angus have a lifetime to write their novels together.

It never seemed like Marty had any fun writing. When I've got a brush in my hand, I lose hours, and there's nothing I'd rather be doing. Marty must be a great writer, or he wouldn't be a Nobel, but did it give him any joy? If not, why was he doing it?

I've never read anything he's written. As far as I know, none of us have. Did the others ever ask to read his stuff? Because I never did. Why didn't I? It might've helped him to hear some positive feedback.

I don't know if I'll ever get the chance, but I have a way to get a glimpse into how his mind works. I go to my desk, where I'd stashed the two crinkled pieces of paper I never got the chance to return. A surge of excitement hits me as I begin to read Marty's work. It's good. Really good.

At the time when we either become a faint imitation of our dreams or a concrete image of our nightmares, I was rescued. It was not a religious epiphany. It was not a pragmatic realization. It was not a ridiculous philosophical declaration. It was a girl. And while the world crumbles and malice rules the universe, I am undismayed, because I love the girl with hair the color of sunshine.

Corruption descended on the prairie like a cloud of locusts, and for the first time I learned what my family really believed in. Not all that much. The church was a club of suckers and sadists, and only the fake sinners paid. To the others—the ones who would cut your throat to take your grandmother's wedding ring and catch up with the Revival a few days later—it was a breadbox. An unholy deception of the worst kind, and I loved everything about it. Because she was there.

The wandering cow came home that night, and I just knew we'd make it. We sat around the fire—more smoke than heat, due to the wet forest—and little Sally hooted, and damned if she didn't call down an owl, and Rance took it with the bow, and we cooked it and were about as happy as we could be, 'cause we knew there'd be mice around. And then the blond girl gave me this look, and it all went away: the fire and the forest, the dreams and the darkness, and the unexplainable need to stay alive.

You could feel the heat. The fire was closing in. It had crossed the river to the south and made it all around Lake Duroy. It was only a matter of time before the Town vanished into ash, and all its sins with it. The smart folks were gone with the last train, along with any semblance of order. There was no way out, and the only thing standing between her and a life she deserved was him. The only thing.

Every afternoon I walk to the park, and if she's there, I watch her. Her blond hair catching in the breeze; her reddened cheeks tightened in laughter; just the glow of her. I know when she has a hard day. I know because it's hard for me. It's hard for everyone else, too. I make sure of that. She is the sun I revolve around. And I hope she never finds out.

I'd tapped out all the relatives, friends, and church-goers; pressed all the people that owed me dough; hit the plasma clinic; and sold Granddad's stock in the Green Bay Packers. For the first time in my life, I knew who I was and what I cared about. I knew what I had to do. My life would matter, and I would never leave her alone again. I would follow love.

How many other first paragraphs has Marty thrown away? Dozens? Hundreds? He was writing a love story. Is there a special girl waiting for the day when he's allowed to see her again? Will someone tell her Marty may never come home?

We've got to get him back so he has the chance to finish his novel. And I want to help him understand that the thrill of being an artist comes from reaching beyond what we think we're capable of, not achieving perfection. I also want to learn if there really is a girl he loves.

My eyes catch on Lake's canvas, leaning against the wall. Until today, she's never let me into her place, so I've never hung it for her. The bottom third is still blank, since Alex broke up the party before she could finish it. He's got to be scared to death that they can't figure out how to help him. I vow to start hanging out with him more. Hear him play the guitar. Make him laugh.

I take the canvas over to the table and grab my oils, but not my brushes. I'll finish it like Lake started it: with my hands. It'll be a pain to get the paint off, but I want to respect her style. Unlike the criminal who painted over the beached whale, I'm not changing a thing about her work. As our paintings brush up against each other's, I want the emotions to merge into something bigger—something that will blow her mind.

Lake

"You're lying!"

"Jules, I'm not the liar here," I say. "*You* lied about Marty's writing. His Mentor never allowed him to move past the ... the beginning part. The first *paragraph*."

The Darwinians have to be questioning why the six of us are sitting in the middle of the crumbling outdoor track, and I doubt they'd believe we're holding cheerleading practice. This one's going to have to be one creative lie—which I'll let Stryker deal with.

Jules twists her hair into a bun. "They told me they were moving Marty from our wing for observation."

"Why would they tell you and not the rest of us?" Alex wheezes. He has a clear tube running from an oxygen tank into his nostrils, and he still got winded getting here. But at least he's well enough to rejoin our meetings.

"Yeah, what's so special about you?" Anna demands.

Stryker catches my eye and lifts an eyebrow to prod me. I understand how Johann Becher must've felt when they debunked his theory that objects combust because they contain phlogiston.

"You're spying for them," I accuse Jules.

"Lake, I hate to sound mean, but you haven't exactly been thinking clearly."

My anger grapples with gut-wrenching shame until I realize she's purposely trying to fluster me. "It's the only, only … *explanation* for why you had that key and why you're aware of things the rest of us aren't."

Jules removes her glasses and wipes the lenses with the bottom of her shirt. "I can't help it if people feel comfortable talking to me."

No wonder it appears as if she barely eats. She's been using food as a prop to justify the hours she spends in the dining hall, prying secrets out of us.

"It's over, Jules." Stryker says. "Since none of us will confide in you again, I hope for your sake you're providing other value to the Darwinians."

Jules's chin juts out, and her eyes narrow, making her resemble a fox readying itself to pounce on a defenseless rabbit. "I'm more valuable than any of the rest of you."

"Then it's true? You're their *spy?*" Anna asks, sounding more upset than I'd expect given her typical aloofness.

Jules says, "I've only been confirming facts so they know if everyone is telling them the truth."

How can Jules live with herself? I grab my journal and jot down, Jules = spy!

"Traitor." Alex shakes his head in disgust, dislodging the plastic tube from his left nostril.

"I told them I was worried about Marty," Jules insists.

"Was that before or after … *Marty's Mentor* seized his body?" I hate that I can never remember his name.

"I didn't know about that part, honest." Jules wipes her eye, even though there isn't a glint of tears.

What would have happened if I'd confided in Jules about Sophie's confusion?

Stryker says to Jules, "What I'm questioning is why they'd lie to you."

"Sarah never lied to me about Marty," she answers, defiantly.

"I thought Sarah is your Mentor," Orfyn says.

Jules's eyes widen, and she looks like she wants to be anywhere but here.

"How would your Mentor know anything about Marty?" Alex presses.

"You haven't merged with her yet," Stryker states matter-of-factly.

Of course. It's the only logical answer.

"You've got to be kidding," Alex says.

"I'm right, aren't I?" Stryker asks.

"I'm a little behind the rest of you," Jules answers, avoiding our eyes. "But I'm starting the first phase soon."

Orfyn's forehead furrows. "After what we've learned about Marty, you're still going through with it?"

"My aunt isn't like Angus Doyle."

That's his Mentor's name. I jot it down in my journal.

"Sarah is your aunt?" Anna asks.

"Yes, but—"

"She's been using us as her personal guinea pigs," Alex accuses.

A question squeezes its way into the argument, and I document it before forgetting it.

"Sarah is very ill, but she's waited to merge to protect me." Jules looks at each of us imploringly. "She's only going through the procedure to give me the chance to do great things."

"Keep telling yourself that," Anna snaps.

"You do realize Sarah intentionally hid Marty's condition from you," Stryker says.

"You're all wrong about her!" Jules cries out before sprinting back to The Flem, leaving her glasses on the ground. Was even her studious look a charade?

"She's delusional," Anna says angrily.

"I think Jules believes she was helping," Orfyn says.

"Most of the evil in this world is done by people with good intentions," Stryker says as if it's a Universal Truth.

I give him a questioning look.

"T.S. Eliot," he answers, as if it explains his perspective on humanity.

"Do you think they would've told us the truth about Marty?" Alex asks, adjusting the tube in his nose.

"No," Anna answers. "They wouldn't want us to question if the same thing will happen to us."

"Bat would never try to take over my body," Orfyn says.

Would Sophie? I never thought I'd be consoled because she doesn't realize she has the ability to try. What about the other Mentors? No one is jumping to their defense.

"I told Bjorn what's been happening to some of us." Stryker's eyes fall on me.

I grip my journal tighter.

His eyes move on to Alex. "Bjorn revealed that the Darwinians have been working on a way to extract the second consciousness as a failsafe."

"Are you saying they can unmerge us?" Alex asks.

"In theory."

Could this be what Cecil was going to recommend in his notes?

"Just because they *can* doesn't mean they *will*," Stryker says.

Anna's fury explodes, and not because of phlogiston. "Why the hell not?"

Stryker flings a rock toward The Flem. "They're not going to let Angus Doyle die, and they may not want to risk implanting him into another Candidate's body because he could take over that person, too. Their best option is to allow Angus to remain where he is and see what happens."

"But there's the possibility Marty won't be the one canceling ... I mean, *controlling* his own body," I say.

"Think about it," Stryker says. "Angus is one of the most influential writers of our time, and Marty is a sixteen-year-old nobody. Do you think they'd see it as a failure if Angus had Marty's body to use for another lifetime?"

"Crap!" Alex rasps.

Anna stands and towers over us. "We have to *confront* them and *demand* they remove him from Marty's brain."

"That's the last thing we want to do," Stryker says, calmly. "One problem is manageable. Five problems would cause them to evaluate whether they should start over again with more compliant Candidates."

"They wouldn't dare," Anna says, two decibels lower.

"Think about Marie Curie," Stryker says. "She died of radiation poisoning, but millions of people have been saved because of her discoveries. Most would agree the benefits outweigh the cost of one life." Stryker holds Anna's eyes. "Do you want to risk our lives in order to see which of us is right?"

Emotions battle across her face until she shakes her head in resignation.

"Jules is going to tell them we know about Marty," Alex says.

"Of course she will," Stryker says. "And that's why we're going to act like we believe they'll figure out how to save him."

"For how long?" Anna asks.

"Until we have a better solution."

"What if there were somewhere else Angus could live?" Orfyn asks.

"Tell us where you're going with this, Art," Stryker says.

"Before getting anyone's hopes up, I need to talk to Bat."

"Then it's nap time for you." Stryker stands and brushes off the back of his khakis. "Everybody, continue with your normal routine. And act like you have faith they'll do the right thing."

It didn't used to be an act.

I notice my note to myself. I run to catch up to Alex, which isn't difficult since he's towing an oxygen tank. "You visited Mexico before you came here, didn't you?"

"No, not since I was a little kid. Why?"

I hesitate, but he needs to know that Marty might not be the only one in danger. As I tell Alex about Jules's lie, his breathing gets more and more labored.

Orfyn

These days, Bat prefers to live in the masterpieces. I'm glad he's found a way to escape his basement prison, but now we need to help someone else who's being imprisoned.

Today, Bat is in a painting of Monet's studio in France, filled with paints, brushes, and canvases. I'd love to know what it feels like to hold Monet's tools.

"I think it's too dim in here," Bat says. "What if we lighten it up?"

"Sure." Could my idea actually work?

Bat strolls around Monet's room, slurping a grape soda. "Giverny didn't have electricity until 1909. What do you think, pre-electricity or post?"

"Bat, how is all this happening?" I gesture to the screen where he's now scratching his butt.

"It's what we do."

"I'm not doing anything. You are."

"It's your brain."

Bat shuffles over to an easel and grabs a brush. I cringe as he stabs out a lopsided daisy on one of Monet's blank canvases, in Monet's studio, using Monet's brush and paints. If he can do that …

"Can you help me write your gaming program in my world?"

"Depends on why you need it."

I tell him about what's been going on. "The thing is, we doubt the Darwinians will agree to unmerge Angus if there's no place to put his consciousness. If your program were real, then Angus could keep working, and Marty could get his life back."

Bat scratches his unshaved cheek. "My model predicted this might happen. You can't take the most curious minds, contain their experiences, and then expect them to be satisfied." Bat rotates the canvas ninety degrees and studies it.

"But the Mentors were all dying. This is better than being dead."

Bat paints a yellow sun with a smiley face. "Is this what you were told it would be like?"

"I've gotta admit, when I figured out you weren't an artist—I mean a Master painter—I was pissed. But now, I'm glad you're the one sharing my brain."

He beams at me. "Me, too. But it's not going to work out like this for everyone."

"Do you think the other Mentors will try to take over their Nobels?"

He shrugs. "Depends on the kind of person they were before."

"If the Darwinians can unmerge Angus, is it possible to put him into your program so he can keep living?"

Bat sets down his brush and rubs his stubbly chins. "Software is nothing more than a map for electrical impulses, which isn't that different from how a brain functions. My program is modeled on brain synapses rather than the traditional binary 1's and 0's, and I've developed a matrix of different inputs controlling the amount of electricity that's distributed in each burst ..." Bat continues mumbling techno-geek stuff until finally saying, "It could work."

I've never written software, but if we can do this, Bat and I could save Marty's life. That's a seriously big purpose. And if the same thing starts happening to the others, we'll have a way to save them, too.

As long as the Darwinians agree to it. And the unmerging procedure works. And if their plan all along wasn't to have the Mentors take over our bodies. I recite to myself one of Sister Mo's favorite Bible verses: *Do not worry about tomorrow; tomorrow will take care of itself.*

"What do I need to do to create your program in my awake-life?" I ask.

"Why don't you use the one at my house?"

"Where is it?" I jump up from the recliner.

"Not this house. The other one."

Bat couldn't remember where his real house is. I get on a computer to search for his address, then realize I don't know his last name. Or his first, since I doubt his mother would've named him Bat.

He lives in my head. How could I not know his name?

I type what little I know into the search engine. *Bat video game developer.* Pages and pages of results appear. He was seriously famous!

I hover the cursor over the first entry. Do I want to learn about the old Bat? Will it change how I think of him? But I have to find his house.

I click on a story about how multi-billionaire Bartholomew Wakowski died after a long struggle with ALS. I don't know much about that disease, but I know it destroys the body. The story then lists all the video games Bat has written. I'm not a gamer, but even I've heard of most of them. Bat—the slob who paints flowers that would embarrass a five-year-old—created worlds that entertain millions. What the story doesn't cover is how Bat couldn't leave his house, or how he had no friends or family. I'm glad. I want people to remember the good parts of his other life.

It only takes a few more clicks to find his address. Now the question is: how am I going to get to New Jersey?

Orfyn

I knock on the one Nobel door I didn't paint a hometown on. I tried to find out where Stryker comes from, but his response was, "The past is not the future." He's as elusive as Bigfoot. I've asked, but nobody knows his history. Not where he lived, not which school he went to, and not what made him the perfect Candidate to become the Nobel for Peace.

I half-expect a tuxedoed butler to greet me, but it's only Stryker. I look past him and catch a glimpse of his place. Calling it plain is generous. A nun's room in a convent looks like a Vegas casino in comparison. Why does Stryker choose to live like this? They give us anything we ask for.

"Interested in a game of H-O-R-S-E?" I flick my eyes to the ceiling. Stryker and I aren't friends, but when you need help with an escape plan and want to make sure you're prepared for everything that could go wrong, he's the guy.

"I'll grab my ball."

I hope the person listening doesn't stop to think that Stryker is almost a foot taller than me, and no sane person would ever initiate the trouncing I'm about to face. We head to the basketball court. It's covered in cracks, but at least Stryker got them to install a net. I stand underneath it as he confidently volleys perfect shot after perfect shot.

I don't want Stryker thinking I've got some schmo living in my head. I repeatedly return the ball while explaining—bragging—who Bat was in his other life. Stryker is clearly impressed.

We switch positions, and I half-heartedly throw balls at the basket, telling him about what Bat has been working on. I don't take credit; he knows I'm no computer genius. But I might have let it slip that it was my idea to insert Angus into Bat's program.

"Incredible," Stryker acknowledges, which is the first time he's ever made me feel like I'm not a total waste of space. "We need to get our hands on that program."

My chest swells with pride. None of the other Mentors created a solution that might save Marty. "Then you'll help?"

"I'm not letting you get all the credit." Then he smirks and flicks his chin at me.

I wasn't going to beg, but I'd been hoping he'd offer. I don't know the best way to approach the Darwinians, but Stryker will.

"If something should happen to Bat's program, we've lost our leverage," Stryker says. "We need to be the ones to go and get it."

"It's in Jersey," I say. "Do you have a driver's license?"

"You don't?"

"Nobody in the City drives. Where did you say you grew up?"

"I didn't."

We hold each other's eyes until I break the ice. "Okay. No hometown. Back to the plan. We need to convince the Darwinians to let us leave, and they need to lend us a car."

"Meet me here at eleven tonight. And bring a tube of paint." Stryker has a gleam in his eyes.

"I take it we're not asking permission."

It's late, so I'm hoping everyone is busy with their Mentors. I shut my door as quietly as possible and tiptoe to Stryker's to pick him up. When I turn the corner, Anna is leaning against her doorway, filing her black nails. I get this feeling she's been waiting for me. Damn.

"Is there a reason you're dressed like a ninja?" she asks.

I thought it would be good camouflage, but I look like a black hole in this bright hallway. "Borrowing fashion tips from you." Then I notice, for the first time, she's wearing something non-vampirish. And her eyes aren't smeared with black make-up.

Anna crosses her arms. "Spill it. What are you up to?"

Right. Since she's been such a great friend, I'll confide that Stryker and I are breaking out, and I'm pretty sure we're stealing a car to do it. "Getting something to eat."

"I'll join you."

Crap. "Sure, if you want."

We pass Stryker's door, but I'm not quick enough to think of a stealthy way to let him know I'll now be running late. The thorny silence between Anna and me makes it seem like the dining hall is a mile away. I get a grilled cheese sandwich I don't want, and she grabs a chocolate milk.

"That's all you're having?"

"I'm not that hungry after all."

I hold in my eye-roll as I scarf down the sandwich in less than a minute. "That hit the spot." I get up to go. "See ya later." I'm not too far behind schedule, and since Stryker doesn't know where Bat lives, he can't leave without me.

"Have you ever been to the greenhouse on the roof?" Anna asks, stopping me in my tracks.

"Once." It sits within a Gothic arch. Tall sheets of glass between thin iron bones. It's not easy to get to, since you have to use a rickety fire escape. But I was looking for a new wall that needed an attitude adjustment and dared the climb. When I got there, it was empty, and I didn't end up painting on those walls. Some places are perfect the way they are. "Why?"

"Did you happen to notice that it overlooks the basketball court?" She leans in closer. "Sound can travel far in the wind."

I sit back down and mouth, "Don't." I can't let her sabotage our only chance to save Marty.

"It's time for me to collect," she says, like she's had negotiation lessons from the mob—or worse, Stryker.

"I told you. I don't own anything."

She takes a long, slow sip of chocolate milk. "I want to watch you paint."

"What?"

"I've seen Lake do it."

Yeah, but I don't avoid her. "Why would you want to? It's boring."

Her multi-pierced eyebrow meets the one that looks like a delicate black feather. "Are you telling me I can't?"

"I didn't say that."

"But you haven't said I could, either."

"Anna, why do you want to spend time with me? We're not even friends."

She turns her head toward the wall of water lilies, and after more than a few beats she says, "You're right. Dumb idea."

Oh my God! I think Anna likes me. Is that why she looks so nice tonight? *Double crap!* I might have hurt her feelings. Now she's going to retaliate. "I just meant—"

"I know what you meant." She keeps not looking at me.

"Anna, you've been gearing up to blackmail me from the second we met."

Her eyes look left of my nose. "I didn't know how else to get your attention."

That confession took a lot of guts, and I have a feeling she doesn't let down her guard very often. "I'll make you a deal. If you stop threatening me, we can work on becoming friends."

"Is that all we can ever be?" Her eyes dart around the room.

This is the conversation she's been wanting to have. It feels more surreal than my time with Bat. "I have to be honest. I like someone else."

She scowls. "Lake thinks she's too good for you."

"That's not true. And, it's none of your business."

Anna picks at a hangnail until it bleeds. "I can watch you paint?"

I shoot my eyes to the ceiling. "Do we have a deal?"

She makes a locking motion in front of her lips. For the first time ever, her gaze isn't filled with challenge.

"I'll let you know the next time I start working on something. Promise." And I will.

I think we end on okay terms, but who knows what she'll do after she re-spins our conversation a few dozen times.

Orfyn

"The parking lot is too visible," Stryker says as we conceal ourselves in the shadows outside the back door. "We need to try our luck in the old garage."

"What garage?" I ask.

"It's about a quarter mile away, hidden behind some trees. But there's a camera on the roof that will capture our getaway."

"How do you know all this?"

"I like to get a feel for what I'm dealing with, just in case."

With my artist eyes, I see the fine details that most people never notice. I suppose that a guy who's trying to stop gun violence pays attention to the things put in place to maintain order.

"Is that why you wanted me to bring paint?" I ask.

"You're smarter than you look, Art." He flashes me his grin.

I remind myself this is Stryker's version of a compliment.

He takes the lead, and we stick close to The Flem's ivy-covered walls. When we reach the end of the building, he signals, and we dash across the yard until we reach a bunch of tall, scraggly bushes.

"Head to the big oak," Stryker directs. "Go!"

We're hopscotching our way from shadow to shadow when I hear pounding feet behind us.

"Someone's coming after us," I whisper.

We dart left, toward a strand of birch trees. Adrenaline surges through me like a tidal wave, even though we're not doing anything wrong ... yet.

"Wait!" A girl's voice calls out.

Did Anna follow me? Then I realize it's not her. "It's Lake."

"Why did you tell her about tonight?" Stryker accuses.

"I didn't!"

We wait for her to catch up.

"I saw you guys from my ... my *window*," Lake says. "What are you doing out here at night?"

Stryker says, "We need to leave for a couple of hours."

"Does this have something to do with Marty?" she asks.

I nod.

"Then I'm coming."

"Lake, we're taking one of their cars," Stryker says. "You don't want that kind of trouble."

"I get to decide what kind of trouble I want." The moonlight shines on her determined face, reminding me of a Roman statue.

"Fine," Stryker says, as if Lake hadn't already made the decision for all of us.

We follow Stryker to a line of trees, and as we get closer, I spot the old brick garage. He points to the left corner of the roof. "The camera is mounted there. Make a wide arc and approach from the back. Then climb up and put your paint to good use. Got it, Art?"

"Me?"

"It's your mission. I'm just the driver."

This is the time he chooses to be the sidekick?

I never got caught painting in the alleys, and I'm not about to let it happen now. I zigzag from tree to tree, then make a break across the open field—which is when I spot a bobbing light. I drop to the ground. Someone with a flashlight is heading straight toward me. I say a quick prayer that he can't hear my thumping heart. I'm not sure if it was God's doing or my dark clothes, but the Not-A-Guard, as Lake calls them, passes within feet without noticing me.

I wait until he's out of sight, then make my way to the back of the garage. It's only one story, but the walls have to be ten feet tall. The gutter running along the corner is too mangled to hold my weight, and there's no doorway or window sill to use as a foothold.

As I'm slinking around the building, looking for a way up, I stumble upon a metal barrel in the tall weeds. I roll the rusty barrel to the wall and carefully stand on it. I feel its lid start to give way and leap up, grabbing hold of the roof's edge as the barrel crumbles beneath my feet. It's not lost on me that with Stryker's height, this would've been a cinch.

I pull myself up, but when I stand on the ancient slate tiles, they crack in protest, sounding as loud as a sonic boom—at least, they do to me. I freeze, expecting to see Not-A-Guard returning to nab me, but the only sound I hear is my own heavy breathing. I get down on my hands and knees, splaying as wide as possible, then crab-crawl across the roof. By the time I reach the back of the camera, I'm layered in sweat and covered in decades of rotted leaves and who knows what else. I'm sure I smell terrific, too.

I grab my tube of black paint, squeeze a dab on my finger, add a hefty gob of spit, and smear it on the camera's lens. Just enough to make anything seen through it blurry, but not enough to make anyone think it's anything more than grime. Only then do I allow myself a moment to catch my breath.

I whistle softly and soon hear running feet approaching me. I'm more relieved than I'd ever admit that it's only Stryker and Lake.

"Mission accomplished. Help me down." I hang off the roof's edge, and Stryker reaches up, taking the weight off my fall.

"Nice job," he says. "If the art thing doesn't work out, you can always lead a life as a cat burglar."

Thanks for the confidence, Stryker. And what's a cat burglar, anyway?

As we approach the door, he asks Lake, "Do you still have Jules's keycard?"

"No. I left my room for a bite to eat and couldn't find it when I got back."

I catch Lake's eyes. "Jules must've told them you had it."

My belief in her good intentions drops a few more notches.

"Doesn't matter," Stryker says. "There's no card reader."

I test the handle, and it's locked. I'm debating whether I should try to kick in the door when Stryker saves me the embarrassment. He pulls out his wallet, selects a credit card, and slips it between the door and the jamb. After he wiggles the card and jiggles the handle, the door opens.

"Care to tell us how you learned to do that?" Lake asks Stryker.

"I've met my share of locked doors."

Stryker turns on the flashlight he thought to bring and reveals an old pickup truck next to a van with *The Flemming Academy, Since 1902* on its side. As we approach the truck, a mouse skitters out from underneath, scaring the crap out of me. For the record, even Stryker jumped.

"We need to find some keys," he says, rubbing his hands and eyeing the van.

Lake begins searching the garage, Stryker scours the vehicles, and I rummage through the tiny office. I can't help but notice a calendar with a picture of a girl in a bikini, doing an admirable job of representing July 2002.

I rejoin them. "Nothing. Anyone know how to hotwire a car?" I joke.

"I do," Stryker says.

Lake and I turn to look at him. Should I be surprised anymore?

"The van will be the easiest," he says while opening its rust-pocked driver's door. "Find me a Phillips-head screwdriver, wire cutters, and electrical tape. And work gloves, if you can."

Lake and I collect what he needs, even the gloves. Stryker takes off the plastic casing around the steering column and tosses it on the ground. He spends a moment studying the tangle of wires, then cuts two red ones and wraps them together.

Country music blasts from the radio, shortening my life by a year or two. I lean into the van and turn off the noise threatening to destroy our plan.

Lake pulls out a piece of gum.

"Battery still works," Stryker says calmly. He strips another wire and holds it as if it'll explode. "Just a precaution, but I wouldn't be touching this van right now."

Lake and I lurch away.

Stryker touches the bare wires against each other. Sparks fly, and the engine rumbles to life. "One more step." He grips the steering wheel and starts jerking it to the right and left, grunting with each turn.

"Careful," Lake says. "You'll break it."

"That's the point." He yanks the steering wheel hard, and it lets out a sharp, metallic *snap*. He turns the wheel easily in both directions and flashes his Stryker-smile. "The Flem Van, at your service."

Orfyn

We peel out of the garage, narrowly missing a tree, since we don't have the headlights on. Stryker swerves, and the Flem Van's tires skid over the gravel. I death-grip the passenger door, and Lake looks like she's seriously regretting her decision to come along.

"Bjorn raced stock cars when he was young," Stryker says as he whips us around another corner. "I may be channeling his love for speed."

"Are you serious about channeling?" I ask, every muscle tense as we tear down the road.

"I'm still deciding," Stryker says, as easy-going as if we were all hanging out in Lake's rose garden instead of roaring away in a stolen van.

Am I channeling Bat? I have started playing classical music while I paint.

Out of the darkness, Lake says, "Can we stop somewhere for cigarettes?" Then, "I don't know why I just said that."

I hear crinkling and then smell peppermint.

"We're all a little tense, Lake," Stryker says.

"All part of the fun of stealing a van to bring a life-altering program back to the secret brain lab to keep Marty from becoming a zombie," I add, trying to make her smile.

Stryker catches my eye in the rearview mirror, letting me know I'm not the only one who's worried about her. He told me he tried talking to her like we agreed, but he didn't get far. I'll try when we're alone—and if she ends up mad at me again, I still have to do it.

We finally get to Jersey, then Bat's neighborhood. The homes on his block feel like the kind where families have dinner together and share stories about their day. The yards are mowed, brightly colored flowers line the walkways, and kids' bikes lie in the driveways, waiting for the next carefree summer day of exploring. I always dreamed about living in a place like this, and of being one of those kids. Instead, a corporation intent on changing the course of mankind has adopted me.

Fate can be surprising.

Bat couldn't remember where he put the spare key. Knowing him, he "hid" it under the doormat. As we walk up to the house, I see a high-tech panel next to a door without a doorknob, which looks totally out of place.

Stryker studies it while I grin at the doormat, which proclaims, *Live Long and Prosper.*

"It's a palm reader," Stryker says.

Lake beats me to the punch. "How do you know that?"

"My dad had one installed to keep me out of his home office." When Lake raises her eyebrows, he adds, "Long story."

"I don't mean to sound insensitive here," I say, "but Bat's palm is buried six feet in the ground."

Stryker grabs my hand and pushes it against the panel's black screen.

"That's not going to—"

"Welcome, Kevin," says the security panel ... in Bat's voice.

A chill runs through me, and Lake chews her gum fast enough to dislocate her jaw.

Stryker smirks at me. "Kevin?"

Hearing my name is startling, but hearing it said in front of Lake and Stryker—in Bat's voice—is beyond freaky. It takes a few seconds before I can answer, "Another guy in another life."

Stryker gives me a nod, making me feel like he understands, which I didn't expect.

I lead Lake and Stryker into Bat's home, and the hairs on my arms rise to attention. The living room is exactly like the one in my dreams: worn couch, rose-colored wallpaper with flowers, the photo of Bat's mom on the mantel.

Stryker surveys the room. "Not what I'd expect from a gaming tycoon."

"Shut up," I snap. "You don't know what his life was like."

Stryker looks like I sucker-punched him. "Sorry, I didn't mean any disrespect."

"It reminds me of my Grandma Bee's house," Lake says. "It feels like home."

I smile my thanks to her. "Bat said it's in the basement. The stairs are over this way."

I head down the hallway and am confronted by another high-tech door. Next to it is a screen six inches square with a glowing orange line moving from top to bottom. I place my hand on it and nothing happens.

"It's meant to scan something," Stryker says.

Questions about Stryker's old life swirl through my mind like van Gogh's stars.

We start holding up different things in front of the screen, but nothing works.

"He wouldn't give you access to his house, but not the bathtub … I mean, *basement*," Lake says.

"He'd probably use something he could keep on him," Stryker says while opening a drawer crammed with blue First Place ribbons and Certificates of Achievement.

We try the ribbons. We try photos off the wall. We even try my eyes, which only turns everything orange for a few blinks. "Bat's never without his grape soda," I joke.

"Go see if you can find one," Stryker says.

I head to the kitchen. Like in my dreams, the fridge is filled with purple cans. Could that be it? I grab one and hold it in front of the scanner. When the door slides open, I have to chuckle at the way Bat's mind works.

I head down the orange shag stairs and when I reach the last step, I freeze.

It's all real!

Monet. Degas. Van Gogh. I know everything upstairs looks the same, but I couldn't make myself believe that hidden in Bat's basement is a priceless art collection.

"Holy Picasso!" Stryker says.

"They're not ... what's the word? *Originals*, are they?" Lake asks.

I nod. "They're the real deal."

The same nine screens as in my dreams are mounted on the far wall. But in this basement, there's only one of the most comfortable chairs in the world. Bat was so alone. But now, in his second life, he has me.

"Bat told me to turn on the screens when I got here," I explain.

"Where's the remote?" Stryker starts searching.

"I've never seen him use one." I rack my brain, trying to remember what Bat does. He gets a soda from upstairs, plops down in the left recliner, and then the screens come to life. I sit in his chair, feeling like an interloper. It's as comfortable as the dream version, but something doesn't feel right. It's not usually this quiet. Bat always has music playing.

"Mozart, please," I say. Classical music fills the room, and the screens light up.

I gasp.

In front of me is the electronic version of my painting, *Take This*

Cup, with Christ, his twelve disciples … and Bat, sipping from a plain, clay cup.

When you dream about something that feels impossible, and allow yourself to hope that it really exists, and believe it enough to steal a van with a beautiful girl, and risk your life letting a guy who thinks he's a NASCAR driver bring you to New Jersey—well, even then, you're still not fully prepared when it appears right in front of you.

Bat gets up from the table. "You must be Kevin."

"You know me?"

"Naturally."

He looks like my Bat, pink bathrobe and all. Except his eyes don't have that magic that makes you believe anything is possible. "Are you the same Bat as in my dreams?"

"He is the real Bat. I am a program with a more limited array of thoughts and feelings. But please let me say, I am very glad to meet you. It means the procedure was a success."

Stryker nudges me. "Dude, he's hanging out with Jesus!" he says out of the corner of his mouth.

I'm not sure if it's all the masterpieces, Christ and his hockey player disciples having supper right in front of us, or the replica of my Mentor making polite conversation. Either way, this is the first time Stryker has ever referred to me as *Dude.*

"That's a painting of mine," I say, as if that explains it.

"It looks so real." Lake steps closer to the screen.

Virtual Bat stares at her like he's never seen a girl before. Some things can't get filtered out of a copy.

"Virtual Bat, this is Lake, the Nobel for Chemistry."

"Hello, Bat," Lake says, as if there's nothing strange about this experience.

Virtual Bat pulls back his shoulders and tightens the tie on his bathrobe. "You're pretty."

Stryker slides me a look. I just shake my head.

"Thank you." Lake gives him a smile.

"And this is Stryker," I say, trying to salvage Bat's cool. "Peace." Virtual Bat holds up two fingers. "Peace back at you. Now, how may I help, Kevin?"

"I'm Orfyn now."

"We thought you would choose that name."

The warmest feeling floats through me. I really do have a guardian angel ... or two. One who seems as much man as computer, and one who probably acted more computer than man.

I tell Virtual Bat about what Angus is doing to Marty, and our plan to insert Angus's consciousness into Bat's program. "Real Bat said it's here."

"Yes. The prototype is in this room."

"Do you think it will work?"

"In theory. This version has extensive capacity and an impressive range of sensitivity algorithms." Bat rubs his stubbly chins, like my Bat does. "I estimate the current prototype could hold the memories and impulse patterns of twenty mature human minds."

"Then there's the possibility to save those other kids, too," Lake says.

This isn't the time to bring it up, but if her memory keeps getting worse, she may need to be next in line. Would she consider it?

"If it works, Angus Doyle can keep working in Bat's prototype for, well, forever," I say, hoping Lake understands that her Mentor won't have to die if Lake chooses to unmerge.

"This is brilliant, Orfyn," Stryker says.

"Bat and I make a good team," I say, trying to hide how much his compliment means to me.

"Thank you," Virtual Bat says.

"Will you give us the prototype?" I ask him.

"Yes," he says, swiping a piece of bread from Jesus's plate.

Stryker's jaw practically hits the floor.

"Where is it?" I ask, loving that he and Lake get to experience what my Mentor created.

"You must say the magic words, Orfyn," Virtual Bat says.

"Please," I automatically reply.

"That's not it."

"You've got to be kidding."

"Consider it an extra security measure. Or, perhaps it is just that we enjoy games."

This is so Real Bat. I scrape through my memory, searching for what he'd use as a password.

"Vivaldi," I try.

My painting fades, and in its place materializes Munch's *The Scream*. Virtual Bat sets his cup on the bridge's railing and takes an appreciative look around. "One of my favorites. But, alas, wrong."

"Beethoven," I say.

The scene shifts. A girl is outstretched on the ground, looking yearningly back at an unpainted house in a sea of prairie grass. *Christina's World*. Virtual Bat shakes his head. He reaches for his cup, but it disappeared along with the bridge's railing from the last painting. He frowns, as if he couldn't create another one.

"Bach," I blurt out.

The scene changes to a group of well-dressed people sitting around a table filled with wine bottles and crystal glasses. Boats float on the river in the background. Bat swipes a half-filled glass with a smile.

"Mozart," I say with clenched teeth, and the scene returns to *Take This Cup*.

"Can you give me a hint?" I can hear the frustration in my voice. Virtual Bat has all the time in the world, but Marty doesn't.

"That would not be playing fair," he says.

"Will you do it for me?" Lake asks.

He takes so long to answer, I'm worried she's thrown him into an endless loop. He finally blinks. Then he whirls around, and when he faces us again, he's wearing a football jersey. "Does this help?"

I smile, thinking back to the first time I saw Bat in the dreamspace.

He's as big a fan as me—as big a fan as Sister Mo. "The New York Rangers."

The overhead lights dim, and one of the paintings slides to the side, revealing a hidden compartment. Tiny LEDs turn on and highlight a platinum-colored cube the size of a mini-microwave. It's strangely gorgeous. The shimmering metal. The shape. The sense of power—twenty brains' worth. In a room lined with masterpieces, this is the most amazing thing here.

I carefully remove the cube from the compartment. It's lighter than I expect—and it's giving off a low hum. "Is this thing dangerous?"

"Not as long as you do not drop it," Virtual Bat answers.

"Seriously?"

"The power source is somewhat unique."

"We need to show this to Alex. It might help him with his renewable energy project." Stryker flicks his chin at me, which I guess in rich-person speak means *well done*.

"I could kiss you, Bat," Lake says.

Virtual Bat's glass slips from his hand, shattering on the floor and splashing wine all over him and the white tablecloth. He grabs for the cup, tripping on his own feet, bumping into the table, and sending a plate crashing to the floor. Christ doesn't flinch, which I've got to admit is a huge relief. I couldn't handle the Son of God coming to life and losing his cool.

Virtual Bat wipes his hands down his robe. "Is anyone else in your class exhibiting signs of distress?"

I make a point of not looking at Lake. "Alex is having problems breathing."

"How about any of you?" he asks.

"Nothing's wrong with me," Stryker says, with a little too much emphasis.

"I'm good, too," I say. Because I am.

"I'm fine." Lake's eyes are glued to the embroidery on the white tablecloth.

Virtual Bat glances at me, and I give a tiny head shake.

He watches Lake pretend nothing is wrong, and sighs deeply. "Orfyn, from what appears to be happening, I must insist that you unmerge from Bat."

Leave Bat? I've never considered it. Not for a second. I've come to love spending my dreams with him. He's not only my Mentor, he's like an older brother. Why would I live without him? Nothing's wrong with me.

"No way."

"The scenario you are describing is one we considered might happen, and the projected solution was to immediately unmerge, if such a procedure were validated." Virtual Bat stares at me.

"Nothing is wrong with me. I'm not throwing him out like a botched painting."

"I fear that could be a fatal mistake."

Orfyn

I'm in the backseat of the Flem Van with my arms straightjacketed around the humming cube, mentally sending the Traveling Protection Prayer to Archangel Michael so Stryker's driving doesn't send it flying.

"Now that we have Bat's prototype, do you think the Darwinians will unmerge Angus?" I ask.

"I've been ... *questioning* that, too," Lake says.

"For good reason," Stryker says, not exactly upping my faith in them.

"We can all refuse to tell them what's happening in our dreams unless they do it," I suggest.

"Then we're five loose ends who can easily be made to disappear," Stryker says. "There has to be a different solution."

"I wish there was a way to get a message to Marty," I say.

"And tell him what?" Lake asks.

"What do you think happens if a Mentor gets killed in their dreamspace?"

They both reel around to look at me.

"We are *not* using violence to get our way," Stryker states in a tone that ends all discussion.

After miles of uncomfortable silence and the metallic smell of Lake's gum, I have to ask. "Stryker, how do you know how to hotwire a car?"

"I looked it up on the Internet."

I could've done that, too—if I'd thought about it, which I didn't.

"Why does your dad need a palm reader for his office?" Lake asks, saving me from doing it.

Stryker drums his fingers on the steering wheel for so long, I don't think he's going to answer. "He didn't want me to have access to a computer without supervision." His voice has none of its usual confidence.

"Will you tell us why?" Lake asks.

Stryker's eyes stay glued to the road.

"How about we play an *honest* game of One True Thing?" I say. "If you tell us about you, Stryker, I'll tell you both the truth about me."

I'm done beating myself up for who I was before The Flem. If I hadn't been a street artist, Bat would never have known about me, and I wouldn't be driving back with the solution to unmerging. So what if I didn't go to art school? Like Bat says, no one can teach you how to have natural talent. And just because they can't put a score on artistic intellect doesn't mean I'm not as smart as the others. If being a Nobel has taught me anything, it's that everyone is smart in their own way.

"You go first, then I'll think about it," Stryker says.

That's his idea of fair? I'm sure Stryker's life before The Flem was filled with stories that'll impress Lake. But it's time to come clean.

I lean in closer to Lake. "I was a street artist."

She cocks her head. "You weren't joking about that?"

I make myself look into her eyes. "No."

Stryker says, "He's actually pretty famous."

"You know about me?" I ask.

He nods. "Anna told me after the party."

"But you never told Lake."

"It's your secret. And just so you know, I threatened to divulge *her* secret if she told anyone else."

"Thanks for that." Every time I write Stryker off, he does something to change my mind. But what is Anna hiding? And how does Stryker know about it?

I consider ending it there, but I want Lake to know everything. "They wanted to make an example of me, so I was only days away from getting arrested. If it weren't for Bat, I'd be in jail. For creating *art*."

I've built up my secret so big in my head, I no longer know how to feel about it. I watch Lake's face. She doesn't look shocked or turned off, or even disappointed.

"Why didn't you want me to know?" she asks.

"I didn't want you to think less of me," I admit, feeling my cheeks flame.

"Why would I do that?"

Her reaction helps me reveal the truth. "When I first got here, it felt like everything was stacked against me. Everyone is working on really important things, and you're all so smart. Then you guys talked about how graffiti is disrespectful and—"

"And I said it takes away a city's beauty," Lake adds in a voice so soft I can barely hear her.

That memory still stings. "I wanted a chance to fit in."

"I'm sorry," Lake says, "I … I *judged* something I didn't know anything about, which wasn't fair to you."

It feels like a flock of pigeons flies out of my chest, releasing the shame I've been carrying. How did I let their opinions change what I thought about myself? Before I got here, I was never ashamed of who I am—Sister Mo made sure of it. I'm never letting that happen again.

"Why did you choose the name Orfyn?" Lake asks.

"Instead of being something people can hold against me, I turned

212

the fact that no one wanted me into a name I can be proud of."

"I get that," Stryker says.

He does?

Lake says, "My mom always told me that from the moment she first looked into my eyes, she knew what to call me." She gasps.

"What?" I ask.

"People who have Alzheimer's can perfectly roast ... I mean, *recall* their memories from the past. It's the most recent ones I'm forgetting."

Does she realize what she's admitting?

"You're too young to get Alzheimer's," I say, trying to sound like I know what I'm talking about.

"What about Sophie?" Lake says to Stryker. "That could explain a lot."

"What are you talking about?" I ask.

Stryker answers for her. "Sophie doesn't realize she's been merged. She believes Lake is a grad student she can fire."

Holy crap! Lake never let on. Stryker obviously knew about it. Why didn't she think she could tell me?

"You know how much I trust the Darwinians," Stryker says. "But even *I* don't believe they'd insert someone with brain damage into your mind."

"Thanks. I needed to hear that." Lake reaches over and touches his arm.

My stomach knots up when he gives her a reassuring smile.

"Your turn, Stryker," I say. "What's your One True Thing?" *Please don't say it's that you and Lake are secretly together.*

"If I tell you, my story stays here," he says.

"Deal," I say.

"You don't want to cross me on this one, Art."

"You didn't spread around my secret, and I won't share yours."

He holds my eyes in the rearview mirror and finally nods. "Okay. Last year, I started this blog as an experiment to see if I could get people interested in doing something about our dysfunctional government. It took off after I started managing an online forum where the merits of different ideas were debated. Some pretty important people started to follow it, and at times they even added their opinions."

He slowly exhales. "Then I got the idea to coordinate flash-rallies at the state capitals. I'd select an idea from the forum and tell my followers where to meet up. We got the influencers to start listening, and it seemed like real change was starting to happen."

Stryker stops talking, and just as I'm thinking his One True Thing is more about boasting, he says, "At one of the flash-rallies, this guy showed up with an assault rifle. He killed three people and wounded twelve others." His head drops.

"Oh my God!" Lake's hand flies to her mouth.

I stare at Stryker, trying to match what I just learned with the image of him I've been carrying.

Stryker continues, "I was arrested for inciting violence, but before my identity went public, the Darwinians cut a deal with government officials who didn't want it getting out that they'd unknowingly been following a teenager's direction."

"That's why you want to end gun violence," I say, finally understanding. This is not the conversation I thought we'd be having.

"I chose the name Stryker to remind me that no matter how well-meaning your intentions, there are people out there who will take offense and strike back, so you'd better be ready for the fallout."

"Stryker is your alias," Lake says. "I forgot about that."

"Your secret is safe with me," I promise.

Lake adds, "Me, too. And I'm sorry you had to experience something so heinous."

"There's not a single day I don't regret what I did." He hits the gas, pressing us into our seats. He stares into the miles of road ahead, every so often wiping away a tear.

Lake eventually falls asleep, and I spend the rest of the drive thinking about what I just learned. I thought the others had it so easy, but I'm starting to realize everyone has things from their past they keep hidden. Good or bad, we wouldn't be who we are today without them.

When we creep up the gravel driveway to the old garage, the building is blazing with lights. I really want to believe Anna didn't rat us out, but it doesn't matter. We've been caught.

Lake

Orfyn, Stryker, and I are lined up across from three Darwinians. The polished conference table reflects their angry expressions. A man in a strange-colored suit is seated against the wall. He looks familiar.

After Orfyn explains why we had to borrow the van, and about Bat's prototype, the woman—who looks deathly ill—speaks first. "You're asking us to take one of the most influential people in modern times and insert him into a *machine?*"

"Calling it a machine is like saying fire is an inconsequential discovery," Stryker says.

"I'm interested in hearing more," says the older man with a beard.

"It creates a dynamic environment that can be manipulated to feel like you're actually there," Orfyn explains. "Angus Doyle will be able to work wherever he wants—an 1800s French café, the New York Public Library, a replica of his home. And unlike living in a Nobel's mind, he can write day and night. Best of all, you'll be able to talk with him directly instead of having to rely on Marty as the go-between."

The Darwinians' faces remain impassive. Why aren't they more interested?

"The subject could wake up tomorrow," says the Darwinian with greasy, dark hair.

I finally remember where I've seen him. He's the one who insisted Orfyn's demon painting be covered over.

"Or our friend and classmate, *Marty*, might never wake up and become nothing more than a vessel for someone else's consciousness." Stryker's voice is harder than boron.

"Martin is not in imminent danger," the woman says. "I fail to see the need to risk both lives unnecessarily."

"Your mission is to … to *extend* life," I say. "Existing unconscious on … *life support* isn't living." Did my fumbling lessen the importance of my point? And did the Darwinians notice?

"As we are all quite aware, my dear, there are several forms of living," she says in a condescending tone that grates on my nerves.

"Marty deserves the chance to become the writer he was meant to be," Orfyn says. "He's amazing. Have any of you read his work?"

"I understand he was making great progress," says the greasy-haired man.

Something about what he said sounds off, but I can't put my finger on it.

"That's not quite accurate," Stryker says. "Angus wouldn't let Marty get beyond the first paragraph until it was perfect."

I knew that. It's getting harder to keep up and act like I know what's happening.

"There's no such thing as perfection in art," Orfyn adds.

"If Angus did that *before* he took control, what do you think he's doing to Marty's sanity now?" Stryker asks.

"The Mentors were guaranteed a certain future," the woman says. "One that did not include existing in a *box*."

"I agree," says the Darwinian who seems like he could learn something from Orfyn's demon painting. "We must maintain the integrity …"

I never did ask Orfyn why he painted it. I will next time we're alone. What else have I forgotten? I suddenly realize I'm not paying attention.

"… top of that, a machine doesn't have the capacity to come up with creative solutions that have never been explored before. The core of this experiment has always been to see what our greatest thinkers can accomplish with the benefit of a second *human* consciousness to expand what is considered possible."

"And the added benefit of another lifetime, thanks to us," Stryker says.

"Of course," the older man agrees a little too heartily. "Our underlying premise has always been that life compounded will exponentially increase the leaps in human evolution."

"Exactly," says the woman. "Which is why we shouldn't be considering this ridiculous idea."

The older man waits until the woman stops coughing. "I want to discuss this in private with Richard and Sarah."

"Sarah? You're Jules's aunt," Orfyn says, making it sound like an accusation.

Her aunt is a Darwinian?

Jules's Aunt Sarah looks taken aback. "Yes, but that has nothing—"

"Do your plans include taking over Jules's body like Angus is doing to Marty?" Stryker asks.

"I never liked you." Sarah glares at him.

"Then I should be grateful your approval wasn't a requirement when Bjorn chose me," Stryker says. "He told me what you'll be working on once you've merged. Does Jules know the truth?"

Why would Jules care? A tremor runs through me. I think I used to know these things. What is happening to my mind?

Sarah's glare could melt beryllium. "I suggest that you don't anger me further, young man. You are already in serious trouble."

She rises and opens the door to reveal the two Not-A-Guards. "Return them to their wing."

Orfyn reaches for the cube.

Richard pulls the cube closer to him. "We'll keep this."

Stryker leans back in the leather chair. "I want to discuss something in private. I guarantee it will be worth your time."

The older man studies him, then turns his attention to Orfyn and me. "Return to your rooms. Please."

One Not-A-Guard takes the lead, and the other follows us. It feels like we're being led to the electric chair, but despite their daunting demeanor, they leave after dropping us off. In less than a minute, there's a knock.

"Can I come in?" Orfyn asks.

I step aside, and he sits next to me on the couch. I haven't had a cigarette in hours, so my breath should be fine.

"Can you remind me why Stryker wanted to talk to them without us?" I ask.

"I don't know, but I have a feeling he knows what he's doing."

For once, it's not me forgetting. "He should have told us, but Stryker has problems with toothpaste … I mean, *trust.*"

Orfyn walks over to the window and keeps his back to me. "You didn't trust me enough to tell me about Sophie."

"I never told you? I thought I had."

He comes back over and sits closer to me. When he looks into my eyes, my stomach flutters. "That makes me feel a lot better," he says. "When you really like someone, you want to believe they'd tell you if something is wrong."

This day has been surreal, and Orfyn was by my side for it all. I've never been this wrong about anything. I now believe he's someone I can count on when things get tough. Like, when my memory is getting worse.

Orfyn tentatively places his hand on the back of my neck. "Are you going to run away if I kiss you?"

"Why would I do that?"

He smiles as if I were joking. As Orfyn pulls me in, I recall our amazing kiss on the subway, although I can't remember where we were going. His lips touch mine—and someone knocks on my door.

"I really need to work on my timing," Orfyn mutters while answering it.

Stryker looks from me to Orfyn and back to me. "I came by to return your journal. You left it on the conference table."

"Thanks," I say. "I'd be lost without it." No use avoiding the truth anymore.

"What were you talking about with the Darwinians?" Orfyn asks.

"A good negotiator never shares his playbook."

We tell each other everything. Don't we?

"But they are considering it, right?" Orfyn asks.

"They'll let me know what they decide tomorrow, but I'm confident they'll move ahead with our plan."

"You're really not going to tell us what happened in there?" I ask. "We're a ... a *team*."

"It's nothing to be concerned about, Lake."

I don't remember Stryker ever acting so cold to me, and I don't think it's my failing memory.

When he glances at Orfyn, he clenches his jaw. "I need to go over some things with Bjorn." He leaves without even saying goodbye.

Orfyn says, "I should get going, too. We're both exhausted."

"You sure?"

"I'll come by later today." He lowers his head and gives me the sweetest kiss. His lips are soft and gentle, making my skin tingle like I'm standing in a light rain.

After Orfyn leaves, I touch my lips in wonder. I don't remember feeling this way with Stryker. Is that a problem with my memory, or the reason I'm not with him?

I grab my journal to make sure I remember this moment. I know I'll never forget Orfyn's kiss, but ... I turn to a new page and start and stop a dozen times, scratching through line after line, trying to capture the feeling. I finally give up and write, I like Orfyn.

Stryker

I'm lying on my bed, thinking back through my conversation with the Darwinians. It's something Bjorn and I always do at the end of every exercise, to critique what I did well and what I need to work on. One of Bjorn's tactics in a contentious negotiation is to throw them off by beginning with an inflammatory statement, so I tried it on the Darwinians.

"You know you're losing Lake, don't you?"

Sarah breaks into a coughing fit, the white-bearded man examines his nails, and Richard taps his fingers on the conference table. The only one who appears unaffected is the man in the gray-blue suit who recruited me. One thing is clear; he's not an underling. The question is: who is really in charge?

"The situation is under control," Richard says.

He's the suck-up, not the boss.

Bjorn instructed me to build tension but remain calm. I need to keep my tone civil and not take out that guy's windpipe. No more violence. "It's not only Lake's memory problem. There are times when she's not acting like herself."

The two men at the table exchange glances. After the bearded one nods, Richard says, "We always suspected there might be leakage between the dream sessions and a Nobel's awake-life."

First goal met: Get them to admit to something I didn't know. But his impassive attitude about what's happening to Lake makes me want to knock out his teeth. I fight down my anger. "How are you going to deal with this situation?"

"Deborah is closely monitoring the girl," he says.

"Her name is Lake."

Sarah says, "You're the inaugural class. Of course we expected some unforeseen events."

"The inaugural class, ma'am? Are you sure you want to stick with that statement?"

"It's neither productive nor appropriate for you to suggest we aren't being forthcoming," the bearded man scolds, as if I'm a little boy.

I clench my fists under the table. "Certainly it would be most beneficial for there to be trust between us."

He nods.

"On that note, you never told me your name," I say.

He sits up straighter. "Dr. Price."

The fact that he feels he needs to hide behind his credentials is telling. "*Doctor* Price, if I came across as suggesting you weren't forthcoming, then I apologize. Let me ask it another way." I glare at the obviously dying Sarah. "Ma'am, are you sure you want to stick with your fabricated story that we're the inaugural class?"

Dr. Price says, "I don't see the relevance of your question."

"The relevance is that you've got a room full of unconscious kids on the third floor of this wing."

Sarah starts wheezing and pulls an inhaler out of her pocket. Dr. Price closes his eyes as if not wanting to face the truth.

"I knew those two were up to something," Richard mutters.

Even the guy in the gray-blue suit looks surprised.

"The subjects in the *restricted* wing were involved in a different Program," Richard explains.

"Marty is part of ours, and he's up there, too. So, in the interest of trust and your earnest dedication to being forthcoming, may I respectfully ask, what the hell is going on?"

Dr. Price leans back and steeples his fingers. "We are not at liberty to discuss the condition of our subjects."

The man in the gray-blue suit clears his throat and Dr. Price shoots him an annoyed look.

Interesting.

Dr. Price smooths his beard. "Yes, there have been others. Other Nobels." The words seem to crawl out of his mouth. "The earlier attempts at merging were nearly successful. With the age adjustment, additional protocols, and more thorough vetting, your group is susceptible to a *much* lower level of risk."

"I'm feeling so relieved." *Sorry, Bjorn.* I know sarcasm is rarely productive. Time to change the focus away from Lake, for now. "What's your plan to help Marty?"

"Keep him stable until he reasserts his consciousness," Richard answers.

Lake and Orfyn told me what was in Cecil's notes, and according to him there is no guarantee Marty will win his battle with Angus. But I'm holding back what I know until I see how much they'll freely tell me. And more importantly, what they won't.

"In the remote case that Marty doesn't wake up, is there a Plan B?" I lean back in the leather chair as if I'm merely curious and this isn't a life-or-death conversation.

The three Darwinians look at each other as if waiting to see who will be the first to speak.

Dr. Price finally speaks up. "We'll cross that bridge if it becomes necessary."

"I imagine those kids up there have been unconscious for a while. How long are you going to wait before trying to unmerge them?"

Richard puts on a confused look. He could use a lesson or three from Bjorn. "I don't understand where—"

The man in the gray-blue suit holds up his hand. "Drop it. He knows." I've now learned who makes the decisions. "Do you mind telling me your name?" I ask.

"How did you learn of our work to unmerge a consciousness?" the head honcho asks, still keeping secrets.

I don't see any harm in revealing this one thing. I hope it makes them think twice before lying to me again. "Bjorn."

Dr. Price's calm exterior cracks. "Why on earth would he work against us?"

Maybe because you merged him against his will? And, the fact that Price sees this as us-against-them only confirms what I've been worried about. Tactic at this point in the negotiation process: Assume, don't ask. "Then we're in agreement. If Marty doesn't wake within forty-eight hours, you'll begin the unmerging process so you can insert Angus into Bat's program."

"I cannot condone the ludicrous idea of putting Angus Doyle into a machine," Sarah says, dabbing her forehead with a handkerchief.

Richard nods. "Removing his consciousness from a living host is impossible, unless the life of the host is in danger, which of course would threaten the Mentor as well."

So now we're *hosts*. That one word puts their motivations into perspective. I spent the drive back here working through scenarios to make them agree to the unmerging procedure. The problem is, the Darwinians have the power to lock us up, or worse. They could just let Alex and Lake deteriorate until they end up like Marty and allow those unconscious kids to wither away. They need a better solution, and I have one.

If I do what I need to do, I'm putting my own life at risk. I'm not worried about Bjorn taking over my body—he's not that kind of person—but just because I'm feeling fine now doesn't mean I'll remain healthy.

I still have to do it. Time to make up for my past.

"You need a success," I state.

"I'm certain we'll soon have one," Richard says.

I shift to face the person really in charge. "What if I help recruit the people you need?"

My first reaction was to find a way to shut this place down. But I still believe in the Darwinians' mission, and I'd be denying other sixteen-year-olds the same opportunity I had. The change that needs to happen is they'll sign on knowing they can unmerge if there are problems. And I need to alter the Darwinian's stance that our lives are secondary to the Mentors. In order to accomplish all that, I need more control.

"Go on," Head Honcho says.

"Bjorn and I are the ultimate success story. Not only are we compatible and accomplishing what we set out to do, we've been exploring concepts that go beyond our original goals."

"What concepts?" Richard asks, uneasily.

"Ways to expand the Mentors' experience so they have a more fulfilling second life. They're getting bored in there." I point to my head. "And a bored person is unpredictable. You want Bjorn and me to keep working on this, believe me."

"You never told Cecil about any of this," Richard accuses.

"As you're well aware, that's the problem with your current model. You don't know what's really happening in our dreams." I shrug. "I can help with that. I can also be the face of your success, to both potential Nobels *and* Mentors."

"Won't that get in the way of your work with Bjorn?" Dr. Price asks.

"Bjorn has agreed to limit my sleep so I'll have more time in the day to be your recruiter."

Head Honcho says, "Are you suggesting that if we liberate Marty from the experiment, you'll do this?"

"Alex, too," I say. "And whoever else wants to unmerge." I'm thinking of Lake. I'll need all of my persuasive skills to convince her to even consider it.

Number Two strokes his beard. "We would consider Alex if his symptoms don't improve."

"I have one condition."

Richard says, "You're hardly in the position to—"

"Let him speak," Head Honcho commands.

"I assume you're the Board of Directors. I want a seat at the table."

"You're a child," Sarah says.

"I had three million followers who assumed I was an adult. I also have the consciousness of a Machiavellian genius in my head to guide me."

"And if we don't move forward with your proposal?" Head Honcho asks.

"Then you're back to where you are now: a room full of failures, and no way to save the Nobel or Mentor when problems arise. How many kids are you going to churn through before you can no longer face yourself in the mirror?"

Sarah glares at me, and Richard brushes off a piece of lint from his jacket lapel.

Dr. Price gestures to the door. "We'll get back to you."

"We can make this work," I say, rising.

Thinking through it all, I'd give myself a B+ for my performance. I lost a few points because I didn't learn the name of the man in the gray-blue suit.

The Darwinians

"Wakowski's program is an interesting alternative, although of course, we'd only consider it in extreme circumstances," Richard says, slicking back his raven-black hair.

"We may be at that point," Dr. Price says, solemnly.

"Nonsense," Sarah wheezes. "We need to move forward as planned with the next Candidate in line."

"You mean, Juliette," Richard says.

"She told me she doesn't want to wait any longer."

Richard looks skeptical. "I'd prefer to hear that from her."

"Are you questioning me?"

Dr. Price holds up his hands. "Let's stay focused on dealing with these particular Nobels and Mentors." He looks at Sarah. "For now. Imagine being able to communicate directly with our Mentors without the filter of a sixteen-year-old's perceptions." He turns to gaze at the portrait of the woman with curly, salt-and-pepper hair.

The man in gray-blue leans forward. "I suspect some will choose to be implanted directly into Bat's program and forego merging with a Candidate altogether."

"And I can see how some would still prefer the experience of mentoring the next generation." Sarah coughs violently.

Dr. Price glances at the man in gray-blue, who nods. "We'll begin with Martin," Dr. Price states. "He hasn't been in his current state as long as the others."

"We need to maintain the status quo," Richard argues. "Can you imagine the implications if Martin wakes up and Angus is the one controlling his body?"

"An intriguing option," the man in gray-blue says.

"I will never agree to purposely destroy a child's mind so the Mentor can have use of his body," Sarah says.

"Yet you keep pushing us to begin *your* merging process," Richard says.

They glare at each other.

Dr. Price slaps his hand on the table. "Enough! Let's keep this conversation to our current dilemma. We first need to confirm if Wakowski's program will actually work."

"And consider Stryker's offer," the man in gray-blue says. "Can we confirm that he isn't exhibiting Bjorn's symptoms?"

"Nothing yet, although it's not the kind of thing one can test for," Richard says.

"We'll have to hope," Sarah says.

"We're scientists," Dr. Price says. "Everything we do is because of hope."

50

Lake

"Where are the octopuses?"

Sophie keeps warning me not to think of them as pets, but it's not easy when Lucille, Marco, and Stumpy change color when I pet their skin. Just below their epidermis are chromatophorus cells whose center contains an elastic sac of pigment in various colors. An array of nerves and muscles control which colored sac is expanded or contracted, which changes their appearance. They also have the ability to alter their skin's texture. When they're calm, it feels like velvet.

Sophie answers, "The cephalopods have been taking me down the wrong path."

Because of their ability to regrow limbs and their unique nervous system, she'd been sure they were the key to regenerating human brain tissue. At least we'll no longer need to harvest their body parts. Now that I can't play with them here, I'll ask Deborah if I can have an octopus for real.

Sophie lights a cigarette. It smells wonderful. "Alzheimer's doesn't stem from cellular mutations like cancer," she says. "It's a genetic mutation. That's where I need to focus my attention."

JIM AND STEPHANIE KROEPFL

"You want us to work on correcting someone's DNA?"

"It's too late by then. I want to prevent the disease from ever occurring."

"But we are still working on a way to reverse Alzheimer's damage, correct? You know about Grandma Bee, and how important it is to me that we try to help her."

Sophie shakes her head impatiently. "Once the synapses have deteriorated, memories are lost. Even if we can heal the damaged tissue, the person will never return to who they once were."

My mouth goes dry. Sophie has never taken this stance before. "We can still work on stopping her dementia from getting worse. I've been researching how art and music therapy can stimulate the senses and help trigger memories. And there are promising supplements like coenzyme Q10, coral calcium, and huperzine A."

"I need to fix the cause, not waste time trying to patch the symptoms."

Being able to remember loved ones is *not* a waste of our time.

My grandmother was so proud when I was chosen to work on Alzheimer's. She knew the chances of finding the cure in time to save her were questionable, but she pushed me to come here anyway, even though we may never see each other again. And if one day we do, she most likely won't remember who I am. But I've always held on to my hope that Sophie and I would defy the odds and figure it out in time.

I am not giving up on my grandmother, or the millions of people like her who are suffering.

"Sophie, we can do both. Fix the cause and work on reversing it so we can help those who have it now."

She grabs a file from the cabinet and slides the drawer shut. "The past is the past. I need to focus on building a better future."

I clench my hands to stop myself from screaming in frustration. "The future? Sophie, you think you live in the eighties."

She lifts her head and stares at me in a way that makes me believe she's finally figured out what's really happening. "You say the oddest things. We're done debating. I've made my decision."

The anger I've been holding back explodes like trinitrotoluene. "This isn't only your decision. It's mine, too!"

Sophie slaps down the file on the counter. "You're forgetting your place. I've been beyond patient with you, but if you continue your insubordination, it may be time for you to take your leave. Permanently."

The memory of the all-encompassing fear when Sophie disappeared wraps around me like steel bands. I can't face that nightmare for the rest of my life.

"I don't want to stop working together," I say in a voice as calm as I can manage. "I'm sorry I lost my temper. It won't happen again. But help me understand. You said we were making progress. What's changed since yesterday?"

"Yesterday? We haven't seen each other for a week."

My stomach sinks.

"I don't know why you wanted to spend your spring break in that dreadful Panama City when you could have come to the Côte d'Azur with me. I told you we had plenty of space."

My memory has always been perfect in my dreams, so I know I'm not the confused one here. "You were in France with someone else?"

"My cousin, Francesca. It's her apartment."

She has to be remembering a trip from her first life.

"I love the timelessness of that part of the world," Sophie adds, surprising me with her chattiness. "The art museums there are fabulous. I always end up seeing something that helps me look at a problem from a different perspective, like what happened on this trip."

I pull up a stool and sit across from her. "Is that when you decided to change the direction of our research?" Once I help her understand it didn't really happen, we can return to working on a way to reverse Alzheimer's.

She examines her cigarette as if it contains the answer to the meaning of life.

It smells delicious. "Can I have one?"

"This is my last. Sorry." She takes a deep drag, then lets it out.

I breathe in the secondhand smoke, yearning for more.

"I predict this story will become legend," Sophie says, gazing at the ceiling as if seeing it play out in a movie. "I was in a hall lined with portraits of the royal families that spanned centuries. Every few paintings, a dwarf child would appear among their other normal-sized children. That's how I came up with my breakthrough."

What doesn't compute is if she'd had this breakthrough before we merged, she wouldn't have had us spending all that time on octopus enzymes. But how could her trip to France have happened the way she believes?

I realize she's staring at me expectantly. "You want us to work on *dwarfism?*"

"Don't be obtuse. My point is, people will continue to procreate even when they know there's a genetically based disease in their family history. I want to make it impossible for them to pass on their defects to future generations."

"I don't understand where you're going with this." At least, I seriously hope I don't.

"Isn't it obvious? I'm going to make sure everyone with disease markers is sterilized."

Sophie looks like she's in rapture, whereas every hair on my body is standing on end.

"No one will agree to that," I counter.

"That's why they won't be told. Humans can't be trusted to keep their defects out of the gene pool."

"Sophie, it's impossible to secretly sterilize billions of people."

"We've been vaccinating people against diseases since 1796." She looks at me knowingly, making my skin crawl.

She's given this a lot of thought. When did this happen? It wasn't in our dreamspace, or I wouldn't be blindsided. "I can't condone something like this."

"I thought I made myself clear. You will either do what I require, or you will leave this internship. I hope you understand how monumental this is. My work will end diseases caused when irresponsible parents gamble with humanity's future. Don't make the mistake of walking away from a once-in-a-lifetime opportunity to watch *me* change the world."

Fear grips me so hard, I can barely catch my breath. Sophie is psychotic *and* living in my brain!

"Don't you see?" she says, as if the problem is me being dense. "Not only will people no longer suffer from preventable diseases, it will also rein in our population explosion. In the past, a new plague would appear and wipe out a good portion of those living in densely populated areas. The strongest survived, creating more viable future generations. There was also the added bonus of providing a reprieve to our natural resources. But because of advances in science, we've curtailed this natural cleansing process."

When positioned like that, it almost doesn't seem maniacal—unless one has a conscience. "Sophie, having children is part of the human experience."

"Those people will now have the time and money to pursue other meaningful endeavors. Look at me. I chose not to have children, and I've never regretted it."

"But it was *your* decision. Taking away someone's choice is immoral."

"Don't be so melodramatic. I'm not proposing we end the life of the gene carriers. They'll go on with their selfish lives until their diseased bodies fail. But I'll remove their ability to make future generations suffer. And, once they die, their genetic defect will become extinct."

What she doesn't realize is *she* won't be forever known as the Josef Mengele of my generation. That honor will fall to me—the only one of us who will face the repercussions.

In this form of life, Sophie's and Angus Doyle's behavior is unchecked. When there is no societal judgement or enforceable laws or the fear of hell, is this what happens to someone? Or, would a lack of consequences only corrupt the type of person who is willing to do anything to live a second time?

Did the Darwinians not consider something like this could occur?

"It's a lot to take in," I say.

"I'm confident once you've had time to think about it, you'll realize it's the most effective way to end Alzheimer's, and all of the other diseases lurking in our genes."

This is far bigger than my trying to protect our unusual relationship. It's time to tell the Darwinians the truth about Sophie. They need to know that Angus Doyle isn't the only Mentor who has become a super id.

"Do you mind if I leave early today?" I ask.

"Go on. I'm going to stay here and keep working."

Again, how will she do that without me?

I glance at the clock, then notice the moonlight shining through my window. It's not eleven in the morning. It's eleven o'clock at night. The longest dream session yet. No wonder I'm starving.

I reach for my journal. What were we working on tonight/today? Deborah tries not to act disappointed when I don't have much to report, but clinical research is a slow and methodical process, and it's the exception when something momentous occurs. I remember Sophie and I discussing our cephalopods. I've become a big fan of octopuses. Not only are they affectionate, they contain DNA that no other creature on this planet possesses. Sophie considers them an evolutionary anomaly. But there are a surprising number of scientists who believe the Cambrian Explosion from half a billion years ago—

when most of the planet's species came into existence—originated with viruses from outer space.

But what about the octopuses? *Of course!* I want to ask Deborah if I can have one as a pet. It's not technically allowed, but they don't make noise or a mess on the carpet. Was there anything else? Nothing comes to me. I pull out the drawer in my nightstand and shuffle through the contents. What did I do with my cigarettes?

Lake

Since they're being so persnickety about it not being legal for a sixteen-year-old to smoke, I'm chewing gum—and I'm starting to detest gum. I look down at what I'm wearing and frown. My wardrobe has become so drab. I couldn't find any of my scarves, leg warmers, or bright-colored blazers to add some panache. It's time for a shopping trip in the City.

" … and if Marty's procedure is a success," Stryker continues, "they'll consider allowing anyone with life-threatening complications to unmerge."

They plan to insert Angus into a *machine*. What kind of life is that? And it's a *prototype* that has never been tested. I'd never consider it. Alex, on the other hand, is acting like someone handed him a present tied with a big gold bow.

"I'm doing it," he tells us.

"You're so passionate about renewable energy," the Asian girl with platinum-colored hair says. "How can you give that up?"

I can't seem to remember her name.

"You're allowed to ask me that question the day you black out because you can't get enough oxygen," he says. "And they're still insisting nothing is physically wrong with me."

"I'm sorry. I shouldn't have said that," she says.

I've been half-following the conversation while running my bare feet along the stream's sandy bottom. Why didn't I know about this place? It's a hidden oasis. "Do you have asthma?" I ask Alex.

Stryker's midnight-black eyes land on me. "It's a little more complicated than that, Lake."

He's gorgeous. Why haven't I hooked up with him? With those lush lips, he must be a phenomenal kisser.

"Alex, you need to understand the risks," Stryker says.

"I could die or end up with brain damage," Alex says. "No worse than what I originally agreed to."

Kids these days blow everything out of proportion. I catch a reflection of myself in the water and smile. This place must be agreeing with me because I look so young. But my hair is too flat, and I could use more make-up. I'll pick some up when I go clothes shopping.

"What will you do if Marty doesn't make it?" Orfyn asks him.

"Please don't say things like that," the girl with the rings in her eyebrow says.

"Sorry, but Bat wants to make sure he's thought it through."

"If something happens to Marty, then I'll be the first one who succeeds," Alex answers confidently.

"There's one other thing you need to consider," Stryker says. "After they remove your Mentor, the Darwinians will ensure you'll lose all memory of what happened here."

"If I can't remember unmerging, then I won't ever regret it."

This is precisely why these decisions need to be taken out of the hands of those who can't see the bigger picture. My stomach clenches and sweat breaks out on the back of my neck. I don't believe that, do I?

"Alex, do you regret becoming a Nobel?" that girl asks.

"When I was deciding if I wanted to come here, I was reading a book by John Green. There's this great line: 'What's the point of being alive if you don't at least try to do something remarkable?' I didn't let fear stop me from coming here. I'm proud of that."

"And once you get over your cat ... I mean *cold*, you get back up on that horse." I don't remember ever using that idiom before. I must have heard it from Grandma Bee.

"Lake, what about you?" eyebrow girl asks.

"What about me?" I say, feeling my defenses rise.

"You're thinking about unmerging, right?"

"This is why no one likes you," I tell the little witch. "You're constantly going out of your way to be unpleasant." I catch a look between Stryker and Orfyn. I hate when people judge me. "*She's* the one who's trying to make me feel bad about myself."

Orfyn places a hand on my shoulder and whispers, "Lake, let's take a walk." The image of kissing him flashes in my mind, and my heart beats faster at the thought of spending more alone time with him. It *almost* prevents me from realizing he's trying to steer me away from her. I do not appreciate being manipulated, and I will not let that girl ruin my lovely time here. I shrug off his hand. "I prefer to stay."

Orfyn looks at me as if he doesn't know me. I am who I am, and if he doesn't like that I have a mind of my own, that's his problem. I've long gotten over trying to please everyone. I paddle my feet in the water. Why would I have chosen purple toenail polish?

The girl who will one day regret her piercings rises, avoiding my eyes. "I have to go."

I smile in satisfaction.

"Me, too," Alex says, as Stryker helps him with his oxygen tank.

"I hope they'll figure out how to slow the destruction caused by your emphysema," I tell Alex.

"I don't have emphysema."

If he won't admit to what's wrong with him, it's not up to me to make him accept the inevitable.

Orfyn moves closer until our shoulders touch. "Lake, I don't know what's happened since yesterday, but I think your memory has gotten worse."

"I know I've been forgetful, but I'm burned out. That's why I went to Panama City."

He frowns. "When did you go there?"

"Last week. For spring break."

"Lake, listen to me. You did not go to Panama City."

"Yes, I did. Sophie asked me to come with her to France, but I chose ..." My confidence ebbs when I can't conjure any memories of being in Florida. As I look down at my pale skin, my certainty slips a few more notches. "But Sophie went to France, right?"

He gently taps my head. "Sophie only lives in here now."

I start to tremble. "This is how Grandma Bee acts when—"

"Lake, you need to unmerge and save yourself."

I start kissing him to put an end to his ridiculous suggestion. He gives into it, like I knew he would. Men are so predictable. For a few moments, I get lost in his lips—until my thoughts fill with plans for the new direction of my research. For the future.

I change into slacks and a nice top. I don't feel comfortable walking around in pajamas, like that blond girl with the Buddy Holly glasses does. I haven't seen her in a while. She must be putting in long hours. She's someone I could work with. Next time I run into her, I'll ask if she wants to join my research team.

I'm only going out for breakfast, but I grab my journal, merely out of habit. I step into the hall and hesitate until I recall that the dining hall is to the right. The door opens to the room next to mine, and two men in white lab coats wheel out a stretcher with a body on it. A sheet entirely covers whoever is lying there.

"Go back into your room," the bald one directs.

My eyes take in the painting of a city skyline with *Houston* written below. That boy with emphysema lives here. "Is he—"

239

"We're taking him for observation," the Asian one answers.

"Then why is his face curtain ... cowboy ... *covered?*"

"Precaution against the dust." The Asian's eyes land on my hand. I clutch my journal tighter.

"Go back to your room," the bald one says.

I observe the body under the sheet. His chest cavity isn't contracting and expanding, and if he were exhaling, the sheet would flutter. What is his name? How can I not remember? We've been neighbors for years.

"Let's get going," the bald one says. They wheel the motionless boy down the hall. "Please give his parents my condolences," I yell at their backs.

I slide down the wall until I'm on the floor. Poor boy. Once a person gets that disease, they won't recover, which only reinforces my decision.

Which decision?

Tears spring into my eyes. I've been thinking things that come out of nowhere, and I'm saying things I'd normally never dare. I discussed it with Deborah yesterday—or was it the day before? She assured me the results of my neurological exam and imaging test are normal. But something isn't right.

You're perfectly fine.

I no longer think so.

Don't let others put worries in your head. Nothing is wrong with you. Trust me.

I look up at the door and I recall his name. Alex. And he was planning to unmerge. Time was not on his side. The tears I've been holding back stream down my face. He was too young to die.

Go to sleep.

First, I need to document what happened tonight, so I don't forget to tell the others. I capture the event in the journal, then re-read my notes. I'm so exhausted my handwriting doesn't even look like mine.

I wake with a start. My eyes are throbbing, and my top is twisted around me. Why did I sleep in my clothes? I reach for my journal, but it's not on the night stand. Where did I last leave it? My eyes land on all the usual places, but it's not there. I search every drawer, every nook, every place where it could have fallen, getting more and more anxious. Everything I need to remember is in there.

I search again until finally accepting it's not in my room. I must have left it somewhere. I'll ask the others if they've seen it.

I study my door after shutting it behind me. Why would I have *Pittsburgh* on it? I'll get Orfyn to paint me something more uplifting. Perhaps the Eiffel Tower or the streets of Arles.

I knock on the door with the painting of Houston. When there's no answer, I crack it open and call, "Have you seen my journal?" Who lives here again? *Alex, that polite boy.*

I push open the door and see that his personal effects have been removed. Was today the day he was scheduled to unmerge? It must be. Disappointment takes hold of me.

The maintenance man cleaning a window says, "Is something wrong?"

I sigh. "I never got to say goodbye."

Such a waste of a once-in-a-lifetime opportunity. Instead, Alex will be trying to survive high school unscathed.

The maintenance man nods and packs up his gear, even though there are still smudges on the other windows. I shake my head. It's so hard to get good help these days.

Lake

"May I assume your presence here means you'll continue working for me?"

Sophie can't be aware of the Nobels' discussions about unmerging, not that I'd ever consider it. It might be prudent to test her. "What are your thoughts about what's going to happen to Marty?"

"Who is Marty?"

"You've never personally met him, but—"

"Lake, you know I deplore gossip."

Just as I thought. She's not aware of my awake-life. "I plan to work with you for the rest of my life," I say to emphasize my commitment to her. I know Orfyn and Stryker are worried about me, but I have to keep believing my memory problems are only temporary.

"You have the oddest sense of humor," Sophie says. "But I knew once you had time to consider the new direction, you'd come to appreciate its brilliance."

This must be another one of those situations Sophie imagined, like my trip to Panama Beach. I still can't believe I confused Sophie's reality with mine. "New direction?"

"As I explained to you before, I plan to end all genetically-based diseases."

Ambitious, but I'm up for the challenge. "And we'll start with curing those with Alzheimer's."

Anger flashes across her face. "I told you to stop fighting me about that. I've already decided to abandon that direction to work on a method to sterilize those who have the markers."

Her horrifying idea rushes back to me. The French art museum. The dwarf children. The reason the octopuses are gone. I was going to tell Deborah about Sophie's criminally insane plan, but I never did because my memory when I'm awake is degenerating at an alarming rate. But why?

Sophie holds her cigarette as if it's made from a precious metal. "Nasty habit, but I can't imagine working without them. It calms me so I can think."

"Can I have one?"

Sophie passes the pack and lighter to me. As I'm lighting the cigarette, something occurs to me. My go-to when I'm stressed had always been reciting the Periodic Table. When did that change? My eyes latch onto Sophie's nicotine-stained fingertips. It feels as if someone is squeezing my heart, and it suddenly becomes hard to breathe.

"Are you going to be sick?" she asks. "You should stay at home when you're unwell so you don't infect me."

"I think I'm having a panic attack."

"You're so melodramatic. Drop your head between your knees and breathe deeply. You'll be fine."

This advice from the disembodied scientist who thinks it's a brilliant idea to take away people's ability to have children, and who exists not only in my dreams, but may also unknowingly—or knowingly—be influencing me while I'm awake. I'd bolt out of here if *here* wasn't my own brain. And if Sophie didn't control my sleep patterns.

I need to tell the Darwinians, but until I wake, it's up to me to get through this dream without damaging either of our psyches. I need a cigarette. No, I don't! Smoking is disgusting.

"Sophie, I need your help with something personal." I may be held captive by the woman who sees nothing wrong with secretly sterilizing billions of people, but she is also one of the foremost scientists on memory.

She heads over to the freezer. "It's time to get to work."

"This is important to both of us. I've been having problems with my memory. You probably haven't noticed, because it doesn't seem to affect my work in our lab."

She whirls around. "What does this have to do with me?"

She has transformed into a super id, unless she lacked empathy in her previous life, too. For the first time, I can believe she'd try to take over my body. I struggle to maintain a civil tone. "Since we've been partners for some time, I assumed you'd care enough to help me figure out why it's happening."

She sucks on her cigarette so hard, the tip glows like molten lava. How could I ever have thought it smelled good?

"What are your symptoms?" she finally asks.

"I'm forgetting words, I'm not able to find my way to places I'm familiar with, and I can't remember certain events. It sounds like Alzheimer's, but I'm too young."

Her cigarette stops a few inches from her lips. "Why did you bring up Alzheimer's?"

"Given what I've been experiencing, it's a possible diagnosis, but—"

"My neuroimaging results were supposed to be destroyed. How did you learn about me? Tell me! Who told you?"

My knees buckle as it all comes together. She knew she had Alzheimer's, and she still allowed the Darwinians to implant her damaged memories and broken thoughts into a sixteen-year-old's brain.

My brain.

The reality of what she knowingly did to me makes my stomach heave. I scramble to the wastecan and barely make it before throwing up. My memory problems aren't because I'm tired, and no matter what Deborah says, the Darwinians can't help me, because the only

244

one who has any chance of curing Alzheimer's is the woman who gave it to me.

I have to expunge her from my body. I never considered unmerging, but I refuse to spend the rest of my life with her deranged ideas. I'm already confusing her thoughts with mine. What will happen to me over time? I need this dream to end now.

"Wake up!" I yell out loud. I'm still in the lab. I try pinching myself hard, but it doesn't work.

I watch as Sophie picks lint off her turquoise blue jacket with the over-sized shoulders. "You still haven't answered my question. Who betrayed me?"

A terrible thought emerges. "Sophie, I just got sick, and then I was yelling to wake up. Yet, you're not questioning why."

"You try getting as far as I did—a woman researcher in those times—and see what kind of person you become."

My chest feels like it's being crushed by her admission. "*Those* times? Do you mean, back when you were young?"

She blinks rapidly. "It's always been a man's world, and in order to succeed, I needed to create my own rules."

"You understand what's really going on."

"Of course I do. *I* am the one in charge." She wrinkles her nose, grabs the wastecan, and sets it outside the door. When she returns, her lips are tightly pressed. "It's my fault. I've given you far too much latitude, and now you believe you have the right to question me. Starting now, you will do as I say."

"I am asking for the truth. Are you aware you only live in my mind?"

Sophie looks at me with the intensity of a coiled snake.

Lightning bolts of pain fill my head, and I feel myself blacking out.

"Does she or does she not understand she's been merged?" Cecil demands.

It may be because of the level of pain or my burning anger, but my thoughts are easier to sort through. Unlike the past week, there aren't big holes when I recall this dream. I'm almost positive Sophie never admitted to knowing she only lives in my brain, but I know she made me question it. "I'm not sure."

Deborah told me they heard me scream, and when they found me, I was writhing on the floor and bleeding from my nose. I don't remember it. Now, I'm in the infirmary with electrodes attached to my head. I've never had a headache this painful, but they won't give me anything to relieve it, since they're still trying to determine its cause. And, they want to ensure my brain hasn't been damaged. As Sophie had so callously explained, once that occurs, it's permanent, and I will never be the same again. I'm not a violent person, but if she had a body I could be.

"I can't imagine what you've been going through." Deborah dabs the sweat from my forehead with a cloth.

"Don't condone her actions," Cecil snaps. "She's a subject in a monumental, and extremely costly, experiment. Her decision to withhold vital information invalidates months of work."

Waves of fury sweep through me. "My ... my ..." I hate what she's done to my mind! "My *purpose* is to help Sophie continue her research, which is what I've been doing since I merged. And because of it, I'm losing myself to Alzheimer's. How could you have let this happen?"

Deborah turns away, but not before I see her tear-filled eyes. Cecil, on the other hand, is showing no remorse, which shatters my last vestiges of control.

"Did you know Sophie had Alzheimer's?" I yell.

"No!" Deborah looks horrified. "I never suspected."

"We didn't learn about it until after an autopsy was performed on Sophie's brain," Cecil explains.

"But you withheld that information from me and allowed me to believe my memory loss is temporary," I accuse.

"We hadn't concluded it wasn't," Deborah says. "We didn't want to cause you undue stress until we had definitive answers."

"We've been under the impression that Sophie is lucid in the dreamstate because *you* withheld information from us," Cecil answers. "If we had known the truth, we would have approached your condition from an entirely different perspective."

Cecil and I hold each other's eyes, and my insides churn with conflicting emotions. I thought I was doing the right thing by giving Sophie time to assimilate to her new form of life. And, if Deborah can be believed, they thought they were right in shielding me. Stryker's belief about the best of intentions may be truer than I thought.

I groan. It feels like a screwdriver is being driven into my right temple. Deborah grabs hold of my hand. She admitted to how close she was to Sophie, and Sophie said the evidence of her Alzheimer's was destroyed. At least one person is responsible for intentionally implanting her diseased mind into mine. Was it Deborah? I slip my hand from hers and tuck it under the sheet.

"If Sophie isn't aware she's merged, then she created an array of plausible explanations to justify the abnormal world she lives in," Cecil says. "And if she does realize it, we need to understand her motivation for wanting to make Lake believe she doesn't understand what happened to her."

I need to unmerge, but I can't do it by myself. I have to rely on the Darwinians to perform the procedure—even though I'm no longer sure if I can trust any of them. A blast of fear hits me so hard I fold in half.

"There has to be something we can do to control her pain," Deborah says.

"None of us ever imagined the human consciousness has this level of adaptability," Cecil says. "Sophie came up with her idea to sterilize the population without any participation from Lake. It's beyond our wildest expectations."

"Cecil, a little compassion, please," Deborah implores.

She helps me lie back onto the pillow and places a heating pad across my forehead. The warmth takes the edge off the pain, but I can't stop shivering as I think through my options. I can't keep Sophie in my head; her Alzheimer's is eating away at my mind. But how can I trust that whoever is behind Sophie's deception won't sabotage my unmerging procedure to stop it from happening?

"We need to interview Sophie," Cecil says. "I'll prepare a list of questions I need you to ask her."

I am not returning to her dreamspace. Sophie knows I don't agree with her insane plan. If she's only been acting confused, she has the ability to do to me what Marty's Mentor did to him. Now I believe she'd do it. And if she truly doesn't realize she's been merged, it won't be long before both of us forget who we are.

"I need to get her out of my mind. Now."

"Possibly after we understand the situation we're dealing with," Cecil answers.

I have to make them unmerge me. There was a way. It was Orfyn's idea, and I'm sure I wrote it down in my journal—the one I've not been able to find.

"Deborah, what happened to my journal?"

"You told me you misplaced it."

"I don't remember having that cable ... cartoon ... *conversation.*"

She smiles at me sadly. "Honey, there have been many conversations you don't recall."

Was there something in there they didn't want me to remember, or am I being paranoid? It's not only them I can't trust; I no longer trust my own instincts.

"I'm not sure how long we can allow her to interact with Sophie," Deborah says. "Lake's mind is deteriorating more rapidly every day."

This is the first time I've heard her admit it. Tremors rumble through me.

"That's precisely why we need to begin the interview process immediately," Cecil counters. "Think of the information we can glean."

There's no guarantee I'll make it through the unmerging procedure—especially if the Darwinian who helped Sophie intervenes—but it's my only chance to save myself. I sit up to be on eye-level with them. A wave of dizziness envelopes me. Deborah moves behind me and holds me up.

Once my head stops spinning, I say, "I refuse to be your lab rat while my symptoms progressively get worse."

"You'll do as we say, or else," Cecil threatens.

"Or else what?" I make myself hold his eyes.

"We'll never unmerge you. And as hard as it will be to watch, we will document every moment of your demise for the sake of science."

Deborah says, "I want to discuss this with our superiors."

I can't tell if she's on my side or theirs.

Panic tries to take hold, and I shove it away. I can do this without my journal. I have to. My life depends on remembering how we were going to force them to help Marty. I shut my eyes and rub my finger against the scar on my thumb while picturing my grandmother's smile. My mind begins to unjumble, and I piece together the conversation we'd had in the van.

I hope Stryker can one day forgive me for this. "If you don't unmerge me, I will kill Sophie."

"That's an impossibility," Cecil says.

"Do you want me to test it?"

The Darwinians

"The possibility that Sophie would actually die is relatively low," Richard says. "I recommend we have them prepare the interview questions."

Dr. Price shakes his head. "I am not willing to take that risk."

"You're not seriously thinking of inserting Sophie into a *prototype?*" Sarah asks.

"The documents Bat provided us validate the experience Kevin described. Plus, our best software developers and engineers have reviewed the specs and confirmed there is a high probability it will work."

"Sophie would never agree to this," she insists.

"I'd be able to talk to her again," Dr. Price says. "See her face every day."

Sarah erupts into a coughing fit and holds a handkerchief to her mouth. Red specks dot the cloth when she lowers it.

Richard says, "Sophie's new direction is intriguing. We need to explore how it organically evolves with the benefit of a second human intelligence."

"Which means continuing to keep her consciousness in Lake's body," Sarah says.

"You both have valid arguments, but ultimately it's my decision."
Richard leans forward. "Sir, if I could just add—"

"I'll let you both know what I decide. In the meantime, are you certain the girl doesn't remember the incident?"

"Her memory lapses have been too inconsistent to be sure either way," Sarah says.

"This is not an issue," Richard says. "We put someone in place to monitor her that next morning. And we had Deborah confirm it. The girl doesn't remember seeing him being taken away."

"I still can't believe we lost Alex. You both assured me his condition wasn't critical."

"No one could have predicted that a psychosomatic event would be powerful enough to stop his breathing."

"We were wrong," Dr. Price says. "But it will be far more devastating if the Nobels learn about it."

"Should any of them begin to suspect the truth, a course of action has been put in place," Richard says.

They avoid each other's eyes. Then Sarah clears her throat, letting out a wet noise. "One other thing. Please inform them that I want to begin the procedure immediately,"

"Surely you don't want to put your niece at risk," Dr. Price says. "On top of a deceased boy and a girl who has threatened to kill her Mentor, we have all those unresponsive subjects."

"I've been told I have less than a month."

"I am sorry to hear that, but we need to wait and see if the other Nobels start to exhibit life-threatening symptoms."

"What we need is a success story," Richard says.

"I assure you, I'll provide it." Sarah turns away and coughs into her handkerchief again.

Orfyn

"They're going to unmerge me," Lake tells me.

I know it's the only way to make sure Sophie doesn't do any more damage. Lake will only get worse, and Sophie might take over her body. I've been repeating to myself all the reasons why she needs to go through with it, and now that it's really going to happen, I want to beg her not to.

We're only beginning.

I pull my eyes away from the rose garden Lake saved and look up. The sky is a dense wall of gray nothingness. "How did you get them to agree to it?"

"Actually, you gave me the idea. I ..." She looks down at her hands. "I threatened to kill Sophie." Her voice is a whisper. "I didn't know what else to do." She starts scratching lines in the wooden bench with her fingernail, and a tear slides down her cheek.

"You had no choice, Lake."

She shrugs. "I'm just relieved I never had to try."

I should be proud that I was the one who came up with the solution, but it's why she'll be leaving The Flem. "Does Stryker know?"

She shakes her head. "I don't know how to tell him."

"He'll understand."

"I hope so." She doesn't look convinced.

I reach out and tuck a strand of hair behind Lake's ear, something I've always wanted to do. Her hair feels like silk. "Don't take this wrong, but you're acting more like yourself today."

"They're giving me a dream-suppressing drug. I suspect as a period ... No, that's not right. A *precaution* against my harming Sophie. They told me I could only stay on it for a short period before I start experiencing continuous hallucinations, which is why I need to unmerge as soon as possible." She looks at me with a burning intensity. "I'm so angry at Sophie. Sometimes I think I could actually do it, which only makes me angrier because she's turned me into that person."

"I'm so sorry this is happening to you."

Lake wraps her arms around herself. "How did it come to this? I wanted to save people, and I ended up threatening to kill someone."

"You did what you had to do to save yourself."

She shakes her head as if to push out an unwelcome thought. "Was I that bad?"

How do you tell the girl you love the truth? "What do you remember?"

"The last few days were so strange. I'd be doing something like eating breakfast, and the next thing I knew, I'd find myself in the rose garden with no memory of how I got there. But in my mind, it all made perfect sense, and I created these elaborate justifications for why I kept losing time."

A part of me has been hoping it really was only exhaustion, but I'm pretty sure Sophie was breaking into her awake-life and trying to take over.

Lake places her hand on mine. "I promised I'd start coughing ... I mean, *confiding* in you, so I need to tell you what Sophie wants to do."

Lake describes Sophie's plan to sterilize billions of people. In the rare times when Sister Mo watched the news, I'd hear her quoting Philippians: *What shall it profit a man, should he gain the whole world, but lose his own soul?* What kind of person would Lake turn into if she spent the rest of her life with Sophie in her head?

"You have to unmerge," I say, finally accepting the truth.

Lake leans her head against mine. "I know. But if I do, I'll never see you again."

"When I get out of here, I'll come find you."

"I won't remember who you are."

I wrap my arm around her waist and pull her closer. "You'll fall for me all over again."

She grins. "You are irresistible."

"And persistent."

"Some would call it stalkerish."

"Hey, whatever works."

"It works," Lake whispers as her lips touch mine.

As we get lost in each other, I vow to find Lake and remind her about art and clouds and medieval curses all over again.

Orfyn

Bat is in a well-lit diner on a dark city street. Edward Hopper's *Nighthawks*. He is wearing a hat like the other characters, though they aren't barefoot. Or wearing stained pink bathrobes.

"We're unmerging," he states.

"What are you talking about?"

"You need to go through with the procedure."

The Darwinians told us Alex got so bad, they had to act quickly and unmerge him. I hope he didn't think no one cared enough to say goodbye. We didn't get the chance. And after what Marty's and Lake's Mentors pulled, they don't deserve to keep living in their Nobels' bodies. But unlike them, Bat is the least controlling guy I ever met. I am not letting this happen.

"We're just getting started," I argue. "We can't quit now."

Bat wiggles his fingers, and the color of the girl's dress changes from orange-red to periwinkle. He thinks more creatively than anyone I've ever met. And because of him, I'm starting to think that way, too. He's a great Mentor.

Bat slogs to the front of the painting and puts his hands on his hips. In the greens and oranges of the night scene, he looks like an obscure 1940s superhero: weird, well-meaning, and wired-a-world-away from everybody else on the planet.

"Your friends are suffering from their Mentors' diseases," he says.

I want to believe the tension in his voice is him playing up the drama of the four diners in the painting. "Not all of them. Stryker and Anna are okay."

"You sure?"

"Bat, I feel great."

"Let me see your hands," he orders.

I hold them up. "They're fine."

Bat steps closer and spends a long time examining them. "I didn't plan on telling you this, but I had ALS. It wasn't supposed to affect us after I separated from my body." He flutters his fingers. "I couldn't use the keyboard anymore."

To create his video games, he needed to be able to type.

"I couldn't control my tongue."

Voice recognition software would've been useless. His games were the only thing he had in his life. I look down at my own hands. If they give out, I won't be able to paint anymore. I'd be Kevin, but I'd no longer be Orfyn.

"We don't know if it will ever affect me," I say.

"I won't take that risk."

Bat waves his hands, and the name on the sign switches from *Phillie's* to *Bat's*. He nods in satisfaction. I love watching him in the paintings. I don't want this to end. Bat spent the last eight years alone, and now he has me. We've been together every single night for the past month. He can't let me leave. We're all the family each other has.

"To be great, you have to follow your own dreams, not someone else's," Bat says. "I created my games because I wanted to see if I could. I would never have tried if someone told me how to do it."

"You're not like that," I say.

"You need to be working on your own art, not my latest one."

"You have a new game?"

He spins around. The tie from his bathrobe swirls around him, his grubby toes grab the blue-white city pavement, and his unshaven cheeks tighten in a huge smile. "Crimson Frog."

"Tell me about it."

He grins mischievously. "You'll find out one day."

I look around the Bat Cave, trying to accept that this may no longer be my home. "Can I think about it?"

"It's not your decision. It's mine."

I stomp to the screen so we're nose-to-nose. "It's my brain. I get a vote, too!"

"Don't fight me on this, Orfyn. I'm doing what's right for both of us."

I cross my arms. "I won't tell them you want to unmerge."

"You don't think I planned for that? After the file in my health record activates, they'll unmerge us, believe me."

Since Bat's real house uses *my* palm print for access, I have to believe him. "Bat, I don't—"

"You should get going."

"Can we wait a while before doing it?"

Bat leans his butt against the restaurant's window, giving the customers a special view. "It's already in motion."

My heart feels like it's shriveling into a raisin.

"And don't worry about Rosa," Bat says. "I made sure she and her mother have a good life."

"Then you *were* the one who caused them to disappear."

"I had the means to help them, and I thought it was about time they caught a break. Meeting you was the best thing that could have happened to her."

She's okay. The worry I've been carrying all this time evaporates. "After I unmerge, I won't remember any of this. Or you."

"Don't you love those times when something happens that jogs a memory you think you've forgotten?"

"Are you saying I'll remember you?"

Bat spreads his arms wide, exposing his belly. "I'm pretty unforgettable."

I have to smile. "True that." I take in Bat's basement—my favorite place in the world. "You've taught me so much. Not only about art, but about not being afraid to be who I really am."

"Then stop copying other people's work and start creating your own."

"I will. I promise." My eyes fill with tears, and when I blink them away, Bat is standing next to me with outstretched arms. I fall into them, and we hug for the first and last time.

"I love you, Bat. Thank you for choosing me."

He wipes the sleeve of his bathrobe across his runny nose. "I get to love you forever."

56

Lake

I stroll down our wing, taking my time to appreciate the painting on each Nobel's door. There's now a new one. But instead of Stryker's hometown, Orfyn painted the seven of us at the Jamaican party. The inaugural class—including Jules. Orfyn still wants to believe Jules thought she was helping. He's that kind of person. In the painting, everyone is having a wonderful time, even Anna. Orfyn portrayed me painting with my hands, which makes me wonder once again why I allowed my prejudices to override my feelings for him.

So much lost time.

He finished my abstract painting, and we hung it on my wall. It stops me in my tracks every time I pass it, but they're not allowing me to bring it with me. After I'm back home with Grandma Bee, there can't be any reminders about my being here.

I touch the figure of Alex. Deborah teared up when informing me that he successfully unmerged a few days ago and is already back home. It's comforting to know how much she cares about us, that we weren't merely specimens in an experiment. It gives me confidence that she'll ensure they go through with it and unmerge me. And knowing Alex survived is making it easier for me to face the risks a second time.

I hope some part of him remembers how important it was to him to find a renewable energy source. I'm not worried about losing my passion to cure Alzheimer's; I'll have Grandma Bee as a constant reminder.

The dream-suppressing drug is helping, but I'm experiencing thoughts that I know are Sophie's. Deborah says they won't continue after I'm unmerged. I still get angry when I think about Sophie's betrayal, but strangely, I miss her at the same time. There's a hole in my life that our work used to fill. Alex was right. It's better to forget about what I'm giving up.

They're moving me off the Nobels' floor tomorrow to begin the Blanking Phase, so I need to say my goodbyes today. A tie hangs from Stryker's door handle, but that's not stopping me on my last day as a Nobel. I enter his darkened room and hear rhythmic snores that sound like waves crashing onto a beach. I reach to shake him, then get a better idea. I clamp my hand over his mouth and watch as his eyes fly open in surprise. He grasps my wrist with his long fingers and easily removes my hand.

"Not funny, Lake."

"Fair is fair."

He sits up and turns on the light. My eyes travel down his broad, bare chest. My heart doesn't miss a beat, once again proving that he was never the one for me.

"I'm starting the unmerging … the unmerging *procedure* tomorrow," I say, sitting on the edge of his bed.

"I know."

"Were you going to let me leave without saying goodbye?"

"I'm not good with goodbyes."

"That's the coward's way out. And you're not a coward."

He grimaces. "No, I'm a lot worse."

"Why would you say something like that? You're one of the most courageous and caring people I know."

He shakes his head. "How can you believe that?" He throws off the covers and gets out of bed. "It doesn't matter. You won't remember any of this soon."

I march after him to the couch. "Then what does it hurt to tell me?"

"You don't want to hear this, Lake."

"I do. Please."

He stares down at his bare feet. "I was at that flash rally."

"The one where those people were shot?"

"Passionate people who were trying to change the world. And I led three of them to their deaths." He wipes his eyes with the back of his hand. "The part I didn't tell you is, one of them was my girlfriend."

It feels like someone punched me in the stomach. Poor Stryker. I can't imagine what he's been going through, though I know he'd detest my pity. "She is why you chose to be here, and why you're working to end gun-related violence."

He nods. "Her name was Alicia, and she was the sweetest person I've ever met." Tears stream down his face. "I'll never forgive myself for putting her in danger."

I move closer and tentatively place a hand on his arm. He doesn't shrug off my touch. "No one could predict that someone would do something terrible like that."

His face is filled with anguish. "I was the one who purposely threw gasoline on volatile issues to get people to stand up and challenge the status quo. I loved how important people took me seriously, but I let my ego push things too far. I was naïve to think the protests I coordinated would remain non-violent."

I always thought it was an expression, but my heart truly aches. "Stryker, let me ask you this. Why did Alicia go to … that place? The race. No. The *rally*?"

"I wanted to show her what I accomplished, and because of that, she got killed."

"She was there because she believed in your cause, and she believed in *you*. If she was as wonderful as you say, she'd want you to forgive yourself."

Stryker lets out a breath. "I promised myself I'd never get close to anyone again."

"I also think she'd tell you that you can't keep pushing people away."

His near-black eyes meet mine. "I almost broke my promise with you."

I recall our one hug and how I felt like something was wrong with me. It was never about me. How many times have I misinterpreted situations because I didn't have all the facts? I even convinced myself that someone was right for me because he fit the image I had in my head of the perfect boyfriend.

"We've been good friends," I say. "Other than the fact that you have an annoying habit of telling me what to do."

He smirks. "I may have been told that before."

"Thank you for everything you've done for me." I hold out my hand.

"That's not a decent goodbye." He wraps me in his endless arms. "I could have loved you, Lake. If things were different."

"I wanted to love you, too."

My tears blur Orfyn's face until he resembles a chalk drawing in the rain. "We're going to forget each other."

His light brown hand holds my ivory one—the color of The Flem's walls before he transformed them into works of art.

"I'll make sure we meet again," he promises.

It's a sweet thought, but I can't conceive how it will ever happen. Not only are we returning to our vastly different lives to do vastly different things, neither of us will have any memory of each other.

We arrive at the oak tree, and Orfyn climbs to the lowest limb. He reaches out his hand and helps pull me up. We perch shoulder to shoulder and hip to hip. I vaguely recall being here with him before, but I'm not sure when. Or why. How many other important things have I forgotten?

The sky is clear. Thanks to Orfyn, I now prefer days with ever-changing clouds. I watch as a V of honking birds flies overhead. I can't remember what they're called.

After the procedure, will I be able to recall the elements in the Periodic Table? Will I have the intelligence to unlock the secrets of chemistry? Will I look at a painting and remember how I'm no longer afraid to fall in love with an artist? Stop. I have to quit concentrating on the risks, because I can't keep existing like this. I need Sophie to be gone.

Think of what I can teach you.

I've learned that sharp pain drives her out of my thoughts. I dig my fingernails into my palm.

The saddest part is, she could have taught me so much. I've loved what I was doing at The Flem. Because of Sophie, I was working on experiments far beyond my age. And her lifetime of knowledge and experience would have continued to propel me so we could have done remarkable things together. I have to hope that once she's been implanted into Bat's program, the damage to her neurons is overridden and her brain patterns re-stabilize so she refocuses on her second life's true purpose. Mankind still needs a cure for Alzheimer's.

It's not easy to hope someone succeeds after they've sabotaged your dreams.

"I won't be a groundbreaking researcher," I say.

Orfyn pulls me closer. "Don't tell yourself that. You just need to dream bigger. Bat taught me that."

Again, sweet thought, but as my dad proclaims, people don't get a second shot. My role in history isn't what matters most, though. We haven't discovered the cure in time to save Grandma Bee. I'll be by her side while she still has good days, though. That is the one silver lining about leaving The Flem. I plan to make the most of her limited time, because Grandma Bee won't be challenging the premise that we only get one life.

You don't have to do this!

I bite my lip hard. It's ironic how Sophie spent the last month threatening to replace me, and now she's fighting to keep me in her life. I'm still unsure if she always understood we merged, or if she finally accepted it during our fight, which is why I blacked out. Either way, she realizes we're unmerging.

My mind keeps wandering. I need to make this time about Orfyn. "Why didn't we get together earlier?"

"You don't remember?"

"I'm no longer certain which memories are mine."

"We'll just have to create new ones." He runs his finger along my cheek, as if I were a fine sculpture.

Potassium meets water. *Boom!* My eyes scour his face in an attempt to burn it into my long-term memory. Broad, noble nose. Golden-green eyes. Eyelashes any girl would envy. Masterful, paint-stained hands. I wipe away a tear.

"Do you remember our kisses?" Orfyn asks.

"Yes." Although I'm not sure if they were all real. And I have a feeling Sophie was in control at least one time.

Doesn't she realize if all the people with a genetic marker never had children, she wouldn't have been born? Or so many other world-changing people. Thankfully, no one with an ounce of humanity would allow her to implement her plan in the real world.

I need to stop spinning. This is the last time I'll be with Orfyn. "I may need reminding, after all."

His smile ignites a flame that licks at my skin. Our lips know what to do, as if he's been a long-time boyfriend. I wish we'd spent more time together. I think it was my fault we didn't.

As we kiss, I breathe in his scent. Cinnamon mixed with walnut oil. Smell is one of the strongest memory triggers, and I want to make sure that should we somehow meet again, my subconscious will remember what he meant to me.

You'll regret this decision for the rest of your life.

No, I won't. After the procedure, I'll no longer know that I was once the Nobel for Chemistry.

Orfyn

Lake unmerged two days ago, and Marty was yesterday. We were told their procedures were a success. I have to believe they're telling us the truth, because the alternative is too terrible to imagine. I've not seen Jules since that day we learned she was their spy. She may be in the process of merging, but I hope she decided to follow her own dreams. The Darwinians said they'd unmerge the kids on the third floor after me, and Stryker believes they'll go through with it.

I'm next.

Anna asked if we could hold our last meeting in the greenhouse. It was empty the only time I've been up here, so I don't expect to come upon what I do. The sunny room is filled with potted plants in a spectrum of colors.

"What's all this?" I ask Anna.

"Wheat."

"Did you plant these?"

"Yeah, I did," she says, looking proud of herself.

The wheat plants are neatly labeled with their common and Latin names, and there's a list of dates and measurements. How did the girl with a serious case of don't-mess-with-me-itus become so fascinated with wheat?

Stryker is braver than me when he says, "You've been holding out on us, Anna. When did your life's goal change to involve dirt and manure?"

I expect her to rip off his head, but she says, "Who knew, right? Before coming here, I'd never grown a plant in my life. Then I couldn't get it out of my head that there's a greenhouse up here with nothing living in it. Before I knew it, I was researching strains of wheat from throughout history, and figuring out how to get hold of these rare seeds."

Who is this girl?

Anna points to a stalk with thin, tightly-woven spikes. "This is Einkorn. It's the same species grown by Egyptians two thousand years ago to feed the Roman Empire." She lovingly touches the one next to it. "And this is Turkey. It's the wheat that cultivated America's Great Plains."

"That's pretty cool," I say, and I mean it.

She smiles in pleasure. Anna.

I take some time to appreciate the plants' shades and heights and textures. Some are tall with long, reaching leaves. Some are short with thick, juicy-looking kernels. They're all a work of art.

"I eventually learned that my Mentor grew up on a wheat farm in Montana," Anna says. "She makes it sound like a really nice place."

"She's influencing you in a *good* way." Stryker shakes his head in wonder.

Anna cups a shaft of wheat in her hand with more tenderness than I ever imagined she could. "Wheat is a poison to some people's immune systems, but it's also been the builder of societies across the ages. It showed me that nothing is fundamentally bad or good."

I have a feeling she's not only talking about wheat.

"For the first time since I can remember, I'm at peace," Anna admits. "I don't want to go back to the person I was. I'm not unmerging."

I know what the next five years of her life will be like. Monitored.

Work-obsessed. Isolated. And Anna is choosing to stay because her Mentor helped her discover a better version of herself. We could've become friends if Bat wasn't making me unmerge.

"Good for you, Anna," Stryker says.

"What about you, Stryker?" she asks. "Are you staying or leaving?"

"I'm not going anywhere. I plan to be more famous than Gandhi." He almost pulls it off, but I know the truth about his past. He's not doing this for fame.

I think I finally understand what his private conversation with the Darwinians was about. Stryker must have cut a deal to give them one success, no matter who else unmerged. He sacrificed himself for our Nobel class. I wish I could tell Lake.

"It's kind of saintly what you did for us," I offer.

He nods, acknowledging that I'm not too far off track. "What about you, Art? Are you staying here in Never Never Land with Mother Nature and me?"

I run my fingertips along the stalks of Buckskin-Red Winter— for higher elevations, as Anna's label informs me.

"I'm going to figure out how to change the world on my own."

Orfyn

I step back from the brick wall and admire the painting of the girl. This time, she's balanced on the limb of an oak tree. I can't tell you who she is, but she keeps showing up in my paintings. She has hair the color of a sunrise, and a smile like Mona Lisa's, but not. The world's already got one of those. If you're going to paint, why do what someone else has already done?

It's simpler working in the light of day, and a lot more peaceful. I still paint on walls, but now I get permission first. And the owners have been psyched about having my work liven up their buildings. I'm still a street artist, but now I'm a legal one.

I pull open St. Catherine's door and head to the fridge to grab a grape soda. Sister Mo calls for me to come into her office. When I get there, she's seated at her desk, and in the chair in front of her is the Bishop! Perched at the ready in one of the chairs lining the wall is a man in an ash-gray suit and a blood-red tie.

"Out painting again, son?" the Bishop asks as he gets up to shake my hand, which is a first.

Why is he acting so friendly? We've never said a word to each other. "Every day I can."

"And how is your head?"

"I'm feeling fine, Your Excellency."

I don't remember anything about it, but Father Burke told me how I got jumped while painting one night. They beat me up so bad, I ended up in a coma for more than a month. The kids threw me a party when I came back home to St. Catherine's, which was cool.

Sister Mo gestures to the Suit. "Kevin, this man is a lawyer, and he needs to have a word with you. Come sit down, you."

My past might finally be catching up to me, but Sister Mo doesn't look worried. So why is a lawyer here to see *me*?

The Bishop gestures to the other chair. "Sit next to me, son."

When you're an orphan, and nobody has ever called you *son*, and then our church's top guy does it twice, it stops you in your tracks. What's going on?

"Kevin," the lawyer starts, "I'm with Tennison, Franks, and Stuebmann in Newark. First, let me offer my condolences."

"Why?"

"I'm sorry to inform you of the passing of Bartholomew Wakowski."

"Who's that?"

"He was a big fan of yours."

I'm guessing he doesn't mean me, the guy who was abandoned at the orphanage. This has to be about my paintings.

The lawyer hands me a thick, manila envelope. "This is Mr. Wakowski's Last Will and Testament."

Sister Mo looks as curious as I am.

When the Bishop pats me on the hand and says, "I'm sure it's good news," I don't doubt for a second he already knows what's in that envelope.

Watch out. He's going to take a big interest in you from now on. It sounds like good advice, but I have no idea where the thought came from. It's been happening a lot since I got beat up.

The Suit opens his leather folder and begins to read. "I,

Bartholomew (Bat) Wakowski, being of sound mind and rather unsound body, bequeath my entire estate to Kevin Ward, a resident at the St. Catherine's Home for Children. Tell him to paint the world as it should be, and that he has more family than he realizes." The lawyer chuckles. "Mr. Wakowski could be a little eccentric."

When none of us laugh along, he coughs. "Mr. Wakowski was an extremely successful video game inventor. Interestingly, he was also an art collector. His estate includes a number of very valuable paintings, as well as a substantial portfolio of holdings. There's also a house in New Jersey, although we haven't yet been able to gain access."

I look at the Bishop. He's smiling ear-to-ear. Now I understand why he suddenly wants to become my best bud.

"This has to be a joke," I say. "I've never met the guy."

"Oh, it's quite legitimate," the lawyer says. "And might I add that my firm has counseled Mr. Wakowski in the past, and we would be eager to provide legal services to you … uhm … "

I guess he's not sure how to address me now that this Wakowski guy has turned me into something more than a charity case. At least he didn't use *son*.

"You can call me Orfyn."

When the Bishop and lawyer leave, I say to Sister Mo, "I don't understand."

She comes around the desk and puts a thick arm around my shoulder. "I've been a nun for a long time, and one thing I know is there are angels all around us. And you have one watching over you."

As strange as this all is, I smile at the thought.

Sister Mo smacks me on the head. "And don't be too full of yourself, you. You can't go around disappointing angels."

Lake

My eyes snap open.

Sunshine streams through the floor-to-ceiling windows. My eyes latch onto the painting on the wall next to my bed. There's something about it that gives me the courage to believe I can do anything—which is odd, because it's an abstract. I wish the artist had signed it so I can locate more of their work. I still don't know who sent it to me. It showed up a few months ago without a note or return address.

I stretch and think through my day. My Mathematical Methods of Physical Chemistry class isn't until eleven, so I have time to pick up a bagel and enjoy it in Central Park. Since moving to the City, it's become my favorite thing to do.

On the way to the shower, I stop to pet Watson and Crick, my octopuses, and watch their colors shift with my touch. At first, I'd been worried my cat Pasteur would hurt them, but he avoids them like the plague. I think he senses that the octopuses are undiscovered aliens, and he doesn't want to risk one of his nine lives being abducted. I smile at the ludicrous thought, but a tiny part of me can't help but wonder. One day, thanks to science, we'll know the truth about how life started on Earth.

I luxuriate in the water raining down on me. I don't take my loft for granted; I'm blessed to own it. Still, I'd barter my inheritance if there was any way to save Grandma Bee. I often wish I could ask her how she managed to squirrel away so much money, and why she chose to never spend any of it to follow her dreams. She always talked about seeing Rome. Why didn't she ever go? Grandma Bee is in the late stage of Alzheimer's, and her mind is too addled to provide me with the answers.

Dad might know, but we haven't spoken in a while. He's been on tour with his band and isn't the best at staying in touch. The lawyer who manages Grandma Bee's finances didn't have any answers, either. It may always remain a mystery.

I stop on my stoop and look up. The nimbus clouds are my favorites. I've made it a ritual to always find a new shape, which is childish, but it makes me happy. I wait until the winds shift and spot a cloud that looks like a submarine. Satisfied, I head out. A few blocks from the bagel shop, a crowd has gathered. When I get closer, I notice everyone taking photos. I tap the shoulder of a black girl with intricately braided hair. "What's going on?"

"It's a new Orfyn."

"A new what?"

"An Orfyn." She starts talking rapidly. "He's a super famous artist. He's just a teenager, but he owns this gallery uptown that only sells art created by young people and—get this—he donates all the money to the City's orphanages."

"Isn't graffiti illegal?" I ask.

"I hear the building owners pay *him*."

That's a first. I'm walking away when she calls out, "Don't you want to see it? It's gorgeous."

That's a bit generous for spray paint scribbles, but now she has me intrigued. I squeeze through the crowd to get a look. She wasn't exaggerating.

The painting is of a girl seated on a park bench, and she's

surrounded by enormous red rose bushes. Weighty dewdrops cling to the petals, and the blooms look so real I'm tempted to touch the wall to assure myself it's only paint. There's a hopefulness to the girl. Almost as if she's not seen someone in a while and believes this is the day they'll meet again. I chuckle at my melodramatic thought. How would I know what the artist meant to convey?

"She looks like you," the girl says.

I'd been so lost in what the painting made me feel, I didn't look closely at the girl in the painting. We could be twins!

By now, people are starting to stare at me.

"Is that you?" a businessman with gray hair at his temples asks.

"No."

But the girl has my blue eyes that I've always believed were too close together, my nose with the little bump on the bridge, my pale skin, and her long hair is the same color as mine. My breath catches when I notice her bare feet. Her toenails are painted with my favorite shade of purple. I pull out a stick of gum and begin chewing.

"Come on, admit it," encourages a plump woman with blue hair and a ring in her nose.

"It's not me." They look at me in disbelief, but I'm telling them the truth. I never posed for this picture. I must have a doppelganger.

Without asking, the plump woman takes a photo of me in front of my eerie likeness. "I'm posting this one."

I consider asking her not to, then stop myself. It's one photo. What's the harm?

I know the girl just told me, but who is the artist? Considering I'm supposedly brilliant, I have a terrible short-term memory. I lean in to read the name painted in green, the shade of a new leaf. *Orfyn*.

I need to meet him and learn who that girl is.

Epilogue

Darsha pulls her phone from her Hermes purse.

She has tried everything. Every drug. Every therapy. Traditional and non-traditional.

She will not go softly. There is so much more to do. So much more to accomplish. She has one last chance.

"Darwin Corporation," a flinty, no-nonsense voice greets.

"Darsha Patel. Procedure M-Sixteen. Confirmation code three-beta-five-zero."

"Confirmed."

Darsha ends the call. She can still make a difference. All she needs is more time. And soon she'll have all the time in the world.

Art Referenced by Orfyn and Bat

The Last Supper by Leonardo da Vinci

Completed in 1498, it is found at the Basilica di Santa Maria delle Grazie in Milan, Italy. Its intent was to capture the Apostles' reactions after Jesus reveals that one of them will betray him. Technically not a fresco since it was painted on a dry wall, due to da Vinci's experimental technique and medium, it began to deteriorate soon after it was completed. It was also damaged in 1943 during World War II when a bomb exploded just eighty feet away, virtually destroying the building. Miraculously, the wall with da Vinci's painting remained standing. Despite seven restoration attempts, very little of the original painting exists today.

The Lady of Shalott by John William Waterhouse

Painted in 1888, it is usually on display at the Tate Gallery in London, England. Waterhouse is known for his lavish depictions of women in Greek and Arthurian (i.e. King Arthur and Lancelot) mythology. This painting is a portrayal of Part IV of Lord Alfred Tennyson's 1832 poem of the same name.

The Birth of Venus by Sandro Botticelli

Found at the Ufizzi Gallery in Florence, Italy, it represents the goddess of love and beauty on the island of Cyprus. Venus is standing in a giant scallop shell, and demurely covering herself with her long, blond hair. It was painted in 1485. The fact that she is completely naked was groundbreaking since art in the Middle Ages was typically based on Biblical themes. It was intended to be hung in a bedroom, and was not shown in public for its first fifty years.

Water Lilies Series by Claude Monet

Monet spent the last thirty years of his life obsessed with painting roughly 250 "Water Lilies," which are on display in museums and private collections across the world. One can experience eight of these paintings laid side-by-side in two oval-shaped rooms at the Musée de l'Orangerie in Paris. Monet planted and tended to the real-life water lilies in his Giverny (France) garden, and he imported several varieties from Egypt and South America. Today, his garden is open to the public.

View of Scheveningen Sands by Hendrick van Anthonissen

Painted circa 1641, it has been hanging at the Fitzwilliam Museum in Cambridge, England for 150 years. It was never considered to be one the museum's more interesting pieces since the characters were simply staring at a bleak expanse of empty beach—until a huge beached whale was revealed during its restoration. There is no reference to the whale in historical documents, but it is suspected that either a previous owner found the scene unappetizing, or an art dealer thought the painting would better sell without the dead animal. As explained by the curator, "In the past it would be very common to cut a painting or paint over it to fit aesthetic purposes."

The Starry Night by Vincent van Gogh

Painted in 1889, it portrays van Gogh's view while at the asylum in Saint-Rémy-de-Provence (France) where he checked himself in after having a mental breakdown—although without the bars in the window. Recently, an art historian compared the scene to a re-creation of the night sky in June 1889. It was determined that the "morning star," as Vincent described it in one of his 650 letters to his brother Theo, is actually the planet Venus. This painting hangs at the Museum of Modern Art (MoMA) in Manhattan, New York.

The Scream by Edvard Munch

Munch created four versions in various mediums in the late 1800s/early 1900s. Supposed experts interpret it as representing the universal anxiety of modern man (whatever that means). One can be viewed at the National Gallery in Oslo, Norway and two others are at the Munch Museum in Oslo. Different versions have been involved in high-profile thefts—twice—but were later recovered. The white ghost face mask in the horror movie *Scream* is based on Munch's character.

Christina's World by Andrew Wyeth

Painted in 1948, it was inspired when Wyeth saw his neighbor, Anna Christina Olsen, dragging her body across a field due to her disease, Charcot-Marie Tooth (CMT), a degenerative muscle disorder that prevented her from walking. Wyeth once explained, "I wanted to do justice to her extraordinary conquest of life which most people would consider helpless." The actual farmhouse, known as the Olsen House, is open to the public in Cushing, Maine. This painting is on permanent display at the Museum of Modern Art (MoMA) in Manhattan, New York.

Luncheon of the Boating Party by Pierre-Auguste Renoir

Renoir painted this beloved masterpiece in 1880-1881. It depicts a group of his real-life friends partying at Maison Fournaise, a restaurant, hotel and place to rent rowboats that still exists today. It is located just outside of Paris in Chatou, along the river Seine. The woman holding the dog is Renoir's future wife. The painting can be viewed at The Phillips Collection in Washington, D.C.

Nighthawks by Edward Hopper

Painted in 1942, it is at The Art Institute of Chicago. Debate continues as to whether the diner was real or imagined. Hopper's only admission: the scene "was suggested by a restaurant on Greenwich Avenue (Manhattan, New York) where two streets meet." Interestingly, in the painting there is no door shown that would allow one to enter or exit the diner, which could be interpreted as representing isolation and loneliness.

Science Referenced by Lake

The Periodic Table

In 1869, Russian chemist Dmitri Mendeleev created a table of the chemical elements arranged in order of atomic number so that elements with similar atomic structure appear in vertical columns. Gaps were left for yet to be discovered elements. The first scientific discovery of an element occurred around 1669, which was phosphorus. In 1869 there were 69 known elements; in 2019 there are 118 known elements.

The Scientific Method

Muslim scholars, between the 10th and 14th centuries, are attributed to being the greatest influencers behind the development of the scientific method. Today it consists of a series of steps which include: making an observation, formulating a hypothesis, testing the hypothesis through experimentation, accepting or modifying the hypothesis, and then developing a law and/or theory.

Alzheimer's

An irreversible, progressive disease that slowly destroys memory, thinking and reasoning skills. For most people, symptoms first appear in their mid-60s. It is named after Dr. Alois Alzheimer, who in 1906 identified changes in the brain tissue of a woman with symptoms of mental illness. It is suggested that more than 5.5 million Americans may have Alzheimer's. As of the printing of this book, there is no cure.

Butyric Acid

A saturated fatty acid found in butter, raw milk, ghee, animal fats and plant oils. It is also formed in, and thus found in, our colon. Consuming butyric acid has been shown to aid in digestion, calm inflammation, and improve gastrointestinal health. It is a colorless liquid with a penetrating and unpleasant odor that smells like vomit.

Van de Graaff Generator
Looking like a big aluminum ball on a pedestal, it was invented by American physicist Robert J. Van de Graff around the 1930s. Generally used for scientific experiments, it is basically an electrostatic machine that can generate high voltages, and its purpose is to accelerate subatomic particles. It is also used for entertainment because when touching the sphere, one's hair literally stands on end.

Chemtrail
The visible trail left in the sky by an aircraft. Scientists explain they are man-made clouds formed under ordinary conditions. Conspiracy theorists believe they consist of chemical or biological agents released by the government or a secret agency for purposes such as to modify the weather, population control via sterilization, and even mind control.

The Arrhenius Equation
Created by Swedish chemist Svante August Arrhenius in 1899, it describes the effect of temperature on the velocity of a chemical reaction, such as the souring of milk.

Johann Joachim Becher Theory About Phlogiston
A German alchemist, Becher developed his theory in 1667, which attempted to explain processes such as combustion and rusting. Becher postulated that a fire-like element called phlogiston was responsible for these types of reactions. Phlogiston remained the dominant theory until the 1770s, when it was proved to be incorrect.

Josef Mengele
Known as the "Angel of Death," Mengele was a Nazi doctor during World War II at the Auschwitz concentration camp. He is known for conducting horrific medical experiments on the prisoners. After the war, he reportedly moved to Brazil, changed his identity, and died in 1979.

Acknowledgements

First, thank you to Cindy Uh, who took a chance on us, and is the agent of our dreams: brilliant, supportive, persistent, patient and, and above all, kind. We also have to thank Emily and everyone else at the Thompson Literary Agency. How did we get so lucky?

Next, thank you Georgia McBride, Emily, Tori, Amanda, Katherine and everyone at Month9Books. We can't begin to explain how much this book has grown in your extraordinary hands. The incredible insight, the beautiful artwork, and the thousand other things we aren't even aware of that made this book so special. Also, thank you to the Month9Books authors, a true family who provides so much encouragement and support.

Thank you to our first readers who helped us believe in this story: Tracey (how we wish you could have seen this book in print), Mo, Noah, Madison, Eli, Marcy, Grace and Sue.

To our friends who have experienced this crazy journey with us, including Don and Amy, Barb and Sue, Jim and Karn, Andy and Julie, Steve and Jennifer, Hayden and Tracey, Pete and Laura, Adriane and Jeff, Rob (a teacher and hero, aren't they all), the Grand Lake community, and countless others. Also, thank you to our families who never stopped believing in us, especially to our moms who drove us to the library whenever we liked when we were young. You all are our courage when we're shaken, our energy when we're exhausted, and our inspiration when we can't think of one more cohesive thought.

To Doris Reddick. Thank you for the wonderful, endless hours discussing oil painting techniques and introducing us to amazing paintings.

To Dr. Jill Adams, who widened our understanding of the magnificence of YA Literature, and became our friend and supporter.

You gave us our first chance to share the "Merged" journey with so many teens and young adults. Also, thank you to the entire Metro State University English Department. Apparently, great professors can teach old dogs new tricks.

A sincere thanks to Gage and Finn who missed far too many walks when we were a world away lost in this story.

Believe. Dreams come true.

Jim and Stephanie Kroepfl
Photo by John F. Williams

Jim and Stephanie Kroepfl are a husband-and-wife team who write YA novels and stories of mystery and adventure from their cabin in the Colorado Rocky Mountains. You can find them at www.jimandstephbooks.com.

CONNECT WITH US

Find more books like this at http://www.Month9Books.com

Facebook: www.Facebook.com/Month9Books
Instagram: https://instagram.com/month9books
Twitter: https://twitter.com/Month9Books
Tumblr: http://month9books.tumblr.com/
YouTube: www.youtube.com/user/Month9Books
Georgia McBride Media Group: www.georgiamcbride.com

OTHER MONTH9BOOKS TITLES YOU MIGHT LIKE

THE MISSING

SERPENTINE